I0520047

INSIDE THE MIRRORS
BY
JASON R. DAVIS

SPOOK SHOW PUBLISHING

Published by
Spook Show Publishing
151 N. 4th St.
Suite #4
Dekalb, IL 60115

Please visit us online at http://spookshowpublishing.com

Authors website
http://horrorauthorjasondavis.com

Cover Illustration by
SnS-Photo (Jim Sorfleet)
Cover Model: Kat McGill Mayer
Copyright 2013

Cover Design by
Willy Adkins

Dedicated to my family

Special thanks to my editor,
Glenda Wildeman

PROLOGUE

Luke took a long look down the strip and felt the familiar warmth of a summer breeze. It blew through his hair, smoothing it back. The top was down and he enjoyed the summer warmth, cruising in his new car. He was proud of his dreamboat; no one had a car as fresh and hip as his. It was fitting, his dad, Daniel Collins owned half the town, he should have only the best.

Standard was a small town that had grown dependent on its corn fields once the coal mines were exhausted. Where there was corn, there were corn silos, and that was where Luke's father came in. Luke's father owned the silos. They stood in the center of the town, and controlled the purchase price of the entire town's corn supply.

Luke often wondered when the town would finally change its name from Standard to Collins, or Collinsville, or anything relating to the Collins name. After all, if it wasn't for them, the town would have faded away with the coal mines. They had saved this town, why not some recognition for what they'd done?

Luke eased his new car into the open parking spot nearest the front door of the sweet shop. He was supposed to meet his girl, Katie. They were going to take his new wheels for a test drive out on the back roads. There was a creek only five miles out of town. Luke knew a back way to a place that was nice and private. It was a perfect day to play a little hooky from school. They could take a drive and have a picnic. No one should be locked away in some dusty old school when the air was warm, the breeze light. It was too perfect to waste.

The wind gusted along the street, blowing a storm of red dust from the silos. Luke frowned, looking across the street at the five large silos that stood tall, reaching for the heavens. In a town that small, they stood higher than any building and were the closest thing Standard would ever see to a skyscraper.

Luke turned his attention away from the long- standing landmarks. The sweet shop was Standard's only place to hang, and for any teenager, including Luke, it was their second home. He would say first home, but he'd often go home to sleep. Or so he joked to his friends when they said he was there too much.

Luke was standing in the doorway when he heard a scream. It was a sickening sound that sent a chill down his spine, and froze him where he stood. It sounded like a cat caught in a car engine, but was human. It seemed to start from far away, but quickly came closer, ending with a sickening thud.

Luke turned in time to see people running to the body at the entrance ramp to the silos. The man had hit hard, and Luke didn't have to take a close look to know he was dead on impact. He stepped out of the doorway of the sweet shop and made it as far as his car before nausea overtook him and he had to reach out to catch his balance.

What the hell was that? How the hell would someone fall from his father's silo?

Luke could feel his breakfast coming up, and had to bend over to try to settle himself. He needed to get some air.

He could hear the door behind him and within seconds, a crowd of people surrounded him. They were all clamoring for a look, and soon they saw the man, dead on the ground. Those around him grew silent and stood stunned, watching as the crowd across the street grew.

It was like a bad dream. Luke didn't feel himself move, but found himself crossing the street, to the front loading area of the silo. There was already a large group of employees gathered around.

"Who is it?" yelled one of the employees, running up. Luke looked over, and saw his father standing in the open door of the grain bin's front office. He stayed there, in the doorway, with his arms across his chest, watching everyone gather.

A man at the center of the group looked over at Luke's Dad.
"It's Sammy!"

Daniel Collins held the gaze of the man staring at him. Luke could see the accusation in the man's stare, and he wondered what his father had done to make the man believe this was his father's fault. There was such hatred in those eyes.

Luke turned to look at his dad, only to see that his father's gaze was just as strong. Their eyes were locked in anger, and Luke doubted his father would be the first to turn away. He turned back and forth, watching them both, the only one to notice the battle of wills. Then, Luke looked back at his dad one last time, and he swore he could see orange flame flickering in his father's eyes. Luke looked once more at the other man and watched as a horrified look crossed his face, and he lowered his gaze.

Luke glanced again at his father, and caught his eye. His father gave a slight smile. It was unnatural and it sent chills down Luke's back. His father nodded, the orange flame glinting briefly, as his father turned and stepped back into his office.

* * * *

Samuel Young; it would be a name that Daniel would not soon forget. "Sammy" as his friends called him, had fallen on a dark day. It would be the ruin of Daniel. That cursed wife of Samuel's was going after him for everything he owned. Why wouldn't she just go away, take the life insurance and the "extra" insurance that Daniel had offered her, and just go back to whatever hole she'd climbed out of?

Daniel looked out the window of his office at the stain that remained on the loading dock. They'd tried to clean it up for the last two weeks, but Daniel could see the blood soaked into the cement. He could still smell it. When he left his offices at night he could smell the rotting flesh decaying into the cement.

"We're all sorry."

"Huh?" Daniel turned to see his secretary standing in the doorway looking in at him. "Oh, yes, thank you."

She probably thought that Daniel was feeling sorry for the bastard. Yeah, well he wasn't sorry. He wished the bastard was still alive so Daniel could kill him himself. "Sammy" was going to ruin him. All he'd wanted "Sammy" to do was to go up there and take down that damned Christmas tree.

The lighted fixture in the shape of a Christmas tree had stood atop Silo One since before he'd taken over the grain bin nearly ten years ago. It had stayed up, and every Christmas he followed the tradition of lighting it up for all the idiots in the town to stop and gawk over.

Well he was tired of it.

Two weeks ago, on his way into his office, he'd looked up at that God awful thing sitting up there one more time. He had been talking with some local painters about painting the silos, and the tree would draw everyone's attention away from his beautiful monuments. It would turn his beautiful silos into an eyesore. The damn tree was the eyesore, and it had to go.

Sammy had been pedaling his bike into work at the time, so Daniel had told him to go up there and take it down. There was no special reason to ask him in particular, he just happened to be the first person Daniel had seen that morning.

Daniel didn't realize that Sammy's wife had a brother who was some big city law student. He didn't know the brother would give her advice on how to take everything away from Daniel, that he would give her advice on how to ruin his life.

Daniel looked at the letter on his desk that had arrived from his lawyer less than an hour ago. His lawyer had already warned him it was coming, and that the wife was suing him for making her husband work in unsafe working conditions. His lawyer told him not to worry. There had been no laws broken, and that there was little that Sammy's wife could do.

Daniel reached for the letter and put it away in his top drawer. Yeah, nothing to worry about, but he did. That little bitch was going to try to take him for everything he was worth.

He looked up to see his secretary standing back in the doorway, watching him.

"Yes?"

"A young boy called, he said his name was Tom Morgan?"

"So?"

"He says that your wife is acting strange. He sounded concerned and thought you would like to know."

Damn these people; why wouldn't they just leave him alone? Who the hell was Tom Morgan, and why the hell was he talking to his wife?

"How would he know?"

"He mows your yard. He said she wouldn't come downstairs and the back door was wide open so he went up to get paid. He found her in your room, just staring in her dresser mirror and brushing her hair. He said she never noticed he was there. He also says that you own him a dollar for mowing the yard."

Great, what's up her bonnet? Maybe some of the cinnamon she always used had gotten into her head.

"Fine." Daniel looked back out at the stain in the cement. "I'm going home for the day."

CHAPTER 1

"That better be black, no sugar, or I'll be returning you to the pound!"
Rob called after his new partner from the squad car, just before he disappeared into the bright lights of the gas station convenience store.

"Damn rookies."

Rob looked around the darkened parking lot. Trannie on the corner turning tricks, bum at the side of the building, sleeping on the sidewalk; it was a quiet night. Other than the normal night life of the streets, there hadn't been too much going on so far. Nothing worth the time it would take to process. Yeah, Rob could set up and observe the trannie, but that'd just waste an hour watching him, another hour processing, just to have him back on the street within four hours. What would be the point, other than wasting his time?

Damn getting old. Hell, there was a time Rob would have been all over the idea of dragging the trannie in. He'd have sat there, recorded the plate numbers of all the Johns, dragged her to the station and then busted them all. Not that it ever did any good. The system wasn't terrible, but it sure did have its flaws. In the end, what did it really matter? The trannie never hurt anyone.

Rob turned his attention to the convenience store. Rook was at the counter paying for both of their coffees. A young pup, new to the force, this was his first night out on patrol, and Rob was stuck baby-sitting him. By itself it wasn't too bad, since his partner for ten years had taken early retirement last month, leaving Rob to sit at a desk, and waiting to get back on the street. This Rook was his ticket off the desk, but as with any hotshot, he was on his way to the morgue. Rooks, they were always craving action, itching for it. They were always looking for the big case, the next action scene, as though everything on television was real. They wanted to be heroes, and every minute they were doing paperwork was another minute keeping them from it.

Early retirement. Maybe Rob was getting too old, but after what had happened… He dreaded even thinking about doing that to his wife and kids.

The car shook as the rook pulled too hard on the door, fumbling not to dump the coffee all over him and the car seat.

"You said cream with two sugars, right?"

Rob looked harshly at the nervous kid, glaring his answer until the kid broke into a large smile.

"Just kiddin' with you. Black, no sugar, just like you asked."

Rob took the cup, his hands numb to the heat, numb from too many hot cups of coffee on the streets. He took a long sip, relishing the scent, before setting the cup into the holder.

"Not bad, Rook." Rob said, as reached forward to put the car into gear.

"Tommy."

"What?"

"My name, it's Tommy."

"We'll see, Rook."

Hotshots. They burn hot, but they go out fast.

Rob eased out of the parking lot, glaring at the trannie.

"Should we bust her, I mean, him, um it?"

"You'll learn."

"Learn what."

"Car 112, come in please, car 112, come in." The radios crackled on their shoulders. The rookie reached for his to respond.

"Yeah, car 112 here, dispatch. Go ahead."

"Backup is needed at 3880 N. Milwaukee Ave. They are requesting three units, are you able to assist?"

"Roger that. On our way."

The rookie looked over at Rob, his smile so big that his pearly whites showed in the passing street lights.

"Calm down, Rook. Just because we're going in as backup doesn't mean you'll get to see action."

"Isn't that what backup means? They're getting ready to do a bust and want backup units to follow them in. That's us, right?"

"We'll see."

Hotshots…

* * * *

Rob drove his squad car inconspicuously past the address he was given, and then radioed in his location. Detective Thomas was waiting for them, and filled them in on the situation.

It was a bust. A snitch had informed about a meth lab in a small inn, halfway down the street. It was on the third floor, in the mix with the other vagrants and deadbeats who pissed in the hallway. It was a seedy little place that rented more by the month than by the day, off the beaten path and away from incoming tourists; a perfect home for drug labs and prostitution dens.

Rob could smell the urine the moment he entered the lobby. Detective Thomas already had the clerk subdued behind the glass barrier, keeping him quiet as the men worked their way through the lobby. Rook covered his nose quickly, with an ugly look on his face from the stench.

"Damn, what's that smell?"

Rob looked at him coldy, shutting him up.

Detective Thomas pulled his muscular frame up from the front desk clerk, leaving him with his hands zip tied behind him. He pointed to Rook.

"Keep an eye on him; and don't let the clerk let anyone know we're on our way up."

Thomas looked at Rob and two other officers that lingered by the front door, and then nodded toward the stairwell. Thomas then pointed to one of the other police officers in the lobby and motioned to the elevators.

"Watch over these. Anyone comes down, you keep them here."

Thomas turned to the stairwell and Rob followed him as they worked their way up the trash covered stairs. The stench of urine grew, mixed with the rank odor of stale beer. Rob nudged an empty 40 ounce bottle out of his way, but froze when the bottle continued to roll. It bounced down a couple of steps before it shattered. Rob looked up to see the detective give him a disapproving look before continuing up the stairs.

They reached the third floor, and Thomas cautiously opened the door, scanning the hallway to ensure there was no one there. Rob could smell the stench from the lab all the way out to the stairwell. It was overwhelming, the odor of rotten eggs mixed with cat urine. Rob wanted to gag as it burned his nostrils and his eyes watered.

He let his fingers trace over the service pistol in his holster. He stroked the butt of it, and then flicked his wrist to snap the strap. His heart felt like it was going to explode right out of his chest. Early retirement sounded better and better. Ever since his partner had left, it had been weighing heavily on his mind. Situations like this only made it worse, and made it hard for him not to think about his wife and son. Even a month before that, he hadn't thought too much about it, but now, since his partner left him saddled with a desk job unless he took on someone new...

It wasn't his partner's fault. Still, it was easier to blame him than to think about what happened. No wife should ever have to watch her husband go through that. God, please let his wife never have to go through it. Let his wife never know the pain that he saw in that woman's eyes as he sat with her in the waiting room. Ed survived, but he would never be the man he was before. How could anyone?

"Get ready!" Detective Thomas said quietly. He signaled Rob to stay at the top of the stairwell, and then motioned the remaining two officers to follow him. They quickly eased their way through the doorway and quietly walked until they stopped mid-way down the hall to set up on either side of the door. Thomas looked back and forth between the two officers, and then he leaned in to the door, placing his ear against it.

"You crazy bitch, what the hell do you think you're doing? You nearly bit my dick off!" A man yelled from one of the rooms along the hall, closest to Rob. Everyone turned to look. Rob held his breath, waiting to see what would happen next. Slowly, he turned and looked back at Thomas, who then returned his attention to the door.

Thomas took a quick breath and then glanced over at Rob.

In the next instant, the right half of Thomas's face disappeared in a bloody mess, on the floor. The explosion of a shotgun echoed through the hall. It rang in Rob's ears, but didn't register as much as the sight of what was left of Thomas' face. Half of it, just gone, only lumps of flesh and bone mixing together as they fell to the floor.

Gun shots exploded into the hallway, covering the sound of Thomas's limp body slowly falling to the floor, on top of the remains of his face.

Rob scanned the hallway, looking to see where the shots had come from. There was a door open at the far end of the corridor. It was open just a couple of inches, with only darkness beyond. In those few inches, Rob could barely make out what looked to be the muzzle of a revolver, aiming to fire again. Rob raised his gun and aimed just a hair above the muzzle, figuring that whoever was behind that gun, his head wouldn't be too much higher. He had the space between the door and the doorframe in his sights, and he slowly began to squeeze the trigger. He didn't get a shot off before a flash came from the doorway. One of the two officers fell.

Rob looked up quickly, in shock. The officer had been nearly directly in his line of sight to the door. As far as Rob knew, he could be next. He brought his revolver up again, and took a long deep breath. He held it, steadying himself, as he slowly pulled the trigger. In his entire career, for as many times he had pulled his revolver, he had never once fired it off the range. He watched as the hammer came slowly back.

He never heard the footsteps running up the stairs behind him.

"Police! Put down the gun and step out into the hallway!" Rob yelled, still trying to get up the nerve to finish squeezing the trigger.

A heavy force slammed into Rob, sending his pistol flying, and Rob reaching to recover his balance before sprawling on the floor. In his younger, thinner days, he would have shifted his weight and rolled to the right. However, his body wasn't as limber as it once was, and instead he pulled his weight back, using his hands to reach out, so that instead of sprawling forward, he was able to stand into a run. He quickly dashed to the wall, taking himself out of the line of fire of the shooter.

He worked his way back to the corner, still keeping out of sight of whoever had slammed into him. His breath was burning in his lungs.

He didn't realize that he'd been holding it, and slowly, quietly, he let it out.

No sound came from the stairwell. He listened, but couldn't hear anyone else in or around the hallway. The couple that had been screaming before had gone quiet.

Rob looked over at the two officers lying on the linoleum. The third was on the floor, writhing in pain. He must have been shot as Rob fell, since he hadn't seen it happen. However, at least he was still alive.

Rob saw his gun; it had fallen to the center of the hallway. If he went for it, he would be in the open, easy to take out by either gunman, the one from the room at the end of the hall, or the assailant waiting in the stairwell. He was trapped.

The officer on the floor coughed suddenly, drawing Rob's attention. Smoke had started coming from under the door of the supposed meth lab. There was a crash from inside the room, and the sound of glass shattering on the floor. Someone was cleaning up the evidence, but from the smoke, Rob knew they'd started a fire.

The smoke was spilling out into the hallway, making the little available light from the street, just a grayish fog.

"Shit!" someone said from the stairwell. If Rob had to guess, he would say it was he was African American. He had a heavy street accent and his voice was a deep bass. Rob doubted it was someone he would want to go up against. He wasn't a small man, and he was healthy enough, going to the gym three times a week, but the man around the corner didn't sound like someone Rob wanted to tangle with. He'd already nearly taken him out once; he didn't want to give him another chance.

He heard a heavy thump in the stairwell. It sounded like the man had taken a step down the stairs. Rob waited, and sure enough, he heard another footstep, shortly followed by another. The man had walked back down the stairs. Rob figured he probably didn't want to have to deal with the fire coming from the room, or the firemen and law enforcement officers that would soon be there in much greater numbers.

Rob turned to look back at the other end of the hallway. He could barely see it through the smoke, but he still worked his way along the wall, trying to be silent as he came to the door. He took a quiet deep breath, fighting to breathe despite the smoke. He closed his eyes, and did a mental 1-2-3 count. Then he turned and put his shoulder into the door with as much force as he could muster, hoping to knock out anyone hiding on the other side.

The door slammed open with no resistance, smashing into the wall. The room was empty and the window was open. He could hear footsteps as they rushed down the metal fire escape.

Rob briefly thanked the Lord as he turned back around. He could see from there that the stairwell was clear as well.

"Dispatch, we have three officers down, two probable DOAs. Send one ambulance and a fire team." Rob said into his radio. The smoke rushed past him, filling the open room.

Something smashed against the other side of the door to the meth lab. It was followed quickly by pounding. Inside, people were slamming their fists against the door, trying to escape. He could see the fire begin to lick out from under the door and guessed that the locks were too hot for them to turn.

"Stand back from the door!" Rob yelled, hoping that he didn't deter them from working with him to get them out. He hurried from the empty room to the meth lab door. "This is the police, I'm going to try and break it down."

The air was disappearing as smoke billowed out in a heavy cloud. Rob looked at the door, sizing it up. It looked pretty solid. Amazing, considering how sleazy a hotel it was, he thought. He took a deep breath, and the smoke filled his lungs, burning like hidden flames. It sent him into a spasm of coughing.

He cleared his eyes and bent over, forcing air into his lungs. The hallway wasn't quite full of smoke yet, so he could still find breathable air if he stayed low. He took in a couple of good sized breaths. Then before he could stop himself, he ran to the door, his shoulder lowered, to hit the door midway. He figured the lock should give, hopefully before his shoulder did.

Just before he hit, he imagined he saw his wife and his son. They stood at the end of the hallway. They were dressed in black, his wife holding his son close, as they both stood crying.

Damn, he hoped he didn't just make her a widow.

* * * *

Smoke smothered him. It was everywhere, burning his lungs and pulling the moisture from his eyes. It hurt to keep them open, but burned more when he closed them. The smoke swirled around him as if he was walking in the clouds. His head became heavy and he could feel himself wobble as he walked. He thought he was going to pass out, but the sensation of a million hot needles piercing his skin all over kept him awake.

And then there were the screams. They were filled with such agony. There was no way someone could make a sound like that; no way was it made by a human voice.

They came from all around him, but he couldn't see through the dense smoke. He didn't just hear them; he could feel them. Their screams forced their way into his head, vibrated off of his optic nerves and danced on his inner ear drums before finally settling at the base of his skull. They sent sparks of pain shooting to all his nerve endings.

He didn't want to hold his head up anymore. He wanted it to let it fall to the side and make him fall. The floor looked so comforting, as it lay before him, burning and peeling away.

The shrieks faded as the smoke circled around him, and the fire slipped away into nothing. The heat from the fire disappeared, and was replaced with an icy chill running down his spine.

Shapes began to appear in the smoke. Bodies took form around him, hidden in the darkness, as the light from the room faded.

The shapes moved, slowly, as if they waded in water. They came to him, surrounding him in a tightening circle. Just beyond them, everything was dark; the walls that once made up the room were gone.

Rob looked around, watching as the forms approached. He spun around as they grew nearer.

"Stay away!"

He didn't know why, but he was suddenly afraid of them. He'd burst into the room to save them, but something had changed. It didn't feel like the same room anymore and these didn't feel like the same people.

Rob raised his gun and started swinging it around in different directions.

The screams started again, growing even louder than before, ringing in his ears. It felt like they were trying to tear every cell in his body apart. Pain was everywhere. Every part of him just wanted to get away.

He dropped his gun to grab his head. He doubled over and it felt like his insides were being ripped out.

He screamed, "Stop it! Just stop it!"

The shapes reached out to him.

Their hands came through the darkness, getting close enough to pull at his clothes. The screams grew louder and louder. Blood began to flow from cracks forming in his skin. He began to tear apart on the outside.

Somewhere in the darkness, he could feel that something was coming for him. It was there in the darkness, behind the shapes, and patiently waiting. But waiting for him to do what?

* * * *

Rob still felt the chill in his spine when his eyes burst open and the screams faded back into the nightmare. His sheets were soaked with sweat, but the room still felt cold. The sweat had nothing to do with being cold. He could feel a chill on his back, and confused for a moment, he looked down and saw the open backed gown he was wearing. A hospital gown; he was in a hospital bed, the room very dark around him.

Ah, yes, his hospital room, it came back to him. He guessed that it was probably around two or three in the morning. He didn't know for sure, nor did it really matter. It was just good to be out of the nightmare. To get away from the screams that had kept him awake for the last two months, laying there. The screams that he heard every night, he knew who they were. He never saw their faces, but he always knew. They were the ones he tried to save, the ones on the other side of the door that he'd tried to break down. They died there while he listened to their screams.

Another shiver ran down his spine, as though someone walked over his grave.

He adjusted himself in bed, trying to find more warmth. Damn. Why were hospitals always so damned cold? And all they would give him were those thin little sheets that they called blankets. Whoever said doctors weren't all sadists was someone who'd never been to one.

"Ready for the big day?"

Rob looked over at the other bed occupying the room. An old man, Tom Womanski, lay there looking over at Rob. Tom looked like he was more machine than a man as he had so many different tubes and devices hooked up to him. Rob knew that some of it was life support, but he had no clue what the other machines were doing. When Tom spoke, it sounded more like a cough talking with a heavy Chicago accent than a person.

"Get back to sleep ol' man" Rob said, mocking. Tom and he had been trading playful jabs since Tom had his heart attack three days ago. Out of all the roommates Rob had had in his long stay, Tom was by far his favorite. He was the only one who could keep up with Rob's sarcastic wit. Too many of the others were far too into their own problems to listen to Rob and his. It made it easy to talk to the old man, and they traded insults back and forth like a couple of friendly punching bags.

They took each other's barbs well, but damn it made it hard when he was such a light sleeper. Every time Rob woke up in the middle of the night, Tom was always already awake and there to talk to. It made Rob wonder just how loud his nightmares were becoming.

"You get ... good night... sleep first."

Rob looked over at him. He could see that there was more that Tom wanted to say, but he went into a coughing spasm, sending the machines in a tizzy as they tried to calm his lungs.

"Hell ol' man. Spit it out."

Tom took a deep breath, finally getting in a lung full of air. The machines whizzed behind him, steadying to their rhythmic sounds.

"Nightmare?"

"No." Rob smiled at the old man. Tom was right, but Rob wanted to let the man think maybe that just maybe Rob could enjoy his last night there. That for one night Rob would be able to sleep in peace. He would be released in the morning, so it was his big day. Maybe Tom would believe it was just nerves.

"Yer sheet's wet. Nightmare or not. What the hell is that anyway?"

"Don't make fun."

Rob smiled.

"I'll miss you old man. You get better."

"You too. Take care of that wife and son of yours."

"That I will." That he would. They'd already bought themselves a new house, and their old one was up for sale. Once he was picked up from the hospital, it was going to be off to their new home, far away from this hateful city. It was time for a better life for his wife and son. It was time for a safer life for them.

Feeling unsafe and sleepless nights were becoming a way of life for Rob. In fact sleepless nights had become too common since he had nearly blown himself up. They left him with a lot of time alone with his thoughts. Before Tom, who would wake up with him, he'd lie awake for half the night with no one to talk to.

Of course there had been the television. Old black and whites or racy movies to occupy him somewhat; but that grew old. He always knew when morning came with the morning news starting at four, and that was never inspiring. He stopped watching the television all together days before he and his wife made the decision to leave the city.

A little girl, just a couple of years younger than his son Jake, had been caught in the cross fire of a gang shooting. She went to Jake's school, and it had happened less than a block away from their home.

When Rob had moved there, when he had bought that house, it had been a good school, in a good area. It still was, but the gangs, were moving north, venturing further into the north side. Rob couldn't be sure why, but he knew it was making the streets more and more dangerous for his own family.

Rob had kept the television off since the story had broken, but that didn't stop him from thinking about it. It was even worse for his wife, Robyn as she'd had to see it first-hand. He could see it in her face when she visited. She didn't know that Rob had seen the story on the news, and he didn't tell her that he had. She was trying to hide her worries from him, not wanting him to get worked up over it while he lay there in a hospital bed, not able to do anything about it.

When Rob finally mentioned the possibility of them moving out of the city, she agreed without hesitation. At the time it was just a hair brained idea with no thought behind it. Sure, it was a bad time to sell the house, but for safety's sake, she also wanted out. She did some research and within days she found a house in a town that was also looking to bring on an additional deputy. Plus, it was a small town like she'd grown up in. Rob had always lived in Chicago, but for his wife, it would be like moving back home. All he had to do was say "yes."

He couldn't wait to get away.

So now he had a new job waiting for him, and he was itching to step into the shoes of a small town deputy. It would give him time to separate fact from television fiction and see how small town life really was.

Tom loved to make fun of the whole situation. He loved the idea and wanted to see Rob try to handle the change from the big city to small town life. He thought it was a real treat, a rip-roaring laugh. Rob however, knew deep down that the old man felt it was a great idea.

"You have fun out in Mayberry, be the next Deputy Fife."

"Yeah, well you stay and don't get shot here in the Windy City."

"Yeah, you don't get in no more fires either."

"Ha, I won't. I'll be staying away from burning buildings from now on. Couple months in the hospital will teach any man that lesson."

"Don't let the nightmares bother you. You did the best you can. Silence their screams and get some sleep."

"You do the same."

Rob turned away from Tom and rested his head on his pillow. He didn't want to close his eyes and let the nightmares back in, but he didn't want to continue to lie there, worrying. Anything could still happen; they weren't out yet. In the morning, his wife would arrive with their son and then they would be off to their new life.

"Dear Lord, let it be a better and safer one than this," Rob whispered to himself under his breath. He didn't want Tom to hear. Tom's breathing had gone back to the quiet rhythm of sleep. It never did take him long. Rob, on the other hand was another matter.

He lay there silently, knowing it would be at least another half hour of thinking before sleep would finally overtake him.

Robyn woke suddenly and looked over at the clock on the night stand. In the dark room, the digital readout was the only light. It was just past two a.m.

She had been dreaming heavily, but had heard something that woke her. She looked around the room, trying to pinpoint the noise that pulled her out of sleep. The room was still and quiet.

She held her breath, and waited, feeling someone was there, hiding in the shadows. She couldn't see anyone, but the hair on the back of her neck still stood up, and a chilled breeze drifted through the room. She looked at the window; it was still closed and locked tight, and she wondered where the draft had come from. The house was old, but she didn't recall it being so drafty. In fact, one of the selling points had been how air tight and insulated it had always been.

A slight wind blew outside causing a branch to brush against the window. There were people talking down on the street. Two in the morning, and the street corner hoodlums were still running their mouths. New York was supposed to be the city that never slept. People in the windy city, they slept, but not often. It seemed no matter what time she woke up, there was some activity outside.

She had been waking up in the middle of the night a lot more often since Rob had been in the hospital. However, this time was different; this time her sheets weren't covered in sweat from some nightmare.

Robyn looked over her shoulder to see Jake sleeping comfortably in the bed behind her. He was adorable, sleeping without anything to worry about. In the morning, Rob would be released from the hospital, and off they would drive to their new home. Most of the more crucial belongings were already packed and loaded in the moving van parked outside in the alley. It would be blocking the alley all night, but that was one of the benefits of her husband being a cop. Other officers already knew about the van and had assured her that it wouldn't be ticketed. Robyn had been so grateful that many of Rob's friends from the force came and helped her load the truck when they'd heard of the move.

Since Rob had been in the hospital, his police family had all been very supportive. Most of the officers that knew Rob spent their off shifts at the hospital. Many of the wives spent their time consoling Robyn and Jake, and bringing flowers and get-well cards. Everyone meant well. However, the more support they offered, the more it made Robyn want to get away. It was all, always going to be a reminder of how she nearly lost him, and if he returned to work there, she could still lose him.

She didn't like pulling Jake from his school though. They were taking him away from all of his friends. Still, he had been in six fights after school this year alone. Most of them after his dad had been hurt. Jake had his father's temper, but had yet to learn his father's control. Maybe the change of pace to a smaller town would help him calm down.

There it was again, that sound. She had heard it in her sleep and wasn't sure if she'd been imagining it. It sounded like it was coming from downstairs, like something had been knocked over, and then glass rattling.

Robyn looked over at the display on the wall. The house alarm still showed green. The house should be secure and safe, but there it was again. Something else was knocked over, this time she could hear glass breaking.

She reached over to the night stand to grab the phone off its charger, but it wasn't there. She propped herself up and looked again, confirming that the phone was missing.

"Damn!" she whispered to herself. It was probably down in the kitchen. She had been talking to her mother about the big move earlier and hadn't brought the phone back up with her before bed.

She'd have to sneak herself into the kitchen to call 911. It was either that or chance making it to the other phone in the living room.

She didn't like either option, but sitting around in her room waiting for whoever was downstairs to come upstairs... She refused to finish the thought.

What did she have?

She scanned the room. Everything other than the mattress they slept on and the clock was all packed and in the living room downstairs. The room was empty. She had no weapons, nothing to defend herself.

She had to do it. She had to sneak down to the kitchen, it was her only option.

Robyn stood quietly and made her way to the door on her toes, avoiding the boards she knew would creak in the silence. She stood at the door, realizing that she had been holding her breath, and as she slowly opened the door, quietly released it.

She looked into the hall and looked for any shadows or any sign that anyone was already upstairs or working their way up.

There was nothing; the house had fallen silent.

She stepped into the hallway, taking one last look at Jake before easing the door shut behind her. She locked it to make sure that he stayed safe. She couldn't bear the thought of anything happening to him.

Another piece of glass broke on the floor downstairs.

Robyn stopped on the staircase, listening for footsteps, for anyone moving around below. Nothing. She stood there for what seemed an eternity, and then bent down to see if she could see anything in the living room at the bottom of the stairs. She couldn't see any movement.

She continued gradually down the stairs, and silently reached the bottom. She paused there, still listening, but the only thing she could hear was her own strained breathing.

She decided to take a chance and peek into the living room. She stayed low and close to the wall, trying to remain hidden. Most of the room was packed away in boxes. Only a few knickknacks were left here and there around the room, as well as the array of photos over the fire place. They'd run out of boxes, so Terry, one of Rob's closest friends, was supposed to bring a box for the last of it when he came by in the morning.

Above the pictures was a large mirror that had been her grandmother's and had been left to her. It was a beautiful mirror with gilt framing. It had a very odd design that almost all of their house guests commented on. The mirror always became a topic of conversation at some point when they entertained, as it always looked out of place in their North Chicago home. It looked more like it belonged on some southern plantation or in a mansion. It should be hanging somewhere more fitting for something so beautiful and ornamental.

Her attention lingered on the mirror, before turning to the pictures they kept below it. They had all been there, and standing in place when she had gone to bed, but now three of them had been knocked over, and two of them were missing. There were only two pictures still standing.

They were all her favorite pictures of her and Rob with Jake. Rob's favorite picture still stood there, the picture they'd taken when she was five months pregnant with Jake. She had always begged Rob to let her throw it out, but he wouldn't stand for it. They were both so happy and excited with the baby on the way.

She knew that Rob had a slight superstitious streak to him, though he would never admit to it. She believed that part of the reason that he wouldn't throw away the picture was he was afraid something would happen to Jake, as it was a picture of her when Jake was inside of her. Rob o wouldn't allow her to throw away any of his pictures, for that matter.

As for that particular picture itself, it was probably Rob's favorite because she was so fat and he could poke fun at her for it. Not harshly, but in that fun way that he did sometimes with his offbeat humor and his charming smile.

One of the remaining two pictures shook and then tipped forward, falling to the floor as though someone had thrown it. She could hear it land and knew that the glass in the frame had shattered.

Robyn stepped into the living room and hurried past the rows of boxes to where the picture had just fallen from the mantle. The three pictures lay on the floor, their frames broken, the glass in pieces scattered across the hardwood. She moved carefully, to avoid stepping on any of the shards in her bare feet.

Robyn looked around the room. She was alone. The windows were closed; so no breeze could blow through. It was dark, and silent, yet she had a sudden chill run down her spine again, and felt cold air on her neck. She was alone, but felt as though someone was watching her. She could feel it, a presence, and could see her own breath as she exhaled.

She'd felt this once before, she knew it, but she didn't remember where. It was an odd sensation, and she couldn't help it. Someone was there, hiding in the darkness. It wasn't so much a "who", but a "what", and it frightened her. Something was in her house, and she couldn't see it. It was watching her, she could feel it.

The last photo behind her on the mantle shook violently. She turned to look at it just in time to see it launch off of the mantle and land farthest away of any of the pictures. This one had made it to the other side of the room before it smashed into the wall. The frame exploded and glass was thrown everywhere.

Out of the corner of her eye, a shape moved in the mirror. She turned to look at it and then turned back to look at the rest of the room. There was nothing there.

It was gone.

CHAPTER 2

"Are you ready?" Josh said. He was nervous; he didn't like being out there even if it was him who brought the others.

"Sure." Aaron said. He was looking at the large house, trying to act tough, and not let Josh know just how scared he was. The Cullin's house loomed over them like a large beast getting ready to eat its prey. Aaron didn't like standing next to it.

The house was abandoned and stood in the woods on the outskirts of town. Aaron didn't know how long it had been empty, but he'd heard the stories about it his whole life. It was known as the Dark Place, and the woods, well, no one ever ventured into them after sunset. There had always been plenty of ghost stories surrounding both the house and the surrounding woods.

Aaron's grandmother had especially told him to stay away. She would say that there had been a great evil there once, and that the ground had turned bad. Aaron always thought she was just being spooky and trying to scare him. Now he understood. As soon as he stepped into the woods, it had felt like the warmth of the sun had been sucked away, leaving only the chill of the shadows.

He didn't like it; he had the feeling that they were being watched. The little hairs on the back of his neck stood and his skin felt cold. It was nearly ninety degrees in the shade, and he had to fight to keep from shivering.

"So you have to go through the house, up the stairs and into the master bedroom. You can stand there," Josh was saying. Aaron hadn't been paying attention to him, but he looked up where Josh pointed. In the upper right corner of the house there was a window. Though most of the windows in the house were broken, that one looked untouched.

Aaron thought that he could see someone standing there, looking at them, someone standing back in the room so that Aaron could only see a shadow, but then the form moved, and it was gone.

Aaron turned to look at Josh who was standing there with a big grin.

"So, do you think you're man enough to join the Monsters Club?" Josh asked.

Aaron looked back at the house, feeling a lump of fear build in the pit of his stomach. He was working hard to hide it, and quickly looked back at Josh, forcing a smile of his own.

"Sure thing. Easy."

"Well, okay tough guy. You get to that window and I'll recommend you for the club."

* * * *

Aaron couldn't believe he was doing it, as he stood just inside the doorway of the large house. Josh, of course, stayed outside. He knew that chicken wouldn't be coming in with him. Aaron doubted if any other members had done this either. No, they wanted Aaron to do it, because Aaron wanted in and wasn't part of their clique.

He doubted that they were even fans of horror movies. They would probably all crap their pants if they watched a true horror film.

The Monster Club was one that Josh had put together. They met every week at his house, in the home theater of his basement and they watched what they called, "scary movies." Aaron had been watching horror films for as long as he could remember; his mother was a huge horror buff. For Aaron's ninth birthday, his mother had gotten him a large Freddy Krueger talking doll that he kept in its box in his room. Josh on the other hand, was always talking about the new and latest horror films, the remakes that littered the video store shelves.

Aaron wondered what they would ever do if they actually watched something like "Aliens" or "The Exorcist;" something that would truly scare the pants off them and give them nightmares.

Josh and all his friends were jocks; he couldn't see them actually having the intelligence to enjoy a classic horror film without heckling as they watched. Still, Aaron wanted to find out for sure, and joining the club couldn't hurt. Maybe they would turn out to be decent, and if they accepted Aaron, maybe he wouldn't be looked at as the weird kid in town.

And watching horror films every week was never a bad thing.

Aaron wanted to hurry up the stairs and make it to the master bedroom as quickly as possible. Just get in and get out, then Josh would be forced to let him in the club since he'd have fulfilled all the requirements they'd thrown at him.

Aaron took a brief look around as he neared the stairs. The house was dim, and little sunlight filtered in through the windows. The tree limbs outside shook in the wind. Their shadows looked like giant arms reaching in from outside to grab him. The main source of light came through the living room just to the left of the front hallway. Aaron stopped with his foot on the first of the stairs to look into the room. He thought he had seen something moving out of the corner of his eye. Something had shifted in the shadows.

Aaron held his breath and listened. He could almost hear the dust settling from the slight breeze that had come through the door when he walked in. It unnerved him how still and silent the house was. In the heavy air, he had a strong feeling that something wasn't right. There was evil in the house, and he was walking right into it.

Maybe his mother was right; maybe he did watch too many horror films.

Aaron stepped away from the stairs and slowly crept into the living room. It was in disorder from thirty years of neglect and abuse. The windows were smashed, by rocks which lay there on the floor around the room; rocks thrown by kids throughout the years, many of them too afraid to do more. Aaron figured that most of the rocks were probably from years ago, as for most people in town the house was a distant and long forgotten memory. The couch was torn, and what was once it's insides, was matted and dirty and spread throughout the room, much of it probably carried off by birds and other creatures throughout the years.

Aaron did another scan of the room, a thought occurring to him. It did look like there was a lot of damage done by animals, but nothing else. No animal remains, or waste, no bird nests, no bat droppings below the chimney, there was nothing other than the destruction that would ever have made Aaron believe that they'd been there.

He walked to the broken window and looked outside. Something wasn't right, and he couldn't place what it was.

"Wrong window, Fudgeknocker!" Josh yelled from where he stood a few yards away. Aaron looked at him, but then turned to look at the woods.

The woods were quiet, just like the house. There was nothing moving, no animals skittering about, no insects buzzing, no birds chirping, everything was as silent as if they were in a bubble, and the rest of the world outside.

Aaron backed away from the window. All he had to do was get up the stairs to the bedroom, look down at Josh and wave. Then they could hurry up and get out of there. Just run up the stairs and be done with it. It would take less than a minute; all he had to do was run. Just run.

Aaron glanced quickly at the portrait that hung over the large fireplace. He guessed it was of the family that used to live there. Most of the portrait was badly damaged: the son and the wife were cut up and their faces had become shredded canvas. However, the face of the father, who stood behind them, wasn't touched. He stood there, smiling grimly behind them, his eyes direct and stern. Aaron could see that though the man smiled, it was strained and didn't seem natural.

He felt his skin grow cold, and the man seemed to look directly at him, as though somehow he had changed position to do so.

Aaron crossed the room slowly, keeping his back to the picture. He couldn't shake it. The feeling that the picture itself was watching him, those eyes, looking right at him, was something that while ridiculous, chilled him to his bones. It was crazy and he knew it, but he still couldn't shake the feeling.

He nearly tripped over the stair risers when he backed into the hallway. He had to reach out quickly to keep himself from falling backward into the wall. And it was a good thing he did. The wall was crumbling away, falling in pieces and in on itself, leaving large holes.

He was sure that if he reached out and put any weight against it, he would fall right through.

Aaron stepped onto the first step and listened to the loud creak as he slowly eased his weight onto his foot. Looking again at the walls, he hoped that the stairs were sturdier. He didn't want to have to explain how he fell through the stairs in a house no one was allowed in, either to Renner, the local cop, or his parents. His being there wouldn't sit well with either one.

Besides, who knew how far he would fall. It looked like the stairs going down to the basement ran under the stairway going up to the second floor. He could see the door beside the stairs along the hallway, and guessed that must be where it went, into the darkness and whatever had been trapped down there over the years. If he were to fall through, he'd land on the basement stairs and then continue down to whatever kind of floor laid beneath. Aaron took another slow cautious step, then another. With each step, he held his breath briefly and eased onto the tread, making sure that his foot didn't continue through the hardwood into the abyss below. The wood sagged as he stepped on it, and he could feel it struggling not to give under his weight.

So what if he didn't do this challenge. So what if he didn't go up to the master bedroom and wave to Josh, showing him that he made it. Aaron could still go back home, watch horror movies in his own living room, and never have to think about it. He didn't need some stupid little monster club to enjoy movies with. He didn't need to go over to Josh's house every week just to watch a horror film in his large home theater basement. He didn't need that.

But he wanted it.

Besides, if he were to back out now, he'd have to face them, all of them, when school started back up in August. Sure, they had a couple months to forget about it, but he doubted they would. They already made fun of him for how strange he looked to them, the way he always dressed in black shirts and pants. He didn't need to add anything else to the list.

Aaron swallowed the lump trying to form in his throat.

"You can do this," he said to himself as he took another step. He was nearly halfway up the stairs, and he could feel the steps getting sturdier. He moved more quickly, hurrying the rest of the way up the stairs until he made it to the second floor hallway, and then paused at the top to catch his breath. His lungs burned a little; he'd been concentrating on controlling his breathing even though his heart had been pounding, like it was trying to escape his chest.

He let his heartbeat ease, waited for it to slow and then looked down the hallway to the room at the end.

There it was. All he had to do was walk quickly down the hallway, rush to the window and wave his hand. Then he could hurry back down the steps and run out the door. He would be done. It would over, and he would never have to worry about this house ever again, never have to come near it. He could go home to his own house and play some X-box. Kill a few zombies and forget that he had ever been there.

Aaron began walking along the hallway, each creak in the floor making him step a little faster. He was almost there. He could almost feel the relief of being done and out of there. He was only a couple feet from the door, so he knew all he had to do was open it and rush to the window.

The master bedroom door opened suddenly. No one was there, he was still all alone, but he watched as it suddenly opened inward. The 'whooshing' sound it made was loud in the quiet of the house.

It made him stop. Fear was working its way into him. He'd been afraid to do this, yes, but before, he'd felt, no he knew that his fears were based on nothing. It had always been all his imagination. But now, it was different; doors were opening by themselves.

Aaron backed away from the door, not sure if he wanted to continue. Something opened that door. It wasn't wind. There was no breeze anywhere throughout the whole house. Even though the windows on the bottom were broken, Aaron hadn't felt any breeze his whole time in the house. Strangely, he'd felt the opposite. The air was thick and stuffy as though the house were locked up tight.

Aaron took another step back, and then thought again about what it would mean if he went downstairs. If he just walked up to Josh and told them about the door. Josh would never believe him and then he'd have to face the ridicule.

And that was exactly what he knew Josh wanted. He knew that Josh never wanted him in their club. Even if he did this, Josh would probably come up with some other test, and then another, and another, until finally Aaron did fail. They were never going to let Aaron in.

In fact, they would go so far as to set him up.

Aaron looked back at the door at the end of the hall. The sun shone brightly into the hallway now, the light coming from the bedroom. He tried to see if there was any sign of someone in the room, anything moving. It was hard to tell, but he thought he could see feet moving under the door.

It was probably Eric. Must have been him. Josh probably had his best friend Eric already there, trying to spook him. Aaron now stood up straight, frustrated that they would use some weak trick in an attempt at scaring him. He wasn't going to let them get it over on him.

Aaron stomped down the hallway. He wanted to make his presence known. He wanted them to know that they were not going to scare him. They'd failed, and he wasn't going to fall for some damn game they thought they could play on him.

He rushed into the room turning quickly to look behind the door, ready to yell at Eric. His arm rose to point his finger at him and let him know what he thought about their stupid game and how petty they were. He didn't scare that easy.

He stopped, frozen, when he realized there was no one there. The room was empty.

He spun around, searching the room. It was bright, the sunlight coming in through the unfiltered windows; curtains long faded from sunlight and hanging to the side. Dust flowed and danced around the room. The bed, unmade, sat to the side of the room, and next to it, Aaron could see a large dark brown spot that looked like something had soaked into the carpeting.

Aaron looked back at the door and the large dresser topped with a large make-up mirror above it. It was a beautiful dresser and mirror combo, something Aaron's mother would have loved to have. The white dresser, looking only slightly aged with time, and was faded in areas where the sun hit it every day. The mirror on top was ornamented with gold along its border with a fancy design that Aaron had seen before. He doubted that it was cheap.

He looked to the floor beside the dresser and saw another dark spot similar to what he'd seen next to the bed.

He looked back and forth between the two spots, suddenly realizing what they were. He stepped away from the dresser mirror, not wanting to get any closer to the larger of the two dried blood.

He looked up at his reflection, scared. He was there, standing where two people had died, violently. He felt a rush of nausea working its way up. He thought he was going to be sick, but he wasn't about to let himself throw up in the room. He needed to get out of there.

Aaron went to the window and looked down. Josh was there, playing with a stick, smashing it against a tree. Aaron knocked on the glass below and saw Josh drop the stick quickly and looked up the window. He looked disappointed.

"Good," Aaron thought as he backed away from the window. He had done it, and put that bully in his place. He felt good. He was excited. He wanted to get downstairs and start rubbing it in Josh's face.

He sure as hell better be in that club now.

Aaron started walking back toward the door when he saw something out of the corner of his eye. He turned toward the mirror. He could have sworn he'd seen something moving in the background.

* * * *

Josh couldn't believe it. The little psycho had done it. Why the hell did he ever have to give in to the little twerp? Eric told him he shouldn't. Actually Eric had been all gung ho for it, but had wanted it to be a trap where Eric would be hiding somewhere and scare Aaron.

Josh had opted out of that plan. He thought bringing him to the house would be enough. He didn't think the little nerd had enough courage to make it through.

It was an old house, abandoned for who knew how long. Josh didn't know too much about the house itself. He just knew that something had happened that made no one want to go there. Aaron had said some murders that happened there, but Josh didn't care one way or the other. Aaron knew the stories and believed them to be true, that was enough for Josh.

Josh looked up at the house. It was large, probably beautiful even, back when it was first built.

Aaron stepped back into the upstairs window. He stood there looking down at Josh.

"Come on! Get back down here! You did it, great job, now let's get home!" Josh yelled up at the window. He didn't like being out there in the woods. Too quiet.

Aaron stayed in the window, looking down at Josh. He had a peculiar look on his face, like he was watching him, but wasn't really seeing him.

Then Aaron smiled and he motioned for Josh to come.

"What the hell does he want?" Josh thought to himself as he threw down the stick he had been hitting the tree with and walked toward the front door of the house.

* * * *

The cool night air, a warm fire with fresh eggs cooking in the banjo, and a clear sky above where the stars shined brightly; what more could a hobo long on the rails ask for?

"It was a good day, oh Coolidge," he thought to himself, as he sat there looking up at the sky. It was a peaceful night and he had worked a good hard day, earning him forty dollars cash, of which he now had thirty-four left in his wallet. The other six dollars he had spent on his fine evening meal of bacon and eggs.

It had been a good day. Hell, he wished they could all always be that good.

"Shit, if life was always like that though, it would get boring," he said to himself as he stirred the eggs. Sometimes when he was all alone, it felt good to talk to himself, even if it was just to hear a voice. It broke the silence just enough to make it bearable.

The delicious smell drifted to his nose, and his stomach let out a long moan of anticipation. The smell brought back memories of being a kid, of what it was like to sit down as a family.

As the eggs finished cooking, he stirred them off onto his metal plate, and then quickly ripped open the package of bacon. The bacon started to sizzle as he carefully laid the strips into the pan, its aroma already replacing that of the eggs on his plate. The grease shot out, stinging his arms as he stirred and flipped. The larger pops, sending grease to his face stung, but he was fine with that. He knew it meant a warm meal.

He finished cooking up the bacon and worked it onto his plate. Then he sat back against a large rock and cocked his eyes to the sky. It was a beautiful night, and here he sat, somewhere in the depths of Arizona, or maybe it was New Mexico. From his point of view, a rider on the rails, they both seemed the same.

The only thing missing was the music. Damn, he missed the times he used to ride with Spider John. Boy, that man could play some blues. They would sit back and enjoy a good meal, and Spider John would pick up his guitar and play for what seemed like most the night.

Next time ol' Coolidge hooked up with Spider, he was sure as hell going to have to ride again with him for a spell. Get those songs of his back into Coolidge's head so that Coolidge could remember them again when he was alone.

There were a lot of hobo musicians out there. Sure, not as many as there were in that radio music most people listened to, but compared to how many hobos were out there, there sure were a lot of them that were musicians. Still, Spider was always Coolidge's favorite. Spider had a way of making the blues his own that would just sing to ol' Coolidge.

Maybe Coolidge would get lucky this year, and catch ol' Spider in Britt, come August. Coolidge had missed getting to Britt, to the Hobo Convention last year, but he sure planned on making it back there again.

Coolidge finished off the last of his bacon and eggs, and then cleaned his plate with the thermos of water that he kept in his backpack, making sure not to use too much so he would have some to drink later. He then washed off the banjo and after everything was dried he secured it back in his bag. He tidied up his garbage and put that away as well, with his bag.

Ah yes, the jungle, wherever he found a place to lay his head for the night and catch a good night's sleep. Sometimes it was in a shelter, sometimes near a train yard, since he'd be searching for his next rail. But then sometimes, like tonight, it would be out under the stars. Out in the great wide open desert, where there was nothing around but railroad tracks that often lay silent. It was a true test of living free, to be anywhere, just lying there, living how he chose to. There was truly nothing out there, good nor bad.

Coolidge grabbed his backpack and started to fluff it up as he shuffled away from the rock. Yeah, it would've been nice if Spider was there to play a tune. Still, he had a smile on his face as he laid his head back and closed his eyes. Come morning, there should be an 8 A.M. passing by on that stretch of rail, it would have to slow down to an easily catchable speed when it rounded the bend in the track.

It was his own private spot in the middle of nowhere, and every once and again, when the routes carried him through, he relished stopping off to enjoy it. To lie out and enjoy the silence and solitude, relishing being all by himself, without any sign of civilization for miles.

It was his private heaven.

Gravel shifted nearby as something in the darkness made its presence known.

Coolidge opened his eyes to look across the fire, staring into the open space of the desert. With the clear sky and with the moon and stars bright above, he could see through the vastness of the night to the cacti that lay deep into the desert. In the direction he'd heard the noise, there was nobody looking back, man or animal.

Still, he pulled himself up to rest on his elbows, and continued to look.

Out of the corner of his eye he saw it, something shifting at the edge of his vision, straight across the fire from him. He turned quickly to catch it, but it was gone again, lost in the darkness.

He scanned the desert, his eyes shifting back and forth, trying to find it. The hair on the back of his neck was standing straight, and a cold breeze moved across the desert. The desert gets cold at night, but this breeze was different than a desert wind. Something was carried on this wind, and the shiver it sent down Coolidge's spine shook his whole body. Something was coming for him; he could feel it.

The fire's flame changed color and no longer sent off the waves of warmth it had been earlier. It faded from a bright yellow, until slowly the color disappeared from it altogether, and it was a white flame, flickering toward the sky. The air turned stale and he no longer felt like he was out in the open desert, but instead trapped inside a room, with the smell of mold strong around him.

Coolidge stopped scanning the desert and turned to stare into the fire.

Sudden pains flashed through him making his vision just a white sheet of agony. He clenched his teeth and brought his fist to his temple, his head a burning inferno. His eyes teared up, and he could feel their coolness as they streaked down his face.

And then a figure appeared. At first Coolidge thought it was an illusion through the sheet of agony, but as the pain slowly faded, his vision returned. He could see a man sitting on the other side of the fire.

The man looked at him, his eyes entirely black, his skin old and wrinkled, and white across his visible veins and bones. He smiled at him, displaying stained yellow teeth and dark gums. Coolidge wasn't close enough to to tell for sure, but he thought the smell of mold drifted off the old suit that hung off him.

Strangely, the man looked somewhat familiar to him as he sat there, but Coolidge couldn't quite place him. It was there, just outside of his thoughts, like a word at the tip of the tongue. Something he wanted to pinpoint, a memory he wanted to place, but he just couldn't grasp it.

Coolidge stared into the man's eyes, not wanting to, but feeling there was nothing he could do to escape it. He tried, but somehow, his desire never made it to action. Something was keeping his mind separate from his body. He had to look, and only his own death could have made him look away.

"Damn Coolidge, my friend, don't' even think about that right now," he thought to himself, his eyes locked onto the dead man sitting across from him.

The flames leapt high, briefly blocking Coolidge from the man, but before he could even begin to hope that the man would be gone, the flame settled back down, allowing him to again see across the fire.

The man still sat there, his black eyes burning into Coolidge. Coolidge had never felt such a desire to run, to get away. He didn't know if the dead man was real or a dream, but Coolidge knew that he wanted to get to wherever his old his legs would carry him, to run down the railway to the nearest stop, nearly thirty some miles down the rails, and not look back for fear of what would be following him. He didn't want to know if death would still be there because in his mind, the man sitting across for him was death, and Coolidge knew it was coming for him.

He never ran, and the man continued to stare at him. His wide grin continued to grow, keeping pace with Coolidge's fear as it did.

The man moved closer, and Coolidge had the sudden thought that he was about to jump across the fire and grab him. That he would try and wrestle ol' Coolidge and drag him down into some depths Coolidge didn't want to think about.

"Get home," the man said his voice a raspy whisper barely heard on the night wind. Coolidge never even saw his lips move. It was more like the words came from the air around him.

Coolidge pulled himself away from the fire, leaning back against the large rock behind him.

The man was face to face with Coolidge faster than he could see him move. One second, the man was on the other side of the fire, the next; he was hovering just centimeters away from Coolidge's face. Coolidge could now clearly see the black eyes of the man. There were no whites around the irises; they were pure black, and they were fixed on Coolidge's. Their stare was unblinking. "Get home." The stench of the man's breath was foul as it filled Coolidge's lungs. It smelled of rotten garbage, made worse by a faint sweet smell of cinnamon. It turned Coolidge's stomach and he could feel the eggs and bacon threatening to come back up.

Coolidge closed his eyes and turned his face away, finally able to pull them away from the dead man.

"Please Lord! Please," Coolidge said under his breath. He had barely been able to spit out the words, hardly able to breathe in the bad air.

He felt a weight lifting around him, and the air started to clear. Coolidge opened his eyes to find the man was gone.

He let out a long sigh of relief. His chest ached, and his head was reeling from what had just happened. He sure as hell didn't want to be part of any more of that.

Coolidge quickly packed up his stuff, making sure to leave no mess before he started making his way over to the rail. The walk would be long, but his only other option was to just sit there all night, waiting for the morning train.

He could walk it, and hell, with death on his back; he figured the walk would be pretty damned quick.

* * * *

"So ya ready to head out to your new home buddy? Get their early enough, I might be able to get your bed together so you won't be sleeping in a sleeping bag tonight," Rob said to Jake as he eased himself into the passenger seat of the car.

He settled himself in, but damned if it didn't feel wrong, him sitting in the passenger seat. He was never one to ride in the passenger seat, even when he was on patrol. Most times it made him feel car sick, just the fact that he was not in control of the moving vehicle. So what if he border-lined on being a control freak? He knew that and he accepted it. Robyn still loved him, and thankfully, she put up with his crap and his stubbornness. When it came to him driving, she actually preferred it.

Rob looked over his shoulder, to see Jake in the backseat playing his Nintendo DS. Jake loved the thing, but Rob worried that getting it for him for last Christmas might have been a bad idea. Jake was never away from it, it was like an extension of his arm, and it made spending time with him difficult. All Jake wanted to do was to have his dad play it with him, but Rob would rather take him to the park and throw the ball around.

Rob smiled at him and then turned to look at his lovely wife, Robyn, as she lowered herself behind the wheel. She was a terrible driver, who was never comfortable with it. She was always nervous and would often beg Rob to take the wheel. He could tell that even though he was just getting out of the hospital and had undergone so much therapy, she still wanted him to drive. She wore a weak smile which she tried to hide behind, but Rob could see it in the apprehensive way she looked down at the ignition. He could almost hear her mentally cursing at the car, scared to actually start it.

"Do you want me to drive?"

"No, I'm fine. I just don't know how I'm going to drive both the moving van and the car though."

"I'll have to drive the truck."

"You know I can't drive through the city.

"Just get us home, I'll see about renting us a car trailer. We'll just attach the car to the moving truck." Rob laid his head back into the seat, trying to melt into it. He wished he could go home and lie down for a while, rest up a little before they drove for nearly three hours in traffic to their new house. Just getting through the paperwork and forms, and the walk from the hospital had exhausted him; the last thing he wanted to do was drive.

"Is everything loaded and ready to go when we get to the house?"

"Yeah, your ex-partner and a bunch of other cops came by and helped load everything in. All we have to do is grab and go."

He felt some relief with the thought that everything was already packed and ready to go. While he didn't relish the thought of the traffic, he did want to get to their new home. The pictures of the new place that Robyn had shown him on her cell phone looked great. She had done a walk through; sending him pictures room by room. It was a large, beautiful home, more than they would ever need. It was twice the size of where they'd lived, but was only a fraction of the price. There had to be some kind of a catch; either the roof was caving in or the foundation was falling apart. Something had to be wrong with it.

Yeah, this would be best for the both of them.

Sure it would...

"Hey Pickle, how about we swing by for KidsDonalds on the way home, get you a toy and a kids meal?"

Jake looked up from his game, his eyes sparkling with the thought of a kids meal and a toy.

"Can I get a double cheeseburger?"

"Sure can." Rob looked over to see Robyn giving him the evil eye, and knew that she didn't want to do any more driving than she had to.

"If you want me to drive hun, I can."

"I just don't think we should be wasting our money on fast food. Money is going to be tight until we get the house sold."

"Just drive us over to the McDonalds, and I'll drive to the house. I've had nothing to eat but that damned hospital food for I don't know how long. Not even the good crap that they serve in the cafeteria either, but that crap they bring to your room that even the mice won't touch. I need a Big Mac, some fries, and a Shake."

Robyn pulled the car into the parking lot and found the first space that she could to park.

"Thank you," Rob said as he pushed open his door and worked his way to a standing position. His body still ached, but at least he was up and moving.

"Yeah, KidsDonalds!"

"Yep, KidsDonalds," Robyn said, as she reached for her own door.

"Get some grub, and then get on the road, what do you say buddy?"

Rob pulled his seat forward, allowing Jake to work his way out of the back seat.

"Sounds good to me, as long as I get a toy."

Rob rifled his hand through Jake's hair, play fighting with him as Jake tried to get away. Rob pulled his hand back to see Jake looking up at him with a big smile.

"Yeah, you'll get a toy."

* * * *

"This it?" Rob asked, as he scanned the houses along the street, and slowed in front of the first one. It looked like the pictures he had seen. There were only four houses on the right side of the street, and they all looked nearly the same. Woods covered most of the left side, as well as beyond the end of the street. For the most part, the area was away from the rest of the town, away from everyone. Rob didn't think there was a way to get much farther away from the world, and wasn't quite sure yet if that was going to be a good thing.

"That's it."

Rob put the truck into park and leaned back in the seat, closing his eyes for a brief, restful second. With a long sigh, he turned and looked at his lovely wife, a large smile on his face.

"Well, let's go in and check 'er out."

Rob worked himself out of the seat, his body aching in protest from the long drive. His back was stiff and sore, and his legs were threatening to buckle under him. He knew there would have been no way that Robyn could have driven the moving truck all that way, and how he'd been able to do it while being on the painkillers was a mystery, even to him. But now they were standing in front of their new home.

They were far away from the sirens and the crime, and the late nights when he would leave her at home while he was on the job. There were many nights that he'd worry when he left, that he was going to get a call for his own home. The dreaded call of a break in, or shots fired, or any of the many calls he handled at other people's homes. He always worried that one day that shoe would be on his foot, and the evil that he protected the streets from would show up on his own doorstep.

Then there were the other worries. That something would happen to him, that every time he went out on patrol, he would make her a widow, make her struggle to survive on a cop's benefits.

Those worries, he hoped, were all be in the past.

He met up with Robyn and Jake around the front of the truck, and he put his arms around both of them and just stopped to look at their new house.

"Just wait until you see my room." Jake said, staring up at his dad.

"Yeah?" Rob looked over at Robyn, a questioning look on his face.

"Yeah, he says he's taking the master bedroom."

Rob burst out laughing as he released them and started walking to the front of the house.

"We'll see buddy."

Rob tried to walk quickly to the front of the house, but pain shot down his back, and his lower back was throbbing. It made him slow down, to walk with a limp favoring his left side. The smile he was trying to keep on his face became more strained.

"You okay?" Robyn asked as she caught up to him.

"Yeah, I'll be fine. I'll just need to get my back massager from the truck when we get in. You got the keys?"

Robyn reached into her bag and pulled out a large set of keys. She brought them up to the door and started working on the lock. Then the door was open, and they were taking their first steps into the new house.

Rob stopped in the front entryway and just looked around, amazed at how large it was. It was spacious, with a large closet directly to the right. There were two open doorways, one on each side, each leading into a large room. One was a living room, and the other a family room, Rob thought, as he scanned it, taking it all in. He looked past the stairs and down the hallway that lead k into what looked like the kitchen area. The whole house was bright with sunlight, and the kitchen actually seemed to glow with it.

Maybe with a kitchen like that, one of them might actually take up cooking. They could start to have home cooked meals.

"How much did we get this place for again?"

"Let's just say that when we get the other house sold, we'll have plenty of money in our savings, even after we pay off the doctor bills."

Rob cringed and looked at Robyn. Yeah, if their house sold. In a housing market that still wasn't looking its best. He knew they were going to lose nearly forty thousand on the house because of the decline in the market, and he worried about what else they might lose.

Jake was already halfway up the stairs, running at full steam.

"Come on, come on!"

Robyn followed, and she wasn't letting go of Rob's hand, pulling him over to the stairs. Breaking out of his trance, he flashed a weak smile at her and stomped behind, his footsteps heavy on the floor. He made it to the stairs and reached for the railing, glad for its sturdiness beneath his hand. He gave it a quick tug to test it, and then put his weight into it as he started working his way up the stairs. At this point he didn't trust anything.

"What time are the movers coming to unload the truck?" Rob asked, as he neared the top of the stairs and looked down the hallway. There were six doors, and he stopped momentarily, wondering where the hell they all went to. How big was this house? He sure as hell wanted to find out how much they were going to be paying for it.

The pain medication seemed to be fading fast, and he could feel a slight pain in his chest, making it hard for him to breathe. The pain in his lower back had gone from a throbbing pain to a shooting one, sending shockwaves through his nerve-endings.

"I found some local guys who work cheap. They were supposed to be keeping an eye out for when we got here, and they're going to help us unload the truck and get the furniture situated."

Robyn was entering one of the rooms at the end of the hall, and Rob walked slowly toward it. He took deep breaths to keep himself calm, but became a little light headed. The smell of paint fumes was heavy throughout the house, and he wanted to get to the first window as soon as possible and stick his head out for air. They needed to get the house opened up as soon as possible.

"Why not just use the guys who packed up the truck? Were they too expensive?"

"We didn't hire a moving company back in Chicago. It was actually most of your buddies from the force. They knew we couldn't afford anyone, so they all chipped in and helped out."

Rob stopped and looked hard at Robyn.

"Why didn't you tell me?" Rob said, frustrated that no one had bothered to mention it. They had all let him leave without giving them a proper thank you.

The men and women he had worked with, they were more than co-workers. They had become a part of his family. They were his extended family, his brothers and sisters. It had been hard for him to leave them. He'd just wanted out of the damned city, and even knowing he felt that way, they were still willing to help him out. He was going to have to make a lot of phone calls, and say a lot of 'Thank-yous', once they got the phone line put in.

Rob walked into the room, past Robyn, and went to the window. He quickly unlocked it and tried to push it open, struggling, but it was painted shut. He slammed his open palm against the frame, following the edge and trying to break up the paint. Little chips fell from the frame and with a loud creak it finally lifted. The room filled with fresh air, and Rob was quick to take a deep breath.

His head hurt at first, but the slight chill of the gentle breeze felt good in his lungs. Taking deep breaths, the fog lifted, leaving only a slight ache.

"You okay?"
"Yeah."

Rob leaned against the window and used it to help him stay upright. He was getting tired, and needed to find somewhere to sit.

"Where's Jake?" Rob looked around, wondering where their son decided to disappear to.

"He's probably out running around. I'm going down to the truck and keep an eye out for the movers."

Rob nodded, not having the strength to really do much more. He watched as she left the room, then he pushed off the wall to go back into the hallway. He checked each of the doors until he came to the one he was looking for. He went into the bathroom, playing with the switch to turn the light on, but nothing happened.

"Ugh," he let out a loud sigh of frustration and left the door open as he sat down. "Finally a place to sit," he thought to himself as he closed his eyes. Six months ago, he never would have thought that the little effort used to climb stairs would wear him out.

He hoped like hell the movers would get there soon, and that the first thing they took off the truck would be a chair for him to sit in. He didn't want to spend half the day sitting in the bathroom. Why the hell had they had to move right after he got out of the hospital, anyways?

"Because you knew if you stuck around the city at all, you would never be able to bring yourself to do it. You'd keep talking yourself out of it."

Yeah, that was true. He would have. He would have gotten back into his routine life, would have accepted that desk job after his workman's comp ended, and they never would have left.

But that's not what he wanted. It wasn't safe in the city, and all he wanted was Jake to be safe, and in a good school without it having to be a private one; a place where he could walk in and not have to go through metal detectors just to get to class.

Damn, he hoped this was going to work, and they would be able to afford this place.

"Hey, Dad!"

Jake was yelled to him from out in the hallway.

"In here bud."

"With the door open? Ugh, gross!"

Jake stepped into the doorway. Rob looked up, nearly laughing, knowing that Jake thought he was in there doing a number two. Instead, he'd catch his dad just sitting on the toilet.

"Oh. Hey, mom wanted me to tell you that the movers are here." Jake said. He stayed just outside the doorway, not looking into the quaint little bathroom.

"Ok. Tell her I'm on my way."

Jake took off running down the stairs as Rob reached out and used the counter top to get back to his feet.

He walked to the door, but out of the corner of his eye, just there at the edge, something moved. He turned suddenly to look, but the only things he could see were the mirror and his reflection, the rough face that needed a shave, and tired eyes that just wanted to close for a bit.

He turned to leave the room, this time ignoring the shifting in the mirror. It had been a long day; it was probably just his damn imagination. It was a new house, there were sure to be strange shifts of light and sound that he would have to get used to.

CHAPTER 3

Rob eased his way down the stairs and out the front door to find Robyn talking to three large guys near the back of the moving truck.

Jake was pleading with her. "Come on, can I please have my bike out of the truck now?" She, however, was caught up with talking, and not paying any attention. She turned in time to see Rob approaching. She smiled and nodded in his direction to introduce him.

"Hey Hun, This is Steve, Colt, and Jesse."

Rob walked up to them and reached out to shake hands. They each shook his with strong firm handshakes, their hands rough from hard work.

"Hey, thanks for helping us out."

"No problem," the bigger of the men said. Rob thought he was the one introduced as Steve.

"Yeah, they're going to help us get everything in. We just have to get them a couple of cases of Miller Lite and pay them fifty bucks."

"A piece?"

Jesse snorted and gave a small laugh, and Steve smiled.

"No, hell, we'll mainly due it for the beer."

"Ok, help me get my car off the trailer and I guess I'll be heading to the store." Rob turned to look down at Jake, who was still begging to get his bike off the truck. "You 'bout ready to run to the store, bud?"

Jake pushed out his lip and crossed his arms in a sure sign of protest, not wanting to do anything until his bike was out.

"Go on Pickle. Go with your dad, and I'll have them get your bike off the truck and ready for you when you get back."

"Ok."

Jake stomped to the car and climbed in while it was still on the trailer. Rob thought about yelling at him to get out until it was down, but Steve was already starting to ease the car along the ramp.

Rob walked around to the back of the truck as the car rolled down the ramp and onto the road. Jesse was behind the wheel and Steve and Colt pushed as it rolled down; making sure it didn't come down too fast. Rob looked over and saw that Robyn was still stood alongside the truck.

He walked toward her, and noticed someone coming down the middle of the street. It looked to be a young woman in a jogging outfit, but as soon as Rob saw her, his police senses kicked in. She looked like she had been attacked, not physically, as her clothes were all still intact, but the expression on her face, the dazed look, and the way she moved told him something was wrong. She was staggering and wobbling like she would collapse at any second.

"Hey hon, go get a glass of water, quick," Rob said as he walked past Robyn toward the girl.

"But all the cups are still packed."

"Then get one of the sodas out of the cab."

Rob rushed to the girl, moving as fast as he could. His muscles fought against him, and pain shot down his back into his legs.

When he reached her, the pain almost sent him to his knees. He reached, nearly falling against her, and needing her support just as much as she needed his. He put his arm around her and tried to push her up, but both ended by grabbing each other to keep each other up.

"Who are you?"

"Don't worry. I'm only trying to help. Now what happened?"

Her weight pressed down on him. His back screamed in protest as he fought against it to hold her up. He'd helped many victims in his time, and wanted first to get her somewhere where she could sit down. He scanned the area briefly and saw the best spot would be his neighbor's front porch. He hoped his new neighbor wouldn't mind the intrusion, but he didn't want to try and make her go the distance to his own porch.

Rob helped her over, and gently lowered her onto the steps. Robyn quickly came behind them with the soda. Rob turned, wincing from the pain in his back, and took the soda from her. He eased it down to the girl who slowly took it from him and then just sat there with it. The street was quiet; it seemed like the only sound was the fizz coming from the freshly opened can.

"Drink a little."

"Thanks. I was just running and started to feel faint."

"Are you sure? You look like you've been attacked."

"No, I'm fine."

"You probably dehydrated yourself. I wish we had some water with us, but most everything is still packed up." Robyn said from over Rob's shoulder.

The woman may have been telling the truth, but Rob wasn't so sure. He had seen many attacks, and often the victim just wandered aimlessly afterwards. They would be in such a state of shock, they wouldn't even realize at first what had happened.

"Thanks, but I'll be fine now."

The girl slowly tried to stand. Her knees shook, and Rob could tell that she was about to fall back. He quickly reached out and she grabbed his hand to steady herself, flashing him a weak smile as she recovered. Rob then felt her grip loosen on his arm, and he pulled himself back so she could get some air without him hovering over her.

Rob took a quick look down the street in the direction of the woods. They seemed to loom there, dark and hidden on the outskirts of town. Anyone could have been hiding in there, and could have attacked without anyone else even hearing it. The house closest to the woods appeared dark and abandoned, so there would be no one who'd hear.

"Thank you, again, for helping me, but I'm fine now. Really."

She looked over at the moving truck and back to the couple standing in front of her.

"By the way, my name's Erika."

Erika reached out her hand to Rob. Rob shook it gently, amazed at how quickly the woman was rebounding. The woman who'd been shaking and close to passing out had disappeared, replaced by the bubbly, bouncing woman with the lively smile that stood before him.

"Do you live around here? Can we help you get home safely?" Rob asked. He knew she was trying to forget about whatever had happened, and that she was probably just putting on a show to make them feel better. However, he was still convinced that she had been attacked, and he didn't like the idea that someone was creeping around in those woods.

"Oh! Actually this is my house. Or at least it's my parent's." Erika said as she quickly bounced up the couple of steps toward the front door.

"You know, once you guys get settled in, you should come to my dad's party. It's tomorrow. He has one every year on July 29th. It's huge, with people coming all the way down from Chicago for it. Anyone's welcome, and because our backyard stretches just past the city limits by a couple of yards, we get away with having a big bonfire without Renner coming out and harassing us. It's kind of a birthday party for my mom, but also happens to be the date we moved in here. So we've had a party every year since."

Rob looked at Robyn, trying not to laugh. He knew it shouldn't be funny to him, and that small town life was going to be a bit different than what he was used to, but he couldn't help it. Still he was curious.

"What do you say Hon?"

"Fine with me."

Rob turned back to Erika as she neared the door.

"We'll see what we can do. We have a lot of unpacking to do, but we will probably stop by for a minute."

"Cool. My dad starts cooking the Hobo Stew tonight. It's his special concoction; you'll have to wait and see. It's really good though."

"Okay then," Robyn said as they headed back to their own yard.

"Why once y'all gets settled in y'all should come to our party," Rob said, chuckling at his horrible southern accent. Robyn pushed him as they approached the moving truck.

"You're evil. She didn't have any kind of an accent. You're just not used to neighbors actually talking to you."

"True. You know, in the last seven years I don't think I talked to our neighbors once," Rob said as he walked to the back of the truck. Steve and Colt had gotten Jake's bike down, and Jake had emerged from the car to ride it back and forth in the street.

"Jake, you really shouldn't be riding your bike in the street, you might get hit," Rob called out to him.

"Rob, look around, have you seen another car even come down the road? He's fine."

Rob looked around, and realized she was right. For the most part, the whole neighborhood was quiet. Except for the sound from the highway that ran through the main street and the interstate a couple of miles away, the town was pretty quiet for late afternoon on a week day.

"This isn't Chicago."

"No, you're right, this isn't Chicago."

"Now go get the beer."

Rob took another look around. It really was quiet here.

* * * *

Rob stepped into the small market with Jake following close behind him. It hadn't taken long after Rob had gotten in the car for Jake to hurry off of his bike and come running to climb into the car. He made sure he didn't get left behind.

"Can I get a toy?" They had barely entered the store, and Jake was already looking around, scanning the market for any signs of toys. Seeing how small the store was, and that there weren't any toys; he quickly turned back to Rob. "Can I get some candy?"

"We'll see."

Rob quickly made his way down the side aisle. The store itself was dark, grungy and very small, with only three aisles. The isle to the left held coolers all along its length. The center aisle was filled with canned goods, and the third aisle held baked goods and deli items, as well as the checkout counter, which contained all the candy and cigarettes. The aisles were short, making it easy for Rob to see the entire store from the entrance. It didn't really surprise him that, other than the cashier, he and Jake were the only ones in the store.

Rob walked along the side aisle until he made it to the back of the store where there were two sections in the cooler dedicated to beer. Rob filled his arms with what he could carry, figuring that whatever the guys didn't drink, he would finish off before bed. Maybe he could drink some of the pain away, or at the very least he could drink himself into such a stupor that he might actually get a peaceful night of sleep.

Rob thought about the nightmares. He wanted to shake the images of that night out of his mind, the hotel hallway, the smells, the screams; they were a part of his life that he didn't want to remember; or have waking him up every night.

He carried the beer up to the counter, and nodded Jake a quick ok toward the candy bars beneath the register. Jake smiled back and quickly went to the small rack of candy and looked through the assortment. Rob watched him, not paying any attention to the cashier, as she started to ring him up. The beeps of the cash register were loud in the store, and what Rob normally would have thought annoying, he found he enjoyed, the sound a relief from the constant hum of the coolers.

"Hello." The cashier said. Rob looked up, noticing her for the first time. She was a young woman, somewhere in her mid-twenties. She was probably native to the area, as she had a Native American face, with high cheek bones and slightly dark skin. Her skin was smooth, and her hair was dark.

"Hello." He said back, as she reached down for paper bags buried deep under the counter. Rob lost attention in her and turned back to Jake, who was trying to sneak a peek at the nudie magazines hidden behind the other magazines in the rack. Jake looked over at Rob, and realized he had been caught.

"Would you like any bottled water? We have an excellent sale, and you really should stock up."

"No, we're fine. We typically just use a filter on the tap water."

"Don't drink the water. You shouldn't have moved in to that house."

Rob turned to look at the woman behind the counter, shocked by her sudden outburst.

"You should leave. Get out of the area as soon as you can. Your family is in danger here." She looked over at Jake, and Rob followed her gaze.

"Excuse me?" Rob said as he again looked back at the cashier.

The woman was gone.

Standing behind the counter was some young pimple faced kid who looked like he still had a couple of years before graduating high school.

"Your total is fifteen ninety-five."

Rob quickly looked around the store, to see where the young woman had disappeared to. He couldn't see anyone, and turned back to the cashier.

"What happened to the woman who was here before?"

"Uh, what woman?"

"The one who started to ring me up?"

The boy looked at Rob cautiously. Rob recognized that look. The cashier was trying to size Rob up, to see if he was just confused or he posed some kind of a threat.

He took Rob's money slowly, careful not to reach too far across the counter in case Rob reached out for him. When he did, Rob could see bruises on his arm, just under his long sleeve shirt. Rob wondered briefly if the man had been robbed recently, as the bruises looked fresh. It explained why he would be so cautious now.

"I've been here the whole time."

The boy gave Rob his change, and he quickly pocketed it before grabbing his bags. He and Jake walked to the door, and made their way outside.

Rob couldn't help pausing just outside the store. Something wasn't right.

He turned to look back inside, wanting to see if the two cashiers were both in there, laughing at playing with the stranger.

Only the boy was inside, standing behind the counter. He watched Rob as he stood looking in at him. He could see the boy inch closer to the wall phone behind the counter and knew that the boy was getting ready to call for help. He wondered if it was going to be the police or the boy's boss. The last thing Rob wanted was to meet his new boss or any of his new co-workers by having them called on him on the first day.

Rob turned, and it was then that he saw her again, in the reflection of the glass door. She was standing right beside him, looking at him. He should have been able to feel her breath on his neck, she was so close, but all he felt was a strange chill just over his shoulder. She eased closer, moving to whisper into his ear.

"Your family is in danger. You must leave," she said.

Rob spun around, trying to catch her.

"Just wh--? Rob stopped talking as he came to face with nothing but air. Jake was the only one standing behind him.

"Leave." He heard her voice as it spoke to him. This time, he could feel her speaking directly to him, inside his head.

* * * *

Samantha sat staring into her bedroom mirror. It had drawn her to it, and she had been sitting for longer than she could remember. She was lost in her own reflection, her silver hair glowing in the sunlight for most of the day. Now she sat in the darkening room, her hair just a twinkle, illuminated by the little light coming into the room from the street light outside.

"God, how long have I been sitting here?" she thought to herself.

She tried to blink; to pull her gaze away from the mirror, but it was as though she was trapped by some invisible force, bound to her chair, repeating the endless motion of brushing her hair.

Behind her reflection she could see the rest of her bedroom, and it looked just as she remembered it when she had risen that morning. The bed was yet to be made and the clothes she had been in the process of gathering for the morning were tossed onto the sheets. .

She looked back at herself, at the nightgown she was still wearing. She had to have been sitting there for the entire day, but how? She barely remembered seeing something move out of the corner of her eye as she was pulling out her jeans. She had planned on spending the day in the garden. The rabbits had been going after her tomatoes, and she was going to put up a chicken wire fence around them to keep them out. She loved to work in the garden. It gave her something to do and made her feel productive in her retirement.

She had just set her jeans on the bed when she noticed the movement, and she looked up at the mirror. A shadow moved behind her, on the other side of the room. She quickly checked the room and then turned to look back at the mirror.

She stopped when she saw herself. She wasn't sure why, just something in her reflection, and how it seemed to be looking back at her. It made her want to keep staring at it. The look in her eyes, the gaze it held, was so distant.

It was her, but it wasn't.

Then her reflection moved. At first, she thought her reflection was moving by itself, that it had separated from her, and now had a mind of its own. But then she realized that her reflection was leading her, to sit down in front of the mirror. If she hadn't watched herself lowering into the chair in front of the mirror, she wouldn't have known she'd been walking. It was as though she had no control of her body, it was moving without conscious thought.

She hadn't felt scared, but sat in front of the mirror and brushed her hair; never getting tired of the repetitive motion, nor slowing down. She couldn't stop, didn't want to stop. It felt so relaxing, like letting in an old friend lead her.

A door slammed shut somewhere in the house. It sounded like the back door, she could hear the glass shake in the doorframe, but who could it be? It was still dark out, so there was no way it could be her husband. He worked the third shift; he was never home before sun up.

Where had he been all day? Why hadn't he been there this morning when she woke up? Usually he was just going to bed as she was getting up, but he never came home. She'd at first thought he was working late, but then he never did come home.

She could hear heavy footsteps walk through the kitchen, and the dull sounds on the carpeting of the inner hallway. They made their way to the bottom of the stairs, and then worked their way up.

She tried to scream. Beyond anything else, she wanted to call out, to shout at the top of her lungs, hoping that her neighbors would hear her. Inside, she was screaming, putting all she had into it. She could feel her arms tingle, itching to move, but unable to. She was frozen, looking at herself in the mirror, her reflection staring back, mocking her.

"Don't worry," a man's voice said inside her head. She felt a chill on her right shoulder and then soothing warmth that spread down her back. She relaxed again, and she felt like an old friend was was there to comfort her, she could tell.

She should have screamed, but instead, lost the desire to. It wouldn't have mattered anyways. She already knew that no matter how loud she yelled, no one could ever hear her, other than the intruder that was making his way to her room.

Out of the corner of her eye, the door started to inch open. She wished she could turn her head, all she could see was a dark shape as it appeared in the doorway. It was a tall form, with broad shoulders and some kind of orange light around its eyes. She could feel the menace in its being, in the way it stood in the doorway.

The shape stepped forward, moving into the light. She watched as it became her husband, and the feeling of dread became a lump in her stomach.

"Hey Hon," she tried to say, but her lips still wouldn't move and nothing more than a breathy whisper came out. Her husband acknowledge that he'd heard it as he walked toward her. Something was wrong. His body was tense and he was hiding one of his hands behind his back.

He stepped around behind her and stood, hovering over her. Light glinted in his eyes as he glared at her reflection, and for a moment her heart skipped a beat fearing that he was ensnared in the same trap that she was.

Then it was over. He brought the knife he'd been hiding behind his back, up to her throat. In one quick motion, blood began to gush from what had once been her throat. She couldn't even reach up to try to stop the bleeding.

She sat, a statue, as the blood left her body. She could only watch herself die in the mirror. The blood felt hot on her neck as it drained away. She could feel its warmth flowing down the front of her nightgown.

Even as she grew tired, and wanted to collapse to the floor, her body remained stiff, and her mind trapped. Her hand continued to hold the brush and she went on brushing her hair. It was growing sticky from the blood, but still she brushed it over and into the knots.

Behind her, she watched her husband walk over to the bedside, and pull his revolver from the nightstand. He held the gun to his temple, and without hesitation, a flash filled the room and there was a thump, as his body hit the ground.

Her mind began to shut down, as her life flowed away, leaving a statue sitting there, still watching her lifeless reflection. The world faded around her. She knew her eyes wouldn't close, that she couldn't blink or shut them. Life faded from them, as she sunk into the darkness.

CHAPTER 4

Rob sat up in bed, his pulse racing and his brow covered in sweat. He reached back, and he could feel the moisture on his pillow and the sheets below. The room was cool from the air conditioning, but he was covered from head to toe with sweat and his skin felt like it was on fire. His head felt like it was going to explode, and was heavy, fighting him as he sat up in the bed.

He wished the nightmares would be done. The waking up in the middle of the night, the lack of any real sleep, the sheets soaked with sweat, it was all getting old. He was tired of not being able to sleep. He had hoped that leaving the hospital would help, but now there he was, awake again at God only knew what hour.

And what about the gun shot? He could have sworn he had just heard a gunshot and that was what had woke him up.

He almost wished he could remember his dreams, his nightmares. All he remembered of them were the screams, and the dark shapes coming for him. When he woke up, everything faded, leaving him feeling he couldn't tell if he was still in the dreamscape or not. Rob eased out of the bed, looking over to make sure that Robyn was still sleeping peacefully on her side of the bed. The room was dark, but he didn't want to turn on the light. He moved around the boxes that were in various stages of unpacking around the room. The door was partly open in case Jake woke up in the middle of the night, so they could hear him. Yeah, it was treating him like a little kid, but it was his first night in the new house.

Rob stepped into the hallway, but stopped suddenly when the floor creaked beneath his feet. He waited, listening in the still of the night before slowly putting out his foot to take another step forward. He wanted to avoid the center of the hallway, figuring if he walked near the wall, there would be more support and fewer soft spots. Just because he was up all night, didn't mean he had to keep the rest of household up.

He made it to the stairs and moved down, the soft carpeting feeling good beneath his feet. Compared to their old house in Chicago, this house seemed like a palace. He wasn't even sure yet what they were going to use to fill all the rooms. They had nowhere near enough furniture. There was a whole side room on the first floor that they had no idea what to make of. It would have been perfect for an office, but Rob didn't feel the need to have one. He wanted to use it for a game room, maybe have a pool table in there, and a dart board on the wall, but there was no way they could afford it. Besides, Robyn had already put the kibosh on a game room in the house.

She was already saying that she had plans for it. She'd said it with that large seductive smile of hers, and he knew exactly what she was thinking. She wanted it for a nursery. If they were to get their financials all in place, he had no problem going along with her. It all depended of course, on money, and how much he was going to be paid at his new job.

Rob checked the front door, making sure it was still locked and secure. He turned and worked his way around the boxes at the bottom of the stairs and to the back of the house into the kitchen area. He went to the back door and stared out at the large backyard. A back yard, hell he grew up with a back yard big enough just for a small swing set that he couldn't even swing too high on because it wasn't cemented into the ground. If he got too high, the swing set would start to rock back and forth, threatening to tip over on him.

A smile crept onto Rob's face as he imagined the days ahead, when Jake would be running around the back yard, playing with his friends. Jake was getting a little old for hide and seek, but Rob could imagine all the other games he would play. Rob would have to get Jake a laser tag set like the one he had always wanted as a kid. Build some obstructions for him, so they could run and shoot each other. There was so much that they could do with this place, as long as they could keep it.

In the morning, Rob figured he would have to make a call to their realtor about their house back in Chicago. Robyn had been taking care of it so far. Though he loved her, he would like to talk to the realtor himself and find out how she felt about the house selling in this market. He wanted a better idea of where they stood and how long they would have to keep paying two mortgages.

Rob stepped away from the back door and looked back at the front of the house. There wasn't much light, just the little streaks that came through the front window from the street light. This was fragmented by the tree that stood between the house and the light, creating strange shapes that danced along the inner hallway when the wind blew. Once they got the curtains up in the front room, there would be hardly any light, but for now, it was welcome until he learned his way around and Robyn got all her little night lights situated.

Rob made his way back along the hallway to the bottom of the stairs, less concerned about creaking from the flooring. He figured down there the sound wouldn't carry as well and doubted he would wake anyone up.

He got to the end of the hallway and took a quick glance around at how Robyn was already setting up their living room. She already had the couches situated, and there were boxes waiting in piles throughout the room. He was about to turn and head back upstairs to his waiting bed, when a shadow moved across the living room. He only caught it out of the corner of his eye, but when he turned to look, he saw only himself staring in the mirror hanging on the far wall.

The first thing Rob had done was hang Robyn's grandmother's mirror on the wall.

Rob stepped back from the stairs and began to walk toward the mirror. It was his face staring back at him, but when did he get so pale? Sure, he had been in the hospital for months, but even still, the face looking back at him had no color in it. It was as though he could almost see through the skin to the bones underneath.

A shape moved through the shadows behind him, catching his attention. The shadow had been moving in Rob's direction, and moved behind him before disappearing.

A shiver ran down his spine, but it wasn't a chill. He felt a fiery breeze blow through the living room and grab hold of him. It made the hair on his arms tingle as though they were being singed. The moisture evaporated from his eyes, and his skin was suddenly hot to the touch.

He looked up at the mirror and could see the shape behind him. It was a man, but he still couldn't make out any detail. It was getting closer and as it did, the invisible 'flames' around him grew hotter. Just as he could see what appeared to be an arm reaching out for him, the heat grew. He turned to look behind him, to face it.

The shape was gone.

Rob turned and looked back at the mirror, but it wasn't his own reflection any more. There was a man there, or what was left of a man. His skin was half rotted off and the bones underneath were exposed. The skin was so thin, that even on the parts of him that it covered; the bones were still visible underneath. He was wearing what appeared to be some kind of uniform, one Rob was sure he had seen before, but only in pictures. It was an old police uniform, one like the one his dad had worn. Rob looked at the badge that was covered in dirt and rust, but still clung to the man's uniform. He couldn't make it out, but for some reason, he was sure that if he could, it would be his father's badge number. Rob looked up into the man's reflected eyes. They were coal black, dead black. Still, they burned with a heat that felt as if it was melting Rob's skin away.

The invisible fire around Rob grew stronger, and in the mirror, his reflection was again his own. His skin was melting away, becoming liquid, and he could see it sliding off his bones, dripping to the floor in large globs, flesh and hair sizzled as they hit. He watched as they disappeared, dissolving into the floor.

He looked at the mirror and saw that his reflection was reaching for him. His hand came closer to the mirror until it was just about on him. Then, with a ripple, it came through the mirror, and he had a sudden certainty, that if it touched him, he was never going to be to the same. That some evil greater than anything he had ever experienced in the city would take hold of him.

Rob tried to step back, but his feet felt as if they were locked in cement and they wouldn't move. He put all his weight into breaking free, and suddenly he fell back. His feet were still in place, but the rest of his body feel backward, escaping the mirror.

He landed suddenly, onto his bed. His breath was quick, but he really was back in his bedroom. He was covered in sweat, but nowhere near the mirror. He was safe.

He looked over and saw that Robyn was still asleep. He hadn't wakened her. That was good.

* * * *

"So you don't remember what box it's in?" Rob was searching through another of the boxes that had been put in their bedroom. He was trying to find his dress shirt; he already had his best slacks, socks, and tie stretched out on the bed.

"Don't you think you're over doing it a little? You already have the job, right? So you don't have to go in kissing up to the man."

"Yeah, well, he has yet to meet me. I got the job over the phone; I don't want to start off with him by giving a bad first impression."

Robyn walked across the room and placed her arms around him as she nuzzled her face into his chest. She looked up at him, her large eyes wide and her gentle lips curved into a smile. She stayed there, waiting for it. Finally she said, "Where's my love?"

Rob smiled down at her. It was a forced smile. He was upset, but he didn't want to take it out on her. He brought his arms around her and gave her a gentle bear hug, enjoying the warmth of her near him. Her curves felt good against his body, and he could feel himself getting excited. She must have felt it herself as she purred against him.

"I have to finish getting ready."

"I know."

Robyn pulled away from him slowly, and resigned herself to sitting on the bed. She looked around the room, at the boxes scattered everywhere. All of them had their tops open, and the clothes inside were a mess from being rummaged through.

"It must be downstairs, since I don't see the box that had your good clothes in them."

"They wouldn't have been with my pants?"   "No, because your pants were in a dresser drawer, your shirt was hanging up."

Rob hurried out of the room, the towel draped around his waist threatening to come undone as he quickly hurried down the hallway. He made it halfway down before he rushed back into the room.

"Can you look for me, while I get dressed?"

He remembered that the curtains still hadn't been put up downstairs, and didn't want the neighbors' first view of him to be his naked ass searching through the boxes.

"Sure."

Robyn stood up and walked back over to him and again reached out to put her arms around him.

"Besides, I don't want Jake to see his father running around our new house naked." With that, Robyn quickly grabbed the towel and pulled. In a flash, it gave way to her grasp and she was rushing down the hallway with it. Rob tried to catch her, but stopped at the door, and closed it. He could hear Jake stirring in his bedroom.

* * * *

Rob pulled his car next to a building that, according to his GPS, was the station house for the small, Midwestern town of Standard. He couldn't believe it. It was a red brick building that looked more like it belonged in the ghetto of Chicago than in a small town. There were no windows, and where there had once been windows, was now bricked over. There was a single door on the side of the building; the original door on the front of the building was boarded up, and looked like it hadn't been used in twenty years. The bricks were cracked, and badly weathered; in many places along the wall parts of the brick had been chipped away and lay on the sidewalk.

Next to Rob's car was the only sign that he was possibly in the right place- a solitary, unmarked squad car.

It was early and the sun was just separating itself from the eastern horizon as Rob pulled himself out of his car. His back was already aching again, having stiffened up overnight. He knew when he left here that he'd have to go home and start to work on the exercises that the physical therapist had shown him, to help him work away the remaining stiffness that would bother him over the next couple of months. His back cracked loudly as he straightened and slammed the door.

As he walked to the sidewalk, the door opened and a tall, lanky man stepped into the doorway. He looked to be in his late fifties, with graying hair, starting to bald in places. His skin was pale, and Rob wondered if the guy ever got any sun. He was wearing a tight uniform, a straight up, black police officer uniform with all the accessories. How the hell was Rob going to wear one of those belts again with his back as sensitive as it was? He didn't even want to start to think about it.

"Can I help you?" The officer in the doorway said. He sounded tired and the 'help you' did not come out as though it was meant to be an earnest question but more of a statement. The statement being, 'Be quick and go away.'

"I'm looking for Christian Renner."   "Found him. What can I help you with?"

"Rob Alletto, nice to meet you." Rob stretched out his hand for a handshake, and he could see the officer was slow to respond. He looked at Rob, and Rob could tell that he didn't remember the conversation they had on the phone, or was having a very hard time putting a name to the face.

"Remember, we talked on the phone, you had an opening for a deputy. You said to come see you as soon as I got to town, we would go over the position."

The light came on in Renner's eyes and he nodded his head, remembering the name.

"Ah, yes. I said when you got to the area, but that's alright. Come on in."

Officer Renner stepped back into the building, revealing what was the small hallway that made up Standard's Police Headquarters. Rob eased forward, and followed him as he walked into the first door on the right. The hallway itself was in terrible condition and looked like it was in a building set for demolition. The wall on the left was cracked part way down, and the wood floor felt weak, sagging under their feet as they walked.

Rob followed Renner and stepped through the doorway on the right, noticing briefly that the hallway continued on in darkness. He stepped into the office and was amazed at how small it was. It was nothing like he expected a small town police station to look like. It was smaller without the jail cells in the background. He really had watched too much of the Andy Griffith show as a kid.

Inside the room were a small desk, a floor lamp, an old rotary style phone, two chairs, and a four drawer file cabinet off in the corner. One chair was made of nice leather, but the other was a simple metal folding one, sitting in front of the desk.

Renner stepped around to the other side of the desk and worked his way into his seat. A larger man would not have been able to make it but Renner's smaller size allowed him to pull it off. Rob followed suit and lowered himself into the chair opposite and had to adjust himself so it wasn't too uncomfortable.

"So I take it you're ready to start?"

"Ready, willing and able," Rob said with his forced enthusiasm.

"Well that's good, I guess. Is that going to be a problem?" Renner said as he nodded toward Rob's legs.

"I won't be running any marathons for another month, but I can still work the job."

"Yeah, well there's not too much of a 'job' here. Just some speeding tickets along the highway and breaking up a couple of under aged teens drinking. That's about all we get. Coming up we'll have August Days before the kids go back to school. That'll be about the worst time of year for us. We bring in a couple other patrols from Peoria to help out. Other than that, rotation typically works so that you'll work every other weekend, rotating out another officer that highlights from Peoria's PD."

"Ok, and when else do I work?"

"That's it. Two weekends a month. Like I said over the phone, it's just a part-time position."

"Who patrols the rest of the time?"

"Well, you caught me as I was about to sign off for the day. We don't have anyone else until I come back on at seven tonight. There's really not much of a need for anything during the day. I do it Monday through Friday, and then you'll cover like I said."

Rob was silent, not sure what more to say. He saw the nightmare that was about to happen. He and his family moved there thinking he would have a position. Not a two weekend a month part-time position, but three to four days a week on a full police force. He never even imagined a town would not have a full police rotation. How can they function with no one on duty during the day?

"Any chance of more work during the day, I mean, possibly getting any additional shifts? Anything?

Renner sat back into his chair and looked sharply at Rob. Rob, who was always a stand-up guy, one who had been around the block many years, and was a top officer on the streets of Chicago, was sitting there, his back hunched over and his head hung low, the weight of the mistake he had just made falling on him.

"I'll talk to the other officer. See if I can get him to agree to work only one weekend a month. That will give you an extra weekend. Other than that, we just don't have a budget for anything more. I can set you up as the daytime on-call officer. That gets you an additional five dollars a day, but you only come out if there's an emergency, Also, I can talk to Lostant, the next town over. The mayor there doesn't have the budget for a police force; he just pays to have someone patrol the town a couple nights a week. It's not much, but you just drive around and make sure nothing is going on. You see anything, you call me, and I'll come and make the arrest. You don't even have to go in uniform."

"I guess, if that's what I'm going to have to do."

Rob thought his chest was ready to explode, and his lungs fought for every breath. How the hell were they going to survive until their house sold? How the hell were they going to do this? Robyn was going to have to get a job. She was going to have to find something to help pay the bills. He would probably have to get a second job himself. The idea sickened him; he'd been a cop for nearly all of his adult life, and the idea of doing something else to get by had never come up before.

Rob stood, working hard to keep his legs from shaking. Renner followed suit, and reached out his hand, which Rob took and shook.

"I'll give you a call later and let you know what I find out about that additional patrol. Other than that, I'll give Trent your number so he can call you when he goes on patrol tomorrow night. That way you can ride along and get to know the area and the hot spots."

"Sounds good," Rob said, behind his false smile.

Renner walked around the desk, turning the floor lamp off as they made their way out into the hallway.

"This will probably be the last time you see this office. Everything you'll need is typically in the squad, and when we switch rotations, you'll just pick up the car from my house."

Rob left the building in shoes that felt like bricks as he walked to his car. The first thing on his mind was to call their realtor. Their house needed to sell fast, and he needed to know where they stood financially, or else they were going to lose the new house before the end of the year.

Rob got behind the wheel of his car and quickly pulled out his phone. He had to make some calls before he drove home.

CHAPTER 5

Rob pulled into his new driveway, and saw the moving truck still parked out front. He remembered that he had to return it before the neighbor's party that night, because he didn't want anyone to be around it, and getting themselves hurt. The last thing he needed was to get caught up in a personal injury lawsuit for an accident on his property. Besides, he needed the deposit back in his account so he could open a new one in town.

The call to the realtor didn't give him the confidence that he had hoped it would. The house had been on the market for nearly a month, and there'd barely been any interest in it. It was getting to the height of the buying season, and people just weren't interested in their house, even with a price lower than what they had paid for it.

Then there was the stop by the ATM that didn't go much better. Their checking was nearly depleted and their savings was disappearing fast. They had almost nothing left. Soon they would have to live week to week on his worker's compensation checks, and those weren't going to be enough to cover two house payments.

Rob took a deep breath, followed by another, before reaching for his door. He had decided not to pull into the garage as he figured he'd probably have to head to the store soon and get some more groceries. That, of course, meant even more money out of their account that he didn't want to think about.

Next door, he could see the fire pit in his neighbor's back yard was topped with a metal grating and a large metal garbage can sitting on top of that. An older man with short silver hair was standing next to the can dumping in a pot of chopped cabbage. Rob cocked his head to watch him for a moment, before turning to walk into the house.

Inside he could hear Robyn rummaging through a box in one of the rooms. He found her in the living room going through and carefully pulling out much of her glassware, and setting it in the large glass display case that Rob's grandmother had left him when she passed away. It had taken Rob a long time to get Robyn to agree to bring it home from his mother's, but she had finally given in. Now she loved to show off both her glassware and the display case for it. It had taken Rob nearly two weeks to sand the wood frame down and re-stain it so that it would match their living room furniture.

"I talked to the realtor."

"Yeah, what did she say? Does she have a buyer?"

Rob stepped into the room and looked around. He found that she had cleared a spot on the couch. It was barely large enough for someone his size to squeeze into, but he forced himself in.

"When were you going to tell me that we were so deep into our savings?"

Robyn stopped short, with the glass dish she was unwrapping frozen in her hand, and stood silently for a moment. Rob expected her to look up at him any moment and explain to him, make an excuse, or even lie to him. Instead, however, he heard her sniff. It was quiet at first, but then it was followed by another and another. She set down the dish and slowly lifted her head. Rob watched as she wiped away the tears, as they came more quickly.

"I'm sorry. I didn't want to tell you. I was hoping that I could sneak the money back in once you went back to work."

"That's going to be a problem."

Robyn wiped away more tears from her eyes, but her face still shone wetly as she looked at Rob.

"Why, what's wrong?"

"I'm only going to be working weekends."

"Really?"

"Yeah." A twinge of pain shot up Rob's back and he shifted on the couch, fighting to push against the box rubbing against his side. "The house isn't going to sell. Not anytime soon at least. The market is rough and nobody is really even looking right now."

"What are we going to do?"

"I might be able to get some additional patrols, but until I find out for sure, money is just going to be a little tight."

"Jake needs to get registered for school; he'll need books, and new school clothes."

Rob closed his eyes and took a deep breath. His lungs were on fire again, and it felt like he was being stabbed through the heart. He couldn't breathe. He didn't want to breathe and add more oxygen to the flames in his chest. There were tears in his eyes, and he just wanted to release the pent up energy by slamming his fists into something, anything. Robyn stood up and walked toward the hallway.

"Where are you going?" Rob said as he pushed himself up from the couch, working himself to stand.

"I'm going to start to put away the bedroom."

Rob looked at the half emptied box in the living room, and realized he had pushed her too hard.

Rob stood, watching her go up the stairs. He saw something shift out of the corner of his eye and casually turned to look back over his shoulder.

In the mirror above the living room fireplace, a pale figure stood behind him. It was staring at him through the mirror with a large and tooth filled smile. The man's teeth were dark and stained. Rob recognized him as the man from his nightmare, just as the man reached out for him. He was about to grab Rob's shoulder, when Rob turned quickly to look behind him.

No one was there.

Rob looked back at the mirror .He was alone in the room.

* * * *

Robyn heard the loud jingling of the bell over the door as she entered the musty little shop. Outside, it was a sun filled day, but the rays seemed to barely make it through the dirt covered front windows. Though everything seemed clean as she looked around the little shop, the smell of dust was heavy, and her asthma started to squeeze the airways in her lungs.

She reached into her pants pocket and pulled out her little red inhaler. Some days, especially with her allergies in the summer, that little red puff machine felt like her lifeline. Her lungs would often burn and fight her breathing, just clamping closed like they were in a vice. If it wasn't for that little puff of what tasted like battery acid sometimes, many times, she would have just fallen over dead.

She took a long breath from the inhaler and held it in, relishing the slight burning sensation throughout her lungs, knowing that it was working, and feeling her lungs opening up. A smile touched her lips, and she felt like she had opened her eyes anew as she looked around the store, her eyes adjusting to the dim light.

The little shop was crowded with antiques, knickknacks filled the shelves, till they looked ready to fall off the wall. Many of them were overhanging the ends of the wooden shelves and she feared going down the aisles in case she might knock something over.

She eased through the mess and made her way to the nearest space somewhat recognizable as an aisle. She knew that almost anything she saw in there, she would never be able to afford. Especially with the bills and Rob's job as it was, everything in there was off limits. Still, Rob was home working at getting drunk, and she was tired of unpacking. She needed to get out of the house for a little bit, check out the town and its little shops along the main street. There weren't too many of them. Other than a small sweet shop, three bars, a Laundromat, a video store and the library, there wasn't much else other than the little antique store.

The name of the shop was cute. "Things Forgotten," She loved it, and she was sure she could find many things buried in the piles of old objects. Maybe she could even get some information about her grandmother's mirror. It was such a large and beautifully unique design; she would love to know more about it. Maybe she could talk to someone, and they would let her bring it in, see if they knew some details.

What else did she have to do to pass away her Saturday? Sit at home and continue to unpack like she had done all day yesterday? What she would probably be doing all day Sunday?

Robyn stopped to look at a little lamp that was halfway down the aisle. It protruded into the aisle, making it hard for her to get by. It was cute, with intricate little designs running down the shaft of the body to its base. She had never seen anything quite like it; the base was made of wood and she wondered to herself if it was actually hand carved.

It reminded her of the little creations her dad had made. He was always a handyman, and it was amazing how he worked with his hands, the surprising things he would make. He worked in a factory every day, pulling his nine to five shifts, but many nights when he came home he would lock himself away in the basement for hours. Then, many times he would reappear with a gift for her or her mother, made almost always completely out of wood.

Robyn always wanted to ask him why he never tried to sell the stuff he made. She never did though, because she was already pretty sure of his answer. The creations he made, the beauty they possessed were made from love, and he made them just for her and her mother. The trinkets were never meant to be sold; they were special.

Now, with him gone, she wished she still had them. She was sure her mother must still have some of them. Maybe when she got back to the house she would give her a call, and see if something was put away in storage.

Robyn moved past the lamp in the aisle and heard the sounds of beads brushing together. She looked up in time to see a short, plump American Indian woman stepping out of the back room, looking her over. The woman didn't say anything; she just entered the room and kept watch over Robyn.

Robyn turned away and stepped around a corner, finding another hallway. It was lined with mirrors of different shapes and sizes on both sides, making it impossible for a person to walk down and not see their reflection.

Robyn stood on the edge of the hallway, looking of at the mirrors. They were all so fascinating with all differences amongst them all, but she had a strange feeling that kept her from walking forward. It was odd, but she sensed that something was watching her through the mirrors. A presence hiding in their reflections, like something from her nightmares waiting for her. She felt a warm hand touch her shoulder and jumped as she turned to face its owner. Her heart raced from the sudden shock, the wakeup call that pulled her out of her daze.

"You should never stare too long into your own eyes. You might lose yourself," said the shopkeeper as she stood behind her. "A mirror can steal your spirit if you let it."

The shopkeeper turned and walked back to the other room. Robyn watched her for a second and then turned to look back at the mirrors. She saw herself in the mirror at the far end of the hall how frail she looked and how much weight she had lost since Rob had had his accident.

She turned around and headed back into the store, trying to see where the older woman had gone. She couldn't find her anywhere in the store. She was all alone with the antiques, and suddenly she didn't have as much interest in them. A weight formed in her stomach and she wanted to get home and see how Jack and Rob were doing.

The day was getting late, she could tell by the setting sun outside. Just how long had she been in the store? She didn't feel it had been all that long, but her watch said it had been forty five minutes. She had to get home and get ready for the party their neighbors were having. She knew Rob didn't want to go, but it would be good for him to get out, and they really did need to start meeting their neighbors.

"Mirrors. They are the windows to the spirit realm. Don't look too long. Never look too long," she heard the old woman say from behind the beads.

Robyn reached for the door and listened to the bell as it rang. It really was a cute little store; there were a few things she wouldn't mind getting someday, when they had money. Like that was ever going to happen any time soon, she thought, as she stepped into the late afternoon sun.

* * * *

Rob watched as the street in front of his new house went from a quiet small town dead-end street with hardly any traffic, to being filled with cars trying to find an open spot. Cars were even parking in other people's driveways; the street was packed bumper to bumper.

Then there were the motorcycles. They were all parked in the neighbor's front yard and at last count there were over fifteen.

Robyn was in the bathroom, putting on her makeup and getting dressed up. Rob figured that she would be another hour before she was ready to go next door. Only God knows why she was bothering, he thought to himself as he watched the people going to the party next door, no one arriving was dressed up.

"Ready?"

Rob turned away from the window and saw Robyn as she bounced down the stairs. She had her make up on, but to his surprise, she wasn't overdressed. She wore a simple top with just a plain pair of blue jeans. She looked great, and he couldn't help himself and a smile crossed his face as he watched her.

"Jake knows we'll be next door, right?"

"He's already over there. He was playing in the backyard when some kids came, and he went over to play with them."

Rob reached for the door and opened it for Robyn who was behind him.

"Do you have my inhaler?"

"Yes, it's in my pocket," he said as he followed her out, shutting the door behind her.

They hurried across the grass, and stepped into their neighbor's backyard. Like theirs, the yard was huge, and easily accommodated the large group of people that were scattered about. In the far back was the fire pit with the trash can of stew cooking, around which, was a group of people already waiting with plates, ready to eat. In the corner of the yard was the methodic clank of metal on metal, there was a large group of people playing horseshoes. In the center of the yard were a couple of guys sitting on the top of a picnic table, both with guitars. They were currently just talking with people milling around them, but Rob thought he had heard music just minutes ago, and guessed they would be starting back up again soon.

Near the house there was a large tub filled with ice and there were two kegs of beer in it. Rob made his way there first and saw that Erika was behind the tubs talking to what looked like another twenty something girl. They were both laughing and chatting away, but stopped when Erika saw him walk up to the keg. Rob was already reaching for a couple of cups when Erika turned.

"Hey, you guys made it."

"Yeah," Robyn said as she made her way from Rob's shadow.

Erika nodded at the two guys with the guitars.

"The one on the left is my dad."

Rob nodded and after filling a plastic cup, he left Robyn to talk, and headed in the direction of the picnic table. He could already hear Robyn laughing as he walked away.

Rob approached the two men. A woman had brought both of them a full beer, and they were accepting them from her as Rob stepped up.

"Thank you my dear." The man on the left was saying. He noticed Rob and gave a quick nod in his direction.

"Hey, glad you could make it," the man said.

"Glad to have the invite." Rob replied.

"So how was the drive?"

"We walked."

"Walked? You live in town here?"

"Yeah, we just moved into the house next door."

The man paused for a second, and then his face lit up and he straightened his back so that he was no longer slouching over his guitar. The realization of who Rob was had caught up to him and he was quick to reach out his hand.

"Ah, yeah you're the new neighbor. Glad you could make it. I'm Todd; you've met my daughter I heard. Thanks by the way, don't know what happened yesterday. And then this here," Todd said, as he nodded his glass toward the woman standing next to him, "This here is my wife Bonnie. And this hillbilly with a guitar next to me here is Steve."

"Hey Brother," the other man with a guitar said as he reached his hand out to Rob. Rob took it while he examined him. . The man's hair was dirty and matted; his beard was long and had not been cleaned up in a long time. His clothes were well worn, with dirt and fish gut remains wiped on his thighs.

"Okay, well, I'm going to go check on the stew, see if we need to add some more water," Bonnie said as she stepped away from the group, and heading the direction of the fire.

"Hey Hon, I got a song for you!" Todd called after her as she was walking away. Todd didn't miss a beat as he sang, following behind with the guitar.

"Always marry an Ugly Girl,
That's the only kind.
They'll never ever leave you,
And if she does you won't mind"

Rob nearly lost his beer through his nose as Todd sang. He quickly turned to see how Bonnie was going to react, and was surprised to find her laughing, as she walked away. Both of her middle fingers were raised high in the air as she walked backwards. Todd smiled as he turned to Rob and gave him a cheerful nod.

"What the hell had they gotten themselves into?" Rob thought, as he turned and tried to find Robyn in the crowd. There were more people filing into the backyard, and it was getting harder and harder to see through the pack.

A thundering roar tore through the chattering crowd of people talking throughout the yard. It vibrated in the wind, rumbling and shaking the windows in the panes both of their house and their neighbor's. Everyone turned to look where it was coming from, but with the echo along the street, the sound reverberated, and made it hard to tell.

Then suddenly a bike exploded into view from the side of the house. It was a small Harley Davidson Roadster with a large burly man leaned back and comfortable in the saddle. He zigzagged his way through the crowd, skidding back and forth in the grass, and tearing up large chunks. His large dark sunglasses clung to his face as he looked around the crowd running to get out of his way. He had a large toothy smile on his face, and a big cigar hung out of the side of his mouth. The way he was racing around the yard, it wouldn't be long before someone was hurt.

Rob was quick to react. Well, he was quick to try to react. As he turned to run and catch the bike, his leg buckled, and he leaned heavily onto his good leg, reaching out to the picnic table to keep himself upright. Trying not to lose stride, he pushed off of the picnic table and quickly limped in the direction of the bike, trying to keep ahead of it so he could cut it off. Out of instinct, he reached behind his back to pull out his back up revolver, only to find it not there. He was no longer a Chicago Street Officer, no matter how hard it would be for him to get used to that damn fact.

Rob looked around at the crowd in chaos as they scattered, and he calculated the bike's path so he could plan another tactic, and he saw Bonnie rush at the bike. She was waving her hands back and forth, trying to get the driver's attention; however, Rob didn't think it was working as the bike was not slowing.

"Get out of the way!" Rob called out to Bonnie. Pain was shooting down his right leg like electric shock, and he could barely keep his eyes open. The pain ripped through his spine, and made its way up to his skull, where it grabbed the nerves behind his eyes and pulled them back into their sockets.

His legs were fighting against him, starting to buckle.

"Watch out!"

Bonnie heard him call out to her and turned to look just as the bike neared her. It didn't show any sign of slowing, though she had stopped, and now her eyes were locked on Rob like a deer caught in the headlights.

Rob's legs finally gave out. In a flash, a scorching pain went through his entire back and his legs gave under him. His vision blurred, and then went to black as he landed on the soft ground. The last thing he remembered hearing was the roar of the motorcycle, and screams. The screams had seemed to be getting closer, but yet they also seemed to be getting farther away. He realized it wasn't them getting farther away; it was him moving deeper into unconsciousness.

* * * *

"Do you need an ambulance?" Rob heard someone ask. His head felt like a brick and his entire body felt like it was locked in position. He didn't think he could move. All his senses were numb, yet he could feel something cool against his back.

Damn it, he thought to himself. The coolness on his back, made him sure he was back in the hospital. The whole time he thought he had gotten out, the whole last twenty four hours suddenly seemed like a dream. The beautiful house, everything, just a dream that he had conjured up.

A twinge of pain shot down his back, making his toes curl.

His eyes fluttered open. The light was bright, and at first all he could see were shapes hovering over him. Their colors ran together.

Slowly, his eyes adjusted, and he could see his wife was one of the people standing over him.

"No. Hell no. No more doctors. I'm fine." Rob said. He tried to move, but his body was stiff. He was barely able to move his head, but after resituating himself, he was able to turn and see that he was no longer lying on the ground. He had probably fallen hard, but someone or a group of someone's, must have picked him up and carried him to the picnic table. The wood was refreshingly cool against his skin, but was rough on his back. Above him, Robyn and Bonnie were both over him, with half of the party all gathered around.

"Are you alright?" Bonnie was saying. A ringing started in his ears and it sounded like she was at the back of an auditorium yelling to him.

Rob eased himself to a sitting position carefully, as his back tried to fight against him. His body creaked as he moved, and he could feel everyone's hands on him, helping him, which was probably a good thing, since the world had begun to feel like it was on a spindle and swirling around him. He thought he might pass out again; he could feel his lunch moving through him quickly, and everything wanted to fade out on him again.

Then he was up and sitting. The unease was passing and he again focused on everyone around him.

"I'm fine. Really."

"Damn that was the craziest thing I think I ever saw," said a guy at the back of the group. And with that, the group broke up around him.

"What the hell was all that with the bike about? Rob said, looking up at Bonnie, who was rattled, but said she was okay as well.

"That was Roach. He's one of Todd's friends from the Hell's Angels."

Rob's eyebrows perked up of the mention of the Angels and the color seemed to fade from his face. He remembered having an issue a couple of times with some Angels in Chicago. They were not people that a person wanted to mess with.

"No, no," Bonnie started saying, seeing Rob's reaction, "They're not all that bad, not all of them. A lot of them do good things for the community. But, some of them can get rowdy. Roach, he's always been one to make an entrance, but he's getting older, so his entrances often come across more and more as desperate cries for attention."

"Yeah, I'm sorry about that, Hon," said a big burly man dressed mostly in black and sporting a biker's vest. Rob couldn't see the back of it, but he was sure that if he could, it would have the large emblem of the Hell's Angels on it. The man looked down at where Rob was sitting.

"I'm Roach," the man said, as he walked up to Rob, holding out his hand for Rob to shake. Rob waited a long time, his heart racing, and his whole body filled with heat and anger, and he wanted nothing more than to hit this man for the agony he had caused.

Rob wasn't sure where this new found anger was coming from, as he had been a peacemaker for a long time, and proud of the fact that he was always the one to keep a calm head while he was on the force. Yet now, there he was, and if he'd been able, he would have run his fist through that smile and left the man a bloodied mess.

After an uncomfortable amount of time, Rob reached out and took the man's hand and shook it. Bonnie had been talking to Roach; Rob finally paid attention to what she was saying.

"I can't believe you did that. You sure as hell know there are kids here. You could have seriously hurt someone! What the hell were you thinking?"

Roach turned his attention to Rob, and looking like a scared little mouse huddling into himself as he backed away from this woman, that was half his size.

"I'm sorry Bon-Bon, it won't happen again."

"It sure as hell won't!"

* * * *

Roach backed away from them, and Bonnie turned to look down at Rob. Robyn sat down next to him, and put her arm around him. He suddenly felt hemmed in. This was made worse by the fact that they both wanted to mother him.

"Are you sure you're alright?" Robyn asked, as she nuzzled his shoulder.

With a long sigh, he turned and looked her in the eye.

"Yeah, I'll be fine."

Todd, who had stood silently behind Bonnie, finally stepped up and patted Rob on the back. He said, "Yeah, he'll be fine, we just need to give him some room and stop babying the poor man. First time at our house and we're trying to smother him."

Todd walked back to the picnic table where Steve was waiting to hand him his guitar.

"You son of a bitch!" was heard loudly throughout the party before Todd could strum his first cord. Everyone turned, and was just in time to catch a small, thin, black haired woman slap a slightly taller, silver haired man.

Bonnie quickly turned back to Rob and Robyn.

"I gotta take care of this. I'll be right back to check on you."

Bonnie hurried over to the couple, the man now struggling with, the woman, and he had both of her arms in his hands, holding her by the wrists.

Rob was out of ear shot, but he watched as Bonnie walked up to them and separated them both. He was be amazed by how this woman handled things. She had taken charge of everything so far, and her husband for the most part, stayed on a picnic table, making fun of everything with his friends, as they played their music. They didn't care about any of what was going on; Bonnie, however, was in the middle of all of it.

She was talking to the couple, and the woman was very upset, screaming at the man. Then they were done. Rob could tell that the tension was dying, their shoulders slumped, and some kind of resolution seemed to have been reached. The woman turned away, and stalked out of the backyard, heading to the next house over down the street.

"Shit, please don't tell me that kind of crazy is one of our neighbors." Rob said under his breath.

Bonnie was talking to the man, who kept shrugging his shoulders. Rob watched him intently, trying to get a read on him. He could tell even from across the yard that the man was putting on an act. His stance was all wrong, and he was playing the part over the top, trying to gain Bonnies sympathy, hoping she'd take his side. Rob's days as a Chicago cop had trained him well to spot the truth or deceit. The way the man moved, and how he stood, said far more than the words he was saying to Bonnie.

But why would he care, why would he try so eagerly to get Bonnie to sympathize with him? Usually a man only does that when he cares deeply about what someone thinks about them. He obviously had feelings for Bonnie.

Damn, Rob hoped they didn't just move themselves into an episode of Melrose Place or some day time soap opera.

The man suddenly turned and looked over at Rob, sending a painful shiver through his body. He could feel Robyn's eyes on him, and wanted to turn and look at her, to let her know he was fine, but his eyes were locked with those of the other man, who just stood there, smiling, no longer paying attention to Bonnie as she continued to talk to him. He just watched Rob, with a large tooth filled smile. Rob recognized that smile. It was the broad smile of the man who had been staring back at him in the mirror.

Rob's skin became hot, as though liquid fire engulfed him.

Bonnie walked back to them, and Rob turned to watch, finally able to break his gaze from the man. "Sorry about that," she smiled.

"This is becoming quiet an interesting party. Are they always like this?" Robyn asked. She had rubbed Rob's shoulders and he wondered if she had felt the heat as well.

"No, typically there's more blood. Just kidding, typically we never have any problems until everyone leaves; which probably won't be until late tomorrow for some of these people. They'll just crash where they can find soft earth. Its funny how this is my birthday party, but they're all Todd's friends."

"They going to be okay?" Robyn asked, nodding toward the couple that had stormed off to their own house.

"The Pacifico's? Yeah, they'll be fine. In all the years I've seen them together, that is the first fight I've ever seen them have. They're your stereotypical perfect couple, always the happy ones. Ron and Terry are usually inseparable, and to see them fight like that surprises me. Who knows what's going on? Maybe Terry got laid off, I don't know, but she was all in a huff, screaming that he's gone all the time now, and she thinks he's having an affair. Money trouble can turn a normally loving couple into a pair of vultures fighting over the same piece of meat."

Rob thought about how the man, Ron, had been looking at Bonnie. There had been some deep connection there and he wondered if maybe there was some truth to Terry's worries. Something was up between those two.

Todd was starting a new song, and Bonnie looked over at him disapprovingly. Todd didn't care as he belted it out.

> "She's gone, gone, gone,
> Gone, gone, gone,
> Crying won't get her back."

"Hey Hon," Bonnie called out, "I got one for you. Bonnie then yelled out over Todd's singing,

> "Were you born an Asshole?
> Or did you work at it your whole life?
> Either way it works out fine,
> Because you're an Asshole tonight!"

Robyn couldn't contain herself and buried her face into Rob's shoulder to keep from laughing. Rob couldn't help himself either, and let out a small laugh along with a large smile. Where the hell did they move to? He couldn't help but wonder as he shook his head? Where the hell did they move to?

* * * *

A gunshot echoed through the night, and Rob sat up, quickly wide awake. It was an automatic reaction; he reacted even before he even heard the sound. A cold sweat streamed down his face and he could feel its chill. He'd completely soaked through the sheets again, and he was surprised that Robyn hadn't wakened to complain.

Rob looked around the dark room, searching for some sign of where the shot had come from. His eyes seemed sharp and his senses were on edge, just as when he'd been in the fiery depths of that hallway,. He could almost smell the smoke, but wasn't sure if he was imagining it or if it was just traces of the nightmare.

His breath was quick, and his chest heaving with excitement. He tried to calm down, to let the tension flow away, and calm his breathing. He just couldn't do it, his upper back hurt from the tension, and his shoulder blades wouldn't release, no matter how hard he tried to relax.

He looked over at Robyn; she still slept peacefully beside him. The last thing he wanted was wake her up; she deserved a good night's sleep.

Rob pulled himself out of bed and navigated the room, planning to go downstairs and maybe sit and relax on the couch. He was starting to get used to the feel of the place, and that made it a lot easier to navigate through what was left of the boxes. Robyn had done well getting everything unpacked and situated. The house was already beginning to feel like a home instead of the empty shell they'd moved into.

Rob stepped into the hallway and had the feeling that he was no longer the only one awake in the house. He took a quick look back into the bedroom, but Robyn was still asleep. She looked so peaceful as she slept, in the quiet, dark room. The little light in the room from the street light outside made her skin glisten. . He didn't see anyone but he still couldn't shake the feeling someone was there.

Rob eased the door shut behind him, gently settling the door into its frame so that it barely made a sound in the silence. The only thing he could hear was his own breathing, but he felt he was being watched from somewhere.

He turned and looked toward Jake's room. The door was open a crack, but Rob could see that Jake was till in his bed asleep, his nightlight shining from its home in the wall.

Rob crept down the hallway, walking lightly to prevent himself from waking up the household. Maybe the comfort of the couch down in the living room would release some of his tension, and he might be able to drift off to sleep.

He was halfway down the hall, when the cool night air went sour. A strong odor quickly began to fill the narrow hallway and the room turned instantly hot. Smoke billowed out of vents, streaming around him. He could barely breathe, as sulfur and the smoke weighted the air, and with every breath, he fought a coughing spasm. . He could taste smoke and soot covering the back of his throat.

It quickly filled the hallway, burning and filling his eyes with tears. It came at him from all directions, till he couldn't even see the white walls around him. He was forced to drop to the floor, searching for breathable air. The smoke moved toward him, and when he looked up, it felt like the grey cloud it was reaching down and grab him. Rob looked around, trying to see where the fire and smoke were coming from. His eyes were burning and he could barely breathe, but below the smoke, he could see clearly. At the end of the hallway, where Jake's room was, where just moments before the door had been slightly open, it was now closed, and smoke poured from the space below.

"Jake!"

Rob quickly stood and ran as fast as he could, ignoring the pain that jolted down his leg. He made it to the door and without any thought to his training, reached for the handle and ripped it open.

Flames shot out, surrounding him as he stood there, but he was no longer in his son's room. He was no longer in his own house. He was back in Chicago, at 4000 N. Milwaukee, in the sleazy confines of a hotel room that had been used as a Meth lab, and flames were everywhere. He could hear the screams from the people that had been working in the lab as well as the rest of the people who'd been just hanging out and getting high off the process. They were all just victims now, screaming and dying in the flames.

Rob fell to the floor, sure that the flames were finally going to take him and he'd never see his wife and son again. The last two months had all been just a dream brought on by smoke inhalation poisoning,. There was no house, no new job, just this. He was living his last moments, all in a fire.

Rob looked up into the flames, his eyes burning, and the last of their moisture evaporating from them; to see that the skull faced man was there. He was standing in the fire, but though the flames danced around him, they never actually touched him. His smile was as broad as ever, dirty teeth exposed while he watched Rob. His eyes reflected the fire's flames, looking straight into Rob, and he could feel the intensity of them more than the fire burning around him. They reached into his head, burning in his mind. Rob had to close his eyes; the pain was excruciating.

"Kill them all, kill them all and make the pain go away. KILL THEM ALL and make the pain go away. KILL THEM ALL AND MAKE THE PAIN GO AWAY!" The voice inside Rob's head spoke directly to him. It was a dry rasp, pushing at his skull and his head felt like it was exploding.

And then the pain was gone.

The heat and the smoke disappeared.

He could breathe the air again, and he took it in, in large gasps, trying to catch his breath.

He opened his eyes and found that he was no longer in the meth lab. He was back in his house, back in Jake's room.

He looked around, and saw Jake in his bed, his throat cut. Blood was throughout the room, covering everything. The bed was a red mess with a puddle at its center. On the wall, written in blood was, "Kill them all and make the pain go away." It was written on every wall, throughout the room. It repeated, both in large and small lettering. The only place untouched was the mirror on top of Jake's dresser; not a drop marred its surface.

Rob heard a scream pierce the silence, waking him from his shock filled daze. He turned to find Robyn behind him, her face pale and ghostlike. She stood, in the hallway, staring first into Jake's room, and then at Rob. Her eyes reflected something he had never seen before. She looked at him, truly terrified. She shook her head, whispering "no" as she slowly backed away toward the stairway. Rob reached out to grab her, to catch her before she fell down the stairs. He reached to pull her to him, to comfort her, to save her, but stopped dead, when he saw his hands.

In Rob's right hand, he saw the knife, a large butcher knife, covered in blood. Both of his hands were covered as well, and when he looked down at his clothes, he discovered they were completely drenched in it.

He looked up in shock, and saw the horror in Robyn's eyes as she looked at him. She continued to back away from him though he tried again to reach out to her.

Then suddenly, without even knowing what he was doing, he lunged, plunging the knife deep into Robyn's stomach. The shock in her eyes turned to horror as she looked down at the knife. She looked back up at Rob as the pain reached her, and slumped against him.

Slowly she fell to the floor, sliding off the knife as Rob stood frozen in place.

Rob turned to look at the mirror, at the skull faced man who stood where Rob's reflection should have been. . He was there, holding the knife, and he was laughing.

CHAPTER 6

Rob woke suddenly, bolting straight up in bed. His breath was heavy and irregular; the bed was soaked with his sweat. He quickly looked around to see that Robyn was there, beside him in the bed.

"You okay?" she asked as she stirred slightly. Her eyes were still closed, but she turned her head toward him.

"Yeah, just a nightmare." He put his hand on her shoulder to reassure her, and, he had to admit, himself.

She opened her eyes, and the skull faced man's burning eyes stared at him. They again burned into his skull, screaming through his head.

"Kill them all, and make the pain go away!"

Rob screamed and quickly jumped out of bed. When he looked back, Robyn was watching him with a concerned expression. The flames were no longer in her eyes.

"Should I call and make an appointment with the doctor in town?" She got out of bed and came over to comfort him.

Rob worked at getting his breath back under control.

"No, we can't afford it, and the last thing we need right now is another bill."

Rob slowly made his way back to the bed, with Robyn's help, her arms around his shoulders. She eased him in, and he lay back down.

He knew as he lay there, that he was done with sleep for the night. After all that, there was no way he was going to fall back to sleep and end up back in that trap. Robyn went back to her side of the bed, crawled in, and put her arm around Rob to soothe him. In minutes he could tell from the rhythm of her breathing that she was out.

Within a few minutes more, he too, had drifted back into sleep.

* * * *

"Toilet Out of Order-Use Floor Below."
"If You Jerk it, Don't Squirt it."
"Have a Nice Day."

Coolidge read the writings on the side of the stall with slight amusement. They were mixed with a variety of other phrases written and scratched along the stall. He always wondered what would make a man deface the stalls to leave their mark, but he still found most of them amusing no matter how much it upset him that someone would do it. Part of the hobo code was to respect others and their property. Writing phrases on a bathroom stall was far from the worst he had seen, but still, it was something that should never be done.

He looked at the writing he'd just read. He then lifted his feet off the ground and looked at the floor below. His shoes peeled off the ground as he lifted them, with a ripping sound. The floor was an ugly brown, and Coolidge really had to wonder if someone had taken the note to heart. He sure as hell hoped not.

He set his shoe back on the floor and looked at another phrase on the wall. There was one right under the "Call for a good time" number.

"It's better to be pissed off, than to be pissed on."

Yeah, he sure as hell agreed with that. Hell, he was sure getting pissed on now, now wasn't he. He had been running from the Grim ever since it had appeared to him. He had been so frightened, that he hadn't ridden the rails, or caught a ride. He'd been doing nothing but walking, non-stop. He avoided sleep until he was near the point of passing out, continuing to head east. He was always moving east; north east, south east, but always east, east as far as he could go, never west. Sure, he knew going on the westbound was just a phrase, a reference to death, to catching that beautiful railway to the sky and heavens above, but he sure as hell wasn't going to tempt fate.

Not with no Grim on his ass. It wasn't letting him out of its sight. Everywhere he'd gone, the Grim had been there, watching, laughing at him. He'd stand there, wearing an old train conductor's suit that was as new as the first day it was worn.

Coolidge reached for the rolls of toilet paper, trying to ignore the stench of the bathroom stall. Part of being a man on the rails always made him accept the good with the bad. That often meant taking the bathrooms with running water as well as the ones without. Then there were the nights when he would sleep away from any form of civilization, or even just when he slept in the rail yards, where he wouldn't have any form of a bathroom.

As he looked around the beat up stall with the stained floor, he questioned whether the wilderness wasn't a better alternative.

Coolidge looked at the stall's dirt and shit covered wall, ready to grab another handful of paper, when he stopped to read the scratching's above the dispenser. He could have sworn the scratch was fresh, he thought he had read them all.

"Your days are near an end. Hurry up and get home."

His breath caught as his heart skipped a beat. That had definitely not been there when he'd sat down.

It was there now, plain as day, scratched into the wall, but traced in red. It looked like it was written in fresh blood, but he had no way of knowing for sure, and he'd rather not know. Ignorance was bliss, and he'd wished many times that didn't know as much as he did.

The door to the public bathroom slammed open, causing Coolidge to jump and slide a little on the toilet seat before he caught and re-centered himself. A warm, hot breeze rushed under the stalls and felt like it sucked away the air in the room. On the wind came a stench that was far worse than the putrid smell of the bathroom. The smell of rotting meat and decay, of dead things, flowed through the bathroom, mixed with a sweet smell; one that Coolidge couldn't place.

Even with the heat, a sudden chill ran down Coolidge's spine, and the hair along his arm stood on end as he shivered in the hellishly warm room.

He looked down at the bottom of his stall, watching, knowing that there was a presence in the room with him. He could feel it out there, waiting.

It was four in the morning, and he'd been the only one in the all night diner, other than the cook hidden in back making the occasional meal and the tired waitress that had threatened to throw him to the curb until he flashed cash.

Not that it mattered. He doubted whatever had just entered was even human.

With a sweeping sound, the door closed, and Coolidge held his breath as he sat there, listening for a sound. Whatever it was, he had a burning sensation in the pit of his stomach that it wasn't good. No, something evil was in there with him; standing by the door.

Then the breathing started. It was slow at first. Heavy, long, raspy breathing. Coolidge tried to breathe deeply and quietly. He knew the thing knew exactly where he was. It enjoyed his fear. It enjoyed toying with him, scaring him. He didn't have to go out there to see what it was, to know what it looked like. He knew that it was the Grim, in his spotless train conductor's uniform, with his large, tooth filled smile, and burning eyes. He didn't have to see him to know.

He could tell by the stench that had followed him ever since the damn Grim first appeared to him. The odor had followed him since he'd rushed from his camp site days before. It was the smell of rotten meat infested with maggots, of garbage on a hot summer day after the sun has peaked, and cooked the odors together, creating an ungodly stink. A stink that made Coolidge's stomach twist into a knot and what was left of his middle of the night breakfast threaten to leave him the same way it entered.

The Grim had followed him there. It wasn't a surprise. It had been following him since he had left his little piece of solitude, burning his heels with its closeness, at times. Even when he didn't see or feel it, he knew it was nearby.

It was waiting for him too. It was ready to take him on that westbound ride. His time must be coming soon, he thought to himself. The Grim wasn't letting him out of its sight.

And now it had him trapped there in that bathroom stall.

Coolidge looked around the stall, and the little of the bathroom he could see. There was no place to go. The bathroom had no windows, no other doors, nothing. The only way to leave was the bathroom door on the other side of the room, past the Grim that was currently standing guard over it.

Coolidge could hear the Grim shift its weight before it walked further into the bathroom and closer to Coolidge's stall; its footfalls echoing loudly off the tiled walls.

* * * *

As the Grim made its way to the door of the stall, Coolidge held his breath. Thoughts of what it might do flashed through his mind, including his death and beyond, none of them inviting.

The silence stretched endlessly, and what was only a matter of minutes began to feel like hours. He had to shift his weight; he was beginning to lose the feeling in his leg. Eventually, he thought, someone from the diner would have to come in, but no one had yet, and he was still sitting there alone.

"Hello?" It sounded weak in the silence that had become of the bathroom. The echoes that should have bounced off of the walls stopped at the matte finish of the door.

There was no reply. From the other side of the room, Coolidge could hear the deep, raspy breath start again in the silence long and slow, it continued on and on, and then stopped suddenly.

The room was dead silent. Coolidge adjusted himself on the seat of the toilet, beginning to lose feeling in his other leg.

He looked down under the bottom of the door, at the pant legs of the conductor suit, well-tailored and in pristine condition. However, beneath them there were just bones, covered in pale, dirty skin. Maggots dropped to the tiled floor from inside the pants, forming a pyramid of flesh eaters.

The Grim let out a long breath, drawing it out into an unbearable length, and then began to draw a long breath in. The breathing slowly became regular and rhythmic. It was hypnotic, and began to draw Coolidge in. He could feel his eyes getting heavy, pulling, demanding to close. He felt eager to give in, let his eyes drift shut, and all the cares of the world disappear. He'd never stressed much anyways, but the rhythmic pace made him feel as if he floated in a cloud. The moldy bathroom around him faded away into nothing. The acrid smell of urinal cakes disappeared as he drifted into the void.

He let go and closed his eyes, unable to fight it any longer. The darkness surrounded him, and he lowered his head in defeat.

* * * *

Coolidge was suddenly pulled back into consciousness, waking quickly, much faster than his vision could compensate for, the light sending a stabbing pain deep into his temple.

He raised his hand to his face, trying to block the light. Slowly, his eyes adjusted and he was staring into the headlights of a car pulling into the parking lot.

"Parking lot, parking lot where?" he thought to himself.

He spun around, trying to shake the cobwebs, and figure out how he got there. Instead, his head felt as if it was being squeezed, as heavy as cement. He put all his effort into just staying on his feet as he eyed the building he was standing in front of.

It was a dump in the middle of nowhere. A tiny diner near what had once been a major highway. The night around him was still and quiet throughout the abandoned countryside.

* * * *

Coolidge nearly fell down the front steps of the diner as he stumbled back.

The front door of the diner was covered in bloody handprints, the windows broken. Lying limp on the broken glass was the large white haired lady that had been so cold to him when he'd come into the diner. Her hair was no longer white; it was red, thickly matted with blood. Her throat had been cut and the blood flow had created the streaks of red through her hair. The eyes that had looked at him with such disdain when he had entered were now gone. In their place were gouge marks where someone had dug into the sockets and clawed deep to pull them out.

Coolidge gagged at the sight. He could feel his dinner rise and stick in his throat, fighting to come up. The wave got stronger, and eventually there was nothing he could do, it was just too strong.

He turned just in time to avoid losing his dinner all over the woman, and let it go over of the rail of the front stairs of the diner. It came in wave after wave. His disgust at the smell that hit his nostrils after the first wave, kept bringing more and more, until he thought that his stomach must be somewhere in the mess below.

He brought up his hands to wipe away the remains from his mouth, and for the first time noticed that they were covered in blood. It was everywhere, throughout the wrinkles of his knuckles, even under his finger nails. He stopped and studied them, amazed that there could be so much. He looked down at his clothes and saw that he was drenched in it. His skin was red, and his clothes were stained a dark shade of brown. He couldn't see it, but he could tell that his soul, buried deep inside, had also been deeply stained.

He looked over the rail at what he'd just expelled, and saw the dark burgundy color, the orbs of white, that were buried in his vomit.

Her eyes! He had swallowed her eyes!

A new wave hit, though how he could have any more left, he didn't know, and he leaned over the rail, gagging.

* * * *

A door crashed open. It made Coolidge jump and he nearly fell off of the toilet seat. The seat was wet, covered in piss, making it slippery.

"You die in here or what?" A loud female voice bellowed, echoing off the walls of the bathroom. He recognized it as belonging to the waitress. A flashback of her dead body sent an unsettling chill through him and his body shook.

The door slammed shut.

A fiery chill went through Coolidge's arms and legs, working up to his spine. There was pain, and he could feel it growing. It was hiding there, behind his eyes, and he could feel tears along with it.

He looked down and saw that he'd pissed over all over himself and the seat. Everything was soaked, his clothes, himself. There was urine running down his legs in streaks, into his socks and shoes.

He could imagine what it must have looked like to the waitress; he was sure that she'd tried to look up under the stall to make sure he was still alive, not dead of an overdose, or sleeping.

As he reached for a handful of the stiff, thin tissue that passed for toilet paper, he wondered briefly what she would do if she did find his dead body in a stall. Visions of "Motel Hell," with human sausage being served to paying customers danced through his head as he reached for another wad, trying to soak up as much of the piss from his legs as he could.

He had another pair of pants in his backpack, hanging on the inside hook of the bathroom door. He looked up at it, grimacing at the thought that he was actually going to have to change out of piss clothes. What kind of man has to change out of piss clothes?

"He sure better not be getting too old to be on the road," he thought, as he flushed the toilet, watching the clean water fill the toilet. He reached for another handful of toilet paper and reached between his legs to wet it with the clean water. Once it was well soaked, he brought it back up and began to wipe down his legs. The last thing he wanted, when going back into the diner, was to smell like urine.

He looked at the door again, at the writings scrawled there. He was tired, and wanted nothing more than to sleep, but he knew that he still couldn't. So instead, he wasted more time with the sayings.

He read the writing on the back of the wall twice. The first time through, it didn't really sink in; his head was starting to throb. The second time, he stopped and sat quietly, contemplating what he saw.

"Get Home Now, Boy!"

It wasn't funny or catchy. In fact, if Coolidge didn't know any better, he would think that it was for him. After all, why would something that random be there for him? It didn't matter why. He knew it was there for him. He knew where the Grim wanted him to be, and it wasn't going to stop until he went there.

"Yes dad," Coolidge said under his breath.

He knew he wasn't alone. It was there, waiting, ready for the moment that Coolidge opened that door.

* * * *

Rob eased himself into the passenger seat of the car, wincing from the pain shooting through his back. The front seat of the Standard squad car was a tight fit, not comfortably equipped to have someone riding shotgun. The car was actually set up more like a state trooper vehicle. The on board computer was mounted just over the glove compartment, sticking out so that Rob had to maneuver around it to fit his long legs inside. The keyboard was set low in the mount, and rested heavily on his left leg, leaving little room to situate his legs. The center space was cluttered with the shotgun mount and car radio, and Rob had to "hold" all of the paperwork that would have been better kept in a file cabinet at the station. Unfortunately, the only "station" they had was Officer Renner's makeshift office.

"Get the main vein all cleared out?" Office King asked, over his cup of hot coffee as he sat in the driver's seat. King was driving Rob around, showing him the ropes and the back roads of what would be Rob's new "beat." They'd already been out to what King said the kids called, "Ol' Cumberland." It was a cemetery nearly five miles outside of town, down dark back roads that made it hard to find. King said it was one of the three major "hot spots," and that on any given night the local kids might be out there "boozin' it up."

Rob could tell that King really didn't mind the kids doing what they did all that much. They were just local kids having fun, and unlike the kids out late in the streets of Peoria where King was from, these kids never did any damage and weren't into drugs. For the most part they were just doing some harmless backwoods drinking.

"Sex and Beer" was all that they were after according to King, and to him, that was permissible. Not legal, but it was sure as hell better than a lot of other things they could get their hands on.

Rob could see where the man was coming from. In Chicago, he had gotten used to what was safe to get into and what wasn't. Was it better to harass a man who littered, or catch the drug dealer peddling trash? Rob learned long ago, the man who littered was a nuisance, the dealer was a killer.

A pain shot through Rob's side and he had to adjust himself in his seat. Damn, it was stiff as hell, and made it hard for him to stay in one position for too long.

It didn't make him feel any better that he felt like a rookie all over again. He knew King was trying hard not to make him feel that way, but he did. Rob knew very little about the area, and had no idea what to expect from the people. Hell, there he was, moving from a city with over fifty thousand stoplights to a town that didn't have even one. How in the world was he ever going to relate to these people?

Officer King reversed the squad car out of the parking lot of the truck stop. After midnight it was the only place left open, and besides trying to catch drunks speeding home, this was the main stop on their late night rounds.

The truck stop was just off the interstate on the outskirts of town. It was open twenty four hours, with a diner off to one side, making it a great stop for the long haul trucker or the late night drunkard. With a lot of the trucks using the large gravel parking lot to pull off and sleep for the night, it made it home to more violence than any of the bars at the center of town. If fights didn't break out at the bars, often they did at the all night diner where they came to sober up.

"Well, you ready to head out to the field?"

"The field?" Rob asked, trying to keep a smile on his face, as his back grew progressively more painful. "We're surrounded by nothing but fields; how can you identify anything as, 'THE field?'"

"I guess you can't, but the kids can. They have their party spots named. There's 'Ol' Cumberland, which you've seen, but then there's 'THE' field, and then there is 'THE' bridge. I don't know what drew them to these three spots, but for the most part, it's where they go. The field is actually the hardest one to sneak up on, and Renner, he's all about sneaking up on 'em. Me, though, I like to let them know I'm coming. Like I said, they're not bad kids. Hell, if I could just sit there and watch 'em, and make sure that they're all safe, then I wouldn't mess with them. The field though, there's really no way to just sneak up on them, so you just have to break it up when they're out that way. Hell, I bet the farmers wouldn't even mind, if it wasn't for the mess and the litter they leave behind."

Officer King eased the car off the main highway that paralleled the interstate, onto a small side road just past a set of railroad tracks. It was definitely hidden. If King hadn't made the turn, Rob would never have known the road was even there. It fell disappeared into the darkness, and the headlights barely penetrated it. Rob was amazed that

King was able to keep track of the turns; Rob never even saw them coming until they were already sliding through them.

"It's actually easy to get back here," Officer King said, as he let his foot off the accelerator and let the engine idle down. "It might seem confusing, but everywhere you need to turn, there are landmarks. These kids, they're not rocket scientists, they wouldn't be able to find the place if it was too hard."

King slowed the car as they neared a small cement bridge. They were far out in the middle of nowhere, yet they kept coming across those little bridges. Now that they were out in the country away from the lights, the full moon lit the darkness, and Rob could see the vastness of the fields. He could see along the side of the road and the little creeks that cut across the corn fields. The bridges covered the network of creeks that ran throughout the country.

King suddenly turned into one of the corn fields just before they reached the bridge, and Rob turned to look over at King. Rob couldn't even see where he was turning, until they had exited the small access road into the middle of the field. The corn wasn't high, only about three feet, but they could still barely see the field as they drove.

"I'm going to get myself lost out here," Rob said, as he looked back at the disappearing road.

"Then don't worry about it. You don't have to come out here. Like I said, the kids don't hurt anything, so until you get used to the area, just don't come out this way. I usually just patrol the town, and then stay around the truck stop. You try to find all the hidden spots out along the back roads, especially when you're new and doing it at night, you will get yourself lost. So like I said, don't worry about it. I'm just showing you where to go, so when you get used to it, you can."

They came to a large hill, the access road disappearing on the other side. Rob looked around and saw that all the corn fields around him stopped there, and the access road was the only way to get to the other side. He held his breath; it felt like they were going nearly straight up and the car's headlights shone out into the stars.

When they reached the top of the incline, Rob could see that it was railroad tracks they were driving over. He worried briefly about being stuck there when a train came, but his thought was interrupted when he turned to talk to King and saw the large bonfire just over the hill. There were already a handful of trucks there, and about a dozen people standing around the fire.

"Damn, this is a perfect hiding spot. You can't see the fire from the road, and you can't see it through the field. If you didn't know they came out here, you would never find it."

"Hell, we didn't know about it for the longest time. Not until the farmer who owns the property complained."

King eased the squad car to the side of the field and flipped on the flashing lights. He'd made sure to park the car in such a way that it blocked anyone from trying to driving past them, and out of the field.

"Ugh, time to go talk to them. Talk tough, sometimes give them a ticket, but for the most part, you just want to make sure they get home safe," Officer King said, as he reached for the door handle and started out of the car. Rob waited a second, and then decided that now would probably be a good time for him to make his introductions. He wanted to find out the trouble makers now, before he had to work it out on his own.

He eased out of the car, working hard not to let the pain that was going through him show on his face. He walked around the car and met up with Officer King. He was already talking to the group of kids all of them barely seventeen.

* * * *

The kids had separated quietly, with Rob and King following them out. Rob wasn't happy with how drunk a lot of the kids were, and the thought of letting them drive frightened him. He knew if it was him, he wouldn't have let them all go. The ones that were drunk he probably would have ticketed, but he could see why King didn't. If he ticketed them for Drunk and Disorderly, then it would not hold up in court. If he did anything with a DUI, then the kids would lose their license, and he thought King was right; at heart they were all good kids.

Rob looked at the dashboard clock in the car as they pulled onto the highway. It was just past one in the morning, and Rob was growing tired. He rubbed his eyes, and wondered how he was going to make it until five.

"Let's go get some coffee." Rob looked over at King and saw he was tired as well. King met his gaze, "It's a long shift."

Rob nodded in agreement.

"For the most part, the shift is pretty much over once you break up the kids. Just patrol the main street every now and again, and check on the truck stop. After that, just find a place to set up a speed trap. Just don't get caught sleeping."

"What do you do to stay awake?"

"I stay at the truck stop mostly. At this time of night, it's the only place with activity."

The lights of the truck stop shined brightly, and they got closer.

"Coffee sounds damn good about now. I haven't been up this late for nearly five years."

King turned the squad car into the far parking lot. The lot was filled with trucks and sleeping drivers. King eased along the perimeter of the trucks, turning on his spot light and shining down the rows, trying to avoid shining it through any truck windows.

Rob already felt his attention drifting. This place was definitely not going to be like Chicago.

* * * *

Rob pulled himself out of the squad car, trying to avoid twisting in such a way that would send jolts of pain down his leg. His head ached, his eyelids were heavy, and his neck felt stiff and weak. It had been a long night, and he sure as hell was glad he was done. It was over, and his bed upstairs was calling his name. Damn, it had been one hell of a long night.

He watched as the squad car pulled away from the curb and into his neighbor's driveway to turn around. The lights shined into his eyes briefly as the car swung back out onto the street and then headed back to the downtown area. Not that there was much of a downtown.

The car faded away, and Rob turned to look at his new house. The full moon shone on the windows and cast long shadows across the front yard. In the dark haze of a tired mind, Rob stopped briefly to look at them, and could have sworn they looked like fingers reaching out to him. His stomach was queasy from so much coffee and his head felt like a cement block; the last thing he wanted was to think about anything but sleep.

He stood there, listening, trying to get his feet to take him to bed. He was too tired; he didn't even want to do that. If he could get away with just lying down on his front lawn, and sleeping right there, he would have.

As he stood, the silence weighed on his mind. The night, with the squad car now gone, had become quiet, and he could hear the distant sounds of cars passing on the interstate. Farther along, there was the lonesome sound of a train whistle, probably slowing down to pass by the fields.

A gentle breeze blew through his hair, and in the hot summer night, it felt cool on his skin. , as tired as he was, it was relaxing to stand there and just let the breeze blow. The coolness of the breeze made the fog back off a little. He closed his eyes, enjoying it until it died away.

He looked down the long stretch of dead-end street. A feeling rose from his stomach, twisting it in agony on the way, it was more than just the coffee starting to go sour. There was something in the trees, watching him, its gaze piercing his skin and taking fiery hold of his heart.

He took a long, deep breath and held it as he looked up at his house. The light from the moon faded and darkness seemed to cascade into the street. The streetlights seemed to fade, and the moonlight that had reflected from second story windows only moments ago was gone as if absorbed by the darkness.

A burning sensation shot up his back and raised the hairs on the back of his neck. Suddenly the outside air felt very stuffy, and he felt as if he were in a vacuum, with all the air being sucked out of him.

He could hear a strong wind begin to blow heavily through trees, and turned to look at the end of the street. The trees shook wildly as a savage force tore through them. He waited to be buffeted by the strong wind, but Rob was enveloped in heat, no wind at all blew over him.

He turned and stepped toward the woods. He could smell cinnamon; it assaulted his nostrils in a burning wave, mixed with the stench of something rancid. As Rob walked, it took a couple of deep breaths before he was able to identify it. It was mildew- cinnamon mixed with mildew, and it grew stronger the closer he came to the woods.

Rob reached down for his revolver, hanging on his hip. He could feel he was getting closer to whatever was out there, and doubted that the revolver would have any effect on the unseen presence that kept itself hidden in the darkness of the woods. However, the cold steel gave him comfort, just knowing it was there at his side. It had been with him for a long time, had helped him survive Chicago, and he was pretty sure that it would keep him alive in this little hick town.

Rob made a quick scan of the houses along the street, expecting only the darkness behind the windows. He had the feeling he was being watched but felt alone on the empty street. Hell, it was just past four in the morning, he bloody well expected to be alone.

He soon realized, however, that he wasn't. In three of the four houses between him and the woods, a ghostly shape stood in the open front doorway. Their blank stares were focused on him, with eyes pure black, and skin deathly pale. Emotionless, they watched him as he walked. He stopped in front of the Pacifico's house.

Rob looked back at the house next door to his own. It was hard to believe it was Todd watching him, his eyes dark and expressionless. He didn't look much like the man that offered him a beer just the other day.

Rob turned and looked at the woods. The intense wind that had roared through the trees had stopped. They were silent and still now in the night. The presence was still there, watching him, waiting patiently.

He walked to the edge of the street, to the metal barrier that prevented people from driving into the woods. It was just inches away. Its fury scorched his face and burned the hair from his arms, turning them dark red from its heat. All he could see, though, was darkness.

Rob looked at the house closest to the tree line. It was the only house with no one in the front door watching him. It was completely dark and silent.

Rob stepped away from the edge of the forest, and began to retrace his steps, toward his house. His lungs were on fire, and he let out the long breath that he'd been holding without even realizing it.

As he passed the first house on his return trek, Rob began to increase his pace. He wanted to put as much ground between him and the woods as he possibly could, but then he stopped, as he realized that his neighbors were gone. They had disappeared from their doorways and back to the darkness of whatever was behind their front doors.

Rob quickened his pace and continued down the street. His hold on his revolver was tighter than he thought safe, but was still locked in his holster. Right then it was more for comfort than safety. He hurried to his front door, and quickly into the safety of his house, taking only a second to look back at the street. Out of the corner of his eye, he saw a woman standing directly across the street from his doorstep.

She stood watching, a short, chubby woman in a light colored dress. Because of the way she was dressed, and how she stood, he guessed that she was a Native America. She appeared to be quite old, her spine bent and her posture hunched.

Rob took a step down from the front porch, planning to walk to her. He didn't like the idea of her standing there watching his house at any time of the day, but in the middle of the night was even more disconcerting.

Above him, a bird cried out loudly, rending the night with its shriek. Rob jumped when he heard it, and looked up to see it was perched on the overhang of the front porch. It sat there, watching him intently.

Rob looked back across the street at the woman. She was gone.

It was again the quiet, empty street where he'd been dropped off only minutes ago.

CHAPTER 7

Coolidge sat, listening as the train made rhythmic waves below him. In the past, it would have been a comforting sound that would ease him into a deep sleep. He would have lay there in the railway car, letting it take him to wherever it went, not caring where he ended up.

Now he sat wide awake, afraid to sleep. He didn't dare let his guard down, and was afraid of what would come at him if he took the chance and closed his eyes.

Something shifted in the far corner of the rail car. Coolidge jumped nearly out of his skin; he was sure that he'd been alone in the car. The corner was darker than the rest of the railcar, but there was definitely something there, covered with what appeared to be a rumpled blanket. It fluttered in the wind blowing through the open door of the car. Whatever it was, it moved, shifting slightly under the blanket. His senses were heightened by his fear, and he felt he could almost smell whatever it was under the cloth.

Waves of cinnamon floated through the railcar. It was a strong, stifling smell, mixed with something that had Coolidge choking on its stench. He raised his arm over his nose and mouth trying to block it, but it did little good. It seemed it might smother him, it was so strong. It permeated the fabric of his shirt, forcing its way into his skin.

He looked over his arm at the lump in the corner. It shifted again, this time turning as if someone were rolling over. The cloth slowly pulled away. Coolidge shivered.

In the dim light of the car, a bare leg was revealed from beneath the cloth. Coolidge backed away instantly, terrified of what else would emerge. He imagined what else might be here with him.

He scanned the car quickly. For the most part it was empty, probably being transported from one rail yard to another, or returning from a run. Empty cars always made the best ride, they had the most space, and, typically, rail workers didn't bother to check each one. Some would argue that a half filled car was better; giving more room to hide, however, Coolidge always liked the space in the empties. If you had a good crew on a good line, they often wouldn't bother him, as long as he didn't bother them.

There were a few areas of the car that he couldn't see, but from what he could, there were just a couple of boxes scattered randomly around the edges.

He could hear something sliding across the floor, and quickly turned back to the body in the corner. The blanket was pulled even farther back and he could see the naked backside of a man lying there. His leg moved across the floor, and the body slowly rose. Coolidge shifted away from the corner of the car; working his way to the far side. His stomach grew heavy. Even on the hottest of nights, Coolidge wouldn't be caught dead sleeping naked in a car. Whoever he was, the guy was very pale and thin, not much more than bones. The ribs in his back were easily visible, and the skin sank deeply between each one. His arms and legs were stick thin, and Coolidge couldn't see any muscle at all; how the man could even move, let alone push himself up, was beyond him.

Coolidge looked at the shape across the car working its way up, and was reminded of those fund-raising commercials on late night television. The commercials with that Brady Bunch girl, he could never remember which one it was; maybe it was Marsha. Who knows, but the people in those commercials were always beyond skinny.

The man suddenly turned to look at Coolidge. It was such a quick move it made Coolidge pull himself deeper into the farthest corner of the car, trying to disappear into the wall. In the dim light of the car, the man's eyes glowed, burning a fiery red as they studied him. Then he smiled, his teeth were scanty but the few that remained were stained yellow and rotted black.

"Hello Billy," the man said, his voice a raspy growl.

The color drained from Coolidge's face. No one had called him that in nearly twenty years. Not since he'd left home had he even once been called by his birth name. There were maybe a handful of people on the rails that even knew what it was, and none of them would have called him by it. They all had more respect for him than that.

"Hey, Billy boy! How's Billy the Kid doing these days? Robbed any liquor stores? Eh?" The man smiled as he reached out for the wall to keep himself up.

"Billy Boy! Got any liquor for your old man? Eh,Billy boy?"

He walked across the car, feet shuffling along on the floor as he went, with barely enough strength to put one foot in front of the other.

"Come on Boy! Go get your Poppy some beer, won'tcha? Come on Billy Boy."

"Give me some money, ol' man." Coolidge cried out. Memories of his last days at home flooded back to him, and he remembered his father's hands, huge factory worker's hands that regularly came crashing into Coolidge's face.

"Money! I thought you were Billy the Kid!" In Coolidge's mind, he saw his father's hand, slam into his face, knocking him nearly to the other side of the room. In the rail car, the man was still shuffling his toward him, but Coolidge still felt the slap hit his face, as if it had already happened. It stung hot on his cheek and he was sure that if he looked in a mirror, there would be a red mark.

"You want money boy, youse better get out there and either earn some or steal some." Coolidge mentally felt another slap, this time from the other direction. It was a pattern he knew well, first one side, and then the other. Insult, hit and repeat, over and over until Coolidge was a bloody heap in the corner of his bedroom.

Coolidge collapsed, crying, to the floor of the railcar. The old man was getting nearer, and Coolidge shook his head from side to side, and tried to slide along the perimeter of the car, away from the old man.

"No, no, get away from me!" Coolidge mewled, as he positioned himself in the front corner of the car.

The old man turned and began shuffling again in his direction.

"Come on Boy! Don't make me angry!" Coolidge barely had time to register what was said before his head was slammed back against the metal wall of the rail car. The sound echoed loudly as his head bounced back. Pain shot through his head, and he reached up to the back of his skull, he knew it would come away covered in blood.

Coolidge looked up, his eyes stinging, as he looked through his tears at the old man. The specter continued closer. His father's eyes burned brightly, till flames actually began to emanating from them, and they were completely ablaze.

"Yeah, that's right boy! Look in my eyes. Look real deep." Coolidge could feel his father's breath on his face. The man was still not close to him, but he could feel it, hot on his cheek. The foul stench of death mixed with the smell of cinnamon in the rail car made Coolidge want to puke.

He closed his eyes, trying to keep himself from losing control. He counted each breath, working to calm himself. He could taste vomit starting to rise, and he had to slow his breathing, and swallow to keep it from coming up.

"Look deep into these eyes boy. Youse better get used to it. You'll be here with me soon boy. I'm going to take you down here with me boy! You best get used to the heat, cause the fire, it's coming for you boy! The flames be a-comin' for you."

Coolidge looked up at the old man standing over him. The flames in his eyes were reaching out, almost touching him.

He reached out for Coolidge and lifted him off the floor. Coolidge tried to fight back, grasping frantically at the man's hands. They were like vice grips, their hold unbreakable. He pushed and pulled, even tried to bite the man, to make him release him. The old man's hands were immovable; Coolidge was a prisoner in their grasp.

The man dragged Coolidge along the wall of the railcar, closer to the open door. He panicked as he looked from the open door to the old man. He was laughing; his unnatural smile wide, nearly ear to ear, as if it had been cut into his face.

And then there were the eyes; Coolidge was even closer to them now, and he could feel the heat, becoming more intense as the flames licked out at him. He felt the skin on his cheek burning and charring.

The hot night air reached them as they neared the door. It billowed into the rail car, but felt cool only because of the high speed of the train. It soothed him slightly from the heat of the flames licking against his face. Coolidge wished he could take comfort in it, but he knew what the cool air meant, and in moments he was approaching just what he feared.

The old man held him right at the edge of the door for a brief second, and then in the next, Coolidge was hung in the open, over the edge of the rail car. The man, who looked like he had just barely enough muscle to walk, held Coolidge like he weighed nothing. He didn't even strain as he held him, dangling in the night air speeding past. The train was on a long level stretch of track, and from what Coolidge could tell, they were probably doing somewhere around sixty. At that speed, if he was to hit anything, or even if he were just dropped, he knew his body would explode on impact. Once, when he was sixteen, he had hit a deer with his dad's car. He had been doing just forty miles per hour through the woods, but that had been enough. The damage he had done to the deer was extensive; the organs and entrails had been strewn along the highway. The car had taken a lot of damage as well, but there was almost nothing left of the deer. He imagined that the results would be something similar for him. He didn't think it would make a pretty sight on the tracks.

"I'm going to take you down with me boy."

Coolidge looked from the view of the ground passing by quickly below him, to the face of the old man. He was still smiling and he nodded at Coolidge, confirming his worst fears.

"It's time to come home boy!"

Coolidge had just enough time to register what was happening before it did. The train wheels squealed, as the brakes were heavily applied. Coolidge looked along the side of the train and saw that they were coming to a sharp curve, and the train was slowing in order to make it. As it decelerated, he felt the hands that had held such a tight grip on his chest, let go.

Coolidge was free. He fell into the darkness alongside the train.

* * * *

Robyn had heard Rob come to bed, and knew how late it had been. She knew that he hadn't meant to wake her, even as loud as he was; he'd been trying his hardest to be quiet. Still, he was a big guy, and ever since he had gotten hurt; it was hard for him to move, let alone move quietly.

The last thing she wanted to do was wake him, as she eased herself out of bed. He needed his sleep. He'd worked all weekend on late night patrols, and he deserved his rest.

Robyn tiptoed out of the room and made her way quickly downstairs to the kitchen. She knew Jake would be up soon. He never slept past eight in the morning, unless of course it was a school day. Then she practically had to pull him out of bed, kicking and screaming. Not so during summer vacation; he was nearly up with the sun most days, eager to get playing his DS or watch his morning cartoons on the Cartoon Network. She hated the cartoons on that station. None of them seemed appropriate for kids. They were all so vulgar. "Ed, Edy, & Eddie," what was that teaching her son?

Robyn barely had the first batch of pancakes off of the griddle when she heard Jake hurrying down the stairs, stomping his way toward his oh-so-important cartoons. Jake rushed into the room, and quickly she put her finger to her lips and shushed him.

"Your dad's sleeping. He was out all night on patrol, so I don't want you to be making a lot of noise this morning okay?"

Jake quickly nodded as he slid into his spot at the kitchen island. Robyn set the pancakes in front of him and watched as he quickly devoured them. She didn't realize that she was just standing there watching him until the phone ringing in the other room woke her from her trance.

She quickly hurried into the living room and barely made it to the phone before the fourth ring, when it would switch over to their voicemail.

"Hello?" She never liked to identify herself when she first picked up the phone. She was always afraid that it would be some bill collector. She was used to dodging so many of them, and tired of having to keep coming up with excuses as to why this bill or that bill hadn't been paid. It was a constant struggle to come up with reasons. She didn't like to do it, but since Rob had gotten hurt, she hadn't had too many other options, with their money growing ever tighter over the months.

"Ms. Alletto?"

Robyn recognized the familiar voice on the other end, and quickly let her guard down. Maybe this call would be good news for a change; it was the real estate agent from Chicago. Maybe they'd sold the house, and their agent, Denise, was calling to tell them their financial worries were over.

"Yes Denise, how's the house?" Robyn rebounded. She was already becoming anxious. She bounced a little, as she walked around the room.

"Well…"

Robyn's heart sank. She could tell by her tone that there was news, but it wasn't going to be what Robyn wanted to hear. What could be that bad? There was either someone interested in buying the house or not.

"Okay Denise, what's the deal?"

"Well, we have an offer on the house."

Now Robyn was confused. Denise should be calling them in her overly bubbly voice, crying out "Hey your house is sold!"

"Okay, well that's good."

"Not really." Denise let her words hang on the line for a second, and Robyn's dread started to build. Denise was not typically dramatic, so Robyn knew that whatever she had to say, she wasn't stretching it out for effect. Denise obviously wasn't sure of the best way to say it to her, and both of them were uncomfortable as Robyn waited for the news.

"We have an offer, but it is significantly less than what you were asking." Denise finally said from the other side of the line.

"Well, I mean, we can take a lesser offer on the house, that's fine. As long as it covers what we owe we'll be happy."

Denise was silent, and Robyn felt a lump form in her throat as she looked around for the nearest place to sit. Her legs suddenly felt like they were made of rubber, and she began to feel lightheaded. She didn't know how much longer she could stay upright, and started to sway.

"Okay, so we don't take the offer. It's not a big deal; there will be other offers right?"

Robyn eased herself into Rob's easy chair. On any given day it was always so comforting to sit there. It almost felt like she was sinking into Rob, and he was reaching his large arms around her to hold and to protect her. Today, she couldn't bring herself to even sit back in the chair; she stayed on its edge, trying to breathe.

"Robyn, we could. That would be fine; we could keep it on the market. But buyers are becoming few and far between. This was the first buyer who's shown serious interest in the house. The showings are becoming rare. I would like you to at least think about the offer."

"I'll talk to Rob about it later, and we'll give you a call back."

"And remember, it's just their initial offer, we can still make a counter offer."

"I'll let Rob know."

"I'll talk to you soon."

Robyn turned off the phone and set it down behind her in the chair. She sat there in the quiet room, and noticed the sun was rising, forcing light through the pulled shades.

Upstairs, she heard Jake playing his DS. He had probably remembered that the cable wasn't hooked up yet, so he wouldn't be able to watch his cartoons. Rob was still asleep. She wasn't about to wake him to give him the news about the house, it could wait until he woke up. He wasn't going to be happy when she told him, she knew he was already worried about how they would get by with even just the one house payment. He had been hoping for a little extra from the sale to help get them through the rough patch until they found some solution.

Robyn took a deep breath. It was going to be a rough day.

She could smell something burning and remembered the pancakes cooking in the other room. She quickly stood and hurried into the kitchen, cursing herself as she rushed to lift the pancakes from the pan and toss them into the garbage. They were nearly completely black on the bottom, and now the whole kitchen had gone from the sweet smell of freshly cooked pancakes to a sour burned one.

* * * *

Coolidge didn't know where he was, and had only the slightest idea of how he got there. He had a vague sense that he'd fallen, and fallen far, but what happened next was blank.

So where was he now?

He opened his eyes, and the stars exploded into view, and danced around him. It was extremely bright, sending needles of pain into his skull, and down his spine. He closed his eyes, but it did little to help.

He turned his head slightly, hoping movement would reduce the pain, but made it worse, new needles dug in, and now they were everywhere, piercing his skin in a tidal wave.

"Damn, Damn, Damn!" he thought to himself. What the hell had he been thinking? "Get home," that was what he had been thinking. Dammit!

Coolidge slowly shifted his weight and turned onto his side. He could hear the gravel shifting as he moved. His body settled on its side, but his head felt like a rock. Damn, he just wanted to stay there and let himself die. A throbbing pain began in his head, and again, Coolidge slowly, and cautiously, opened his eye, barely enough to see around him.

Everything was a blur of colors and shapes. He tried to push up on his arms, but they had long since turned to rubber and couldn't hold his weight.

Maybe he just didn't want to get up. He suddenly remembered the railway car that he'd been riding in. Sure, he had been superstitious, hell nearly all hoboes on the rails were, to some extent, but he had been trying to avoid going west. For the last week he had ridden every car he could find going only east. Still, that damn Grim found him. Maybe he was supposed to be going westbound. Maybe his time was up, and the Grim was trying to tell him something. Maybe. But bloody hell, damn him anyways!

Coolidge's body was sore from one end to the other, and he could feel moisture leeching through his clothes. He wondered how badly he was bleeding.

"Ugh," Coolidge said under his breath, as he tried to turn onto his stomach. This time he had more success, and made it all the way.

He felt a cool breeze on his face arms. He couldn't see it yet, but he was pretty sure his shirt was torn to hell. Who was he kidding; he was pretty sure he was torn to hell as well.

He was able to open his eyes wider and saw he'd rolled into a little shade. It was still excruciatingly bright, but he was at least able to see where he'd ended up. He was lying in gravel, just as he'd thought, but alongside the gravel ran a small stretch of woods. Just beyond that he could make out what looked like a corn field.

Corn. Corn! Damn, he was getting a lot closer to home than he'd thought. When did he leave the desert, and how did he end up next to this seemingly endless stretch of cornfields?

Coolidge tried desperately to get his arms to work, and finally they lifted him up. His shoulders were screaming in pain, but he got his legs beneath him.

He spared a moment to look up at the railroad tracks, now remembering fully how he had fallen, and he saw the six foot rocky fall that he must have taken. It was a miracle he was only scratched up, and that he hadn't broken anything. Looking down the track, he could see that the tracks were curved, and realized that, thankfully, the train must have been slowing.

He thanked God for small miracles as he stood, uneasily and nauseous. He wasn't sure how far he could walk, but was grateful that at least he was still able to.

He knew he should have stayed off that damned railway.

Coolidge stumbled to the closest tree, and leaned against it. The world was spinning, and he still wasn't sure if he was going to fall off the world, or puke. He guessed it would be the latter, as he didn't really see falling off the earth as a real possibility.

The world began to settle and steady, and Coolidge looked down at his clothes. They were torn nearly to shreds just as he'd feared, and small cuts covered his arms and legs. None were serious, but they sure made him look like hell. He was going to have a hard time finding day work until he had changed and showered.

Coolidge looked around for his bag. Hobo's always had their back with them, and he always made sure to have a change of clothes and his toiletries inside. It was hard to find day work if a person didn't look presentable.

Coolidge looked all over, even behind the tree he rested against, but his bag was nowhere in sight. He doubted the Grim had been kind enough to throw it off after him, so he was probably stuck without it.

Coolidge felt his shoulders slump, sending a wave of stiffness and pain through him.

He would have to beg. Damn, he hated it when it came to that.

Coolidge pulled away from the tree, looking at it briefly as he stood up straight. He stopped and looked again, the color draining from his face as his mind registered the picture carved there.

"Why the hell would that be there?" he thought to himself. Carved into the tree were two vertical lines. There were three lines carved horizontally across each, one slightly apart from the other two.

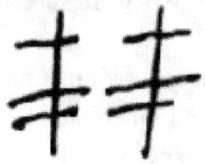

He knew what it meant, but didn't understand why it would be way out there in the middle of nowhere.

Hobo's have their own code. It's sign language that they leave to communicate to others, that most times tells where there's good work, or a nice person willing to help. It can sometimes be a way of marking a place for a good meal or a person willing to give them a place to sleep for the night. But, the two vertical lines, now that was a whole different thing. That was the symbol for danger.

And there it was, out in the middle of nowhere.

Coolidge took a closer look at the tree, and then turned again to take a cautious look around. The track travelled to a sharp curve ahead, the saving grace that slowed the train, and there was a stand of trees with a creek passing through it. All of it seemed so familiar to him. It reminded him of something, perhaps a dream he had once had.

Then it hit him, and he felt a lump form deep in his stomach.

He knew where he was. He recognized the field and the trees, and he knew who had carved that sign. It was crudely done, but he recognized his own handy work. He had carved that into the tree long ago, at the time, not even sure what he was doing. He hadn't really been sure of what it had meant at the time, it had just been something he'd seen in a dream the night before.

That was the night that his father had come home and killed his mother; the same night his father had come home and tried to kill him. He had carved that on the tree where he'd hidden after getting away from his dad. He'd picked the place knowing his father would never come looking for him here. He was safe.

He'd stayed until he saw a train, slowing as it prepared for the curve. He didn't know what he was doing at the time, but just started running to catch the train. He had been running to catch trains ever since.

Now, he was home.

* * * *

Rob was still asleep upstairs, and she doubted he would come down any time soon. She wished he would wake up though. She wanted to talk to him. She couldn't get it off her mind, and she wanted to tell him about the offer, see if he would be interested. She wondered if they'd be able to make it on his income alone, with this house payment and whatever was left over from their old house, if anything...

It must be one hell of a low-ball offer if it didn't even cover what they still owed. They had been in that house for over seven years, and hadn't missed a single payment. She thought they had paid off nearly half of what they'd paid for the house. It would make sense, wouldn't it? It was a fifteen year mortgage, so they should be nearly half there. How could someone offer them less than half of what the house was worth?

She needed Rob to get up, she needed to talk to him, and maybe he could explain it to her. Maybe she was missing something.

"Hey Mom, can I go ride my bike?"

Jake stood in the doorway to the living room. He had his bike helmet under his arm, and was all dressed up for a ride. They hadn't really let him explore too much yet. Their city instincts kept them from letting him out on his own, but every day, Robyn would see kids younger than Jake out riding their bikes freely around the town. Robyn couldn't believe parents would just let their kids ride around the streets by themselves, but Jake had been asking her about it, and she promised him that today she might let him do it.

She didn't want to, she wanted to keep him home, keep him safe.

* * * *

Since they'd moved there, she'd been trying to get used to the quiet. There was no one yelling in the streets, no violence, or kids getting shot. The town was safe. They were safe.

With a long sigh, and against her better judgment, she slowly nodded her approval.

"So, where do you plan on going?"

"I figured I'd take a ride and try to find the park, see what the kids in this town do for fun."

"That sounds good. Do you have your firefly on you? I want to be able to call you if I need to, and if you have any problems just give us a call. Be safe, and be home by five for supper."

"Mom, I'm only going ride my bike."

Robyn stood looking at him. She was amazed at how he was growing up. She didn't know what she would do if anything ever happened to him.

"But you do have your phone on you, right?"

Jake held up his little firefly phone. It was small, and made mainly for kids younger than Jake, but they had gotten it for him when he was younger, and they really couldn't afford to get him anything else. Plus, it kept the phone bill down, since the only people he could call was them, so there wouldn't be any sky high wireless bills to worry about.

"Good!" Robyn said, as she walked him to the door. Her little boy was growing up. She just couldn't get over it. She held the door for him, and watched as he ran outside and picked up the bike that he'd thrown on the lawn the night before.

Robyn watched as he rode away. She didn't close the door until he was around the block and out of her sight. Before turning away from the door, she felt the hair on the back of her neck start to rise and she froze. The room turned suddenly cold as though the air conditioner had suddenly kicked on and was blowing directly at her. She shivered, feeling that she was no longer alone; a presence had entered the living room.

She took a step back and turned to look into the living room. The cold air drifted toward her from there, and it seemed that something waited patiently, but with quiet desperation for her there.   The thought formed in her mind, that if she just stayed where she was, she might somehow be able to escape it forever. She only had to stay in the hallway, where it was safe. Just stay in the hallway… and be safe forever.

"You're never safe."

The voice sprang into her thoughts. It spoke softly, soothingly, but it was raspy, and felt like sandpaper being pulled through her brain. It made her uncomfortable, and   pull away even farther from the room.

She wanted to avoid it. She stood on the threshold wanting only to go upstairs and hide in the bedroom with the door locked, or better yet, escape through the front door into the street. At least out there, nothing could come after her without her seeing it. She remembered the days her parents would leave her home alone. She was only eleven, but more than capable of taking care of herself when her parents went on their nightly trips to local bars. That's what they told her anyway, that she was more than capable, a big girl, more than able to handle herself.

So why was it that most nights she'd be so scared she jumped at every noise, every little knock and ping she heard in the night? There had been nights when she would get so scared she'd go out into the middle of the road, just so she could watch the house and make sure nothing came out after her. It had been her crazy way of making sure she was safe.

"And it would be just as insane now," she thought to herself. What the hell was she thinking? She wasn't a little girl anymore, and she shouldn't be afraid of the rooms in her own house.

Robyn decided she wasn't going to let her imagination get the best of her. She wasn't going to let childhood fears keep her from unpacking and making this old house a home.

Robyn stomped into the living room, not exactly pouting, but forcing herself to believe she was in charge. This was her house, and she was going to get down to business. In Chicago, she never would have thought twice, so why in the hell out there in the boondocks?

As soon as she entered the room, the chill grew even more intense. It was like she'd just stepped into a walk-in freezer. She had to cross her arms to slow her shaking, and her skin was instantly cold to the touch. She breathed slowly to keep from coughing against the chill.

This had to all be in her head, she thought.

Robyn looked around. Her pictures all wore a thick layer of ice. The cup of 'hot coffee' that had been steaming only moments before was now frozen solid. Everything was frozen, everything except for her grandmother's mirror.

Robyn looked up at it and wondered why the cold didn't even touch it. It sat high on the wall, like a window to another world. The reflection was sun filled and cozy. Looking into the reflection, she felt the strong presence on the other side. She absent-mindedly shuffled toward the mirror. She couldn't tear her eyes away from herself. As she got closer, she couldn't help thinking how happy and beautiful she looked. Her reflection was amazing; she looked as radiant as she had on her wedding day.

She'd never been as happy as on that day. Rob had said that she glowed like the sun's rays, and her eyes shone like stars. She was sure he'd stolen the line from somewhere, as he had never been a poet, but it had made her so happy. It was that moment that she knew for sure that she was marrying 'the one.'

Her reflection glowed with that happiness now.

She reached the mirror, and could feel a warmth come through and flow over her. She was so cold, she just wanted a little of that warmth; it felt so inviting, so comforting. Robyn continued to reminisce about her wedding day: her father, walking her down the aisle, her grandmother in the front pew, crying as she watched her little girl being given away, and her mother next to her, holding her hand for support. They all sat and watched her marry the man she loved. Robyn could almost imagine her grandmother here with her now. She hadn't yet fallen sick, diabetes hadn't reached its peak, and she was still able to get around without her walker. She'd worn that beautiful flowered dress that she loved and always wore on special occasions.

Robyn swore she could see her in the mirror, walking up behind her. She was dim but just as she remembered her. She still wore that flowered dress, and her large bifocals.

Her grandmother came up behind her, but unlike Robyn, she was crying.

"Please Grandma, don't cry," Robyn thought to herself. She wanted to say it, but she found that she couldn't speak. She couldn't even move. She was trapped, and forced to gaze at her reflection. Robyn looked at her grandmother, silently pleading for help. Her grandmother seemed to understand, and nodding, quickly wiped away her tears. She reached up to place her hands on Robyn's shoulders. However, they landed not on Robyn's shoulders, but on the one's in the reflection.

Her grandmother began to draw back from the reflection of Robyn, and Robyn watched her smile change to pain, then the colors making up her grandmother's image began to run together. The rest of the reflection stayed sharp, but hers became a swirling mass, moving in different directions.

Suddenly she saw another face, being pulled out of her own. At first, it was indistinguishable, just the silvering that made up the mirror's surface. The silvering began to pull away from her reflection. She could still feel the chill of the room and knew that there wasn't a connection between her reality and the one reflected in the mirror. Still, as she watched her grandmother fighting with her own reflection, it seemed so real.

She had to be losing her mind, she thought. She tried to blink, to pull herself out of it. She still couldn't move. She was still trapped and forced to watch the battle going on in the glass of the mirror.

The silver shifted into another shape, pulling away from her reflection. When the silver finally twisted into shape, it was a face, and she realized that it was that of a man, a very disturbing looking man.

She didn't know if it had anything to do with the way the face had formed, but his skin seemed paper thin, nearly transparent, and the skull and bones underneath were clearly visible. His eyes were large and bulging out of their sockets, his nose decaying into the recesses of a skull. If there hadn't been an overall sheen on the surface of it, she would have been sure that there was no skin at all.

And then there was his smile. Somehow it was larger than his mouth and skin should allow, and it stretched from ear to ear. He stared at her, his smile broad, and allowed her grandmother to finish pulling him in his entirety from her reflection.

Robyn sensed that she recognized him from somewhere. She thought it must be from a nightmare, but couldn't be sure. There was something about him though; she knew she had seen him.

Robyn took a step back, and reached out to the nearby couch to keep from tripping and falling to the floor. She looked away from the mirror for only a second, to make sure that she'd caught herself and had regained her balance, but when she looked back, the man was no longer watching her.

His smile was gone, and he'd turned his attention to her grandmother. The mirror shook violently from side to side as the two grappled, pushing and pulling against each other in a desperate effort to win control

The man threw Robyn's grandmother violently into the couch, causing the mirror to nearly jump off the screws that held it to the wall. Robyn's grandmother was furious. Her brow was furrowed, and her face had turned scarlet. Her eyes burned with a hatred that Robyn had seen her display only once before. Robyn always swore she would never be at the other end of that rage, and she was glad that she never had.

Robyn's grandmother then plowed across the living room, rushing at the man who stood there in its center. He tried to prepare, lowering his stance, and readying for the attack, but she hit him with a force that propelled him across the room, until he slammed into the wall. The mirror shook even more violently, rocking back and forth until it slipped off one of the screws holding it in place.

Robyn watched in disbelief as her grandmother's mirror fell to the floor. When it hit the hardwood, it shattered in an explosion so violent it sent the pieces throughout the room.

Robyn watched the remnants settle. Now that the mirror was gone the room filled again with the July heat, and the specters in the mirror seemed totally unreal.

She just couldn't believe it. The mirror was gone.

CHAPTER 8

Terry watched as her husband stormed out of the house, slamming the door behind him. The door shook in its frame and the dishes in the kitchen sink rattled. She looked at them briefly, and then turned away from the kitchen and walked down the hallway away from the whole mess.

She just didn't know what his problem was. He had been a real bastard lately, screaming at her, starting fights, nearly getting violent with her. As she stepped into the living room and looked around at the mass of clothes that lay on the couch waiting to be folded, she wondered again what had gotten into that man.

The house was a mess. She couldn't remember the last time she'd let the place get like this. Clothes everywhere, dirty dishes in the sink from last week still waiting to be washed, and upstairs, a layer of dirty laundry carpeted their bedroom floor.

Ron was using the mess as a reason to fight with her. Maybe he was right. Maybe it was all her fault. She had kept the house clean and in perfect order for the last thirty years. Kept it spotless while both her sons grew up, and until they were gone, living their own lives. There had never been a smidgen of dust anywhere, but over the last two weeks, she'd had less and less interest in keeping it clean. There was a thin coat of dust on everything.

She knew it upset him, but she couldn't bring herself to do anything about it. She told herself she would start. In the kitchen, there were a couple of dishes in the side rack that she had washed yesterday. On the couch there were a couple of towels that she had folded sitting in the basket beside the couch. She needed to bring herself to finish, but as much as she tried, everything she started just didn't feel like it was what she should be doing. There was something else, but she couldn't figure out what.

Terry stepped up to the front door and looked out the window. She watched as Ron pulled his car out of the driveway, and off to work. Only five more years until retirement, and they were both counting every second. Every day on the news there were stories of more and more companies laying off their employees. A lot of the companies were getting rid of their eldest employees in order to get out of paying pension benefits.

That would put Ron first in line for the chopping block. She didn't know what they would do if that were to happen. Terry put on a good show most of the time, but her medical bills told another story. They had once had the house paid for, and could afford to just live off of whatever they'd get from unemployment and social security, but now they were so far in debt with medical bills, they just couldn't afford it.

Her medical bills. Lately, Ron liked to make sure she was reminded of that. To remind her that he had never been sick a day in his life, and she had been in and out of the hospital for nearly all of the last three years. Her kidneys were failing, constantly filling with stones, and the doctors were at a loss to understand why.

She'd had to have her left kidney removed just a month ago and she was already starting to have the pains again. Now they were more focused on her right side, and she feared that they were going to have to take her right kidney as well.

The last thing she wanted was to be on a machine for the rest of her life.

They'd exhausted their savings to pay the medical bills she'd already incurred. That damn electro-bath, or whatever the damn doctors called it, had cost them just over four grand. The insurance companies had refused to pay, calling the procedure experimental. All that pain, with them shattering those stones inside of her into smaller, passable stones, and she'd still had to have her kidney removed.

She was afraid that they were going to have to take a home equity line of credit against the house just to get them caught up. If Ron were to be laid off, the banks wouldn't give them the loan.

"Bah," Terry sighed to herself, as she stepped away from the front door.

She looked at the clothes stacked high on the couch. Dread settled in the pit of her stomach and she turned away. She was tired. She just wanted to lie down, maybe take a nap. Maybe that would help her to clear her head. She felt so tired lately.

Terry found herself starting up the stairs. She felt like she was losing herself, like she was slipping away. She didn't care about leaving the mess on the couch or in the kitchen. Maybe if she took a nap, it would all go away.

Terry stood in her bedroom but oddly, couldn't remember how she got there. It was as though she'd stepped into a dream and the world around her was no longer real.

She blinked and looked around, and then walked to the bed, but something didn't seem right. If she didn't know better, she would have sworn that she wasn't in her own bedroom, but someone else's.

No, that wasn't quite it. She knew she was in her own bedroom, but she wasn't alone. She couldn't see anyone, but the hair on the back of her neck was standing straight up. Someone was there. No, not someone; something. Something was hiding in the shadows just out of sight.

The sun shone brightly through the window, but the room was cold, and the shadows stretched from odd places in even more odd angles throughout the room. They seemed to be moving toward her, like they wanted to envelop her. She stepped away from the shadow closest to her, nearest the window, moving around it and moved toward the center of the room.

What the hell was she thinking, running away from a shadow? She wanted to laugh at herself, but instead crossed her arms in front of her. In the summer heat she should be sweating, not having the shivers! In the mirror on the dresser, Terry swore she saw something shift just out of her vision, and quickly turned to catch it.

She found herself looking at her own image. It was foreign to her, she'd avoided looking at herself in the last couple of weeks, ever since she had begun to feel contemptible and useless.

She knew her hair had been turning grey, but was surprised at how much more so it was than the last time she'd looked. Her skin had also grown very pale, almost grey, and she noticed additional wrinkles on her face. She also noted the extra skin starting to hang from her arms and from her cheeks.

"My God, I'm getting old," she said to herself as she stood there, contemplating the old lady looking back at her. What happened to the young woman who used to go out dancing with her husband? She used to have to nearly drag him to go, but when she got him out, they both had a fun time.

Her eyes locked on her likeness, and stopped short. Her eyes were different. She had blue eyes. There were a few times when her eyes were mistaken for grey, but, her eyes had always been bright blue. They used to stop her husband in his tracks.

Now she was lost in her own eyes, however, she wasn't lost in love.

Her eyes were black; completely black, with only a small ring of white encircling them.

She walked closer to the mirror, ignoring everything else around her. She leaned in as close as she could, and studied her eyes. It was surreal, how could they turn such a dark color? She lost track of time as she stood there, contemplating her own gaze.

She never noticed when she seated herself in the chair in front of the mirror.

She was completely lost. The mirror had trapped her, and she would never again have control of herself. She became aware of a man standing just behind her, smiling at her. She hadn't noticed him before, but there he was, with his hand on her shoulder. She couldn't take her eyes off of him, nor could she move a single muscle, even a fraction of an inch. He had her.

* * * *

Rob hadn't heard Robyn yelling up the stairs for him, nor did he hear her as she came into the room. She looked at the clock, and saw that it was nearly three. She would have loved to have let him sleep the entire day away, after he had been up all night on patrol, but there was someone downstairs waiting for him.

Slowly, Rob groaned himself awake and looked up to meet Robyn's gaze.

"Hey, honey." Rob said.

"There's someone downstairs."

"Yeah?"

Rob slung his legs over the side of the bed, and sat up. His legs felt like dead weights as they rolled over the edge of the mattress, and every muscle in his body felt stiff. He just sat there for a minute, waiting for the fog to clear as Robyn walked back across the room to the door.

"So who's at the door?"

"Father William. He's from one of the local parishes."

"You trying to get him to convert me? I didn't think you were all into that religious crap anymore"

"Yeah, whatever. No, he's here because Chief Renner told him you were now the officer on call during the day."

Rob pushed himself off of the bed and reached down for the uniform he had left scattered across the bedroom floor the night before.

"Ugh, first day." Rob pulled his pants on in slow and painstaking motions that started and stopped. After two nights of being on long, boring patrols when absolutely nothing of significance happened, the last thing he wanted to do was to be preached to, or worse, stuck on some funeral parade detail. Rob couldn't think of anything that would bring a priest to the door that he'd be interested in taking part in. Especially when he was half asleep and not fully recovered.

With a stress relieving sigh, he pulled on the uniform shirt he had slung over the nightstand and walked to the door, following Robyn as she made her way down the stairs.

He was halfway down when he got his first look at the man standing in his entryway. He was not what he would have expected in a small town pastor.

The man who introduced himself as Father William was short, around the same height as his wife, Robyn, with red hair and a moderately well groomed beard. He was also a little plumper around the middle than Rob would have figured. Father William was also standing there in a suit, not a cassock, which he found surprising. Then again, Rob was never a church going man, so to say that he knew their traditions would have been quite a bit off the mark.

Rob welcomed the Father into the living room, asking him to ignore the mess of boxes that were still scattered throughout the room. Most the boxes were empty, but they had still not been cleared out.

Father William smiled as he took a seat and waited for Rob to do the same.

"So how can I help you today?"

"I'm sorry to wake you. I had called the number and was told that you were now on call. Instead of calling, I figured I would just come over. I hope you don't mind."

Rob had no patience, as tired as he was, and until he had at least some caffeine coursing through his veins, he wasn't going to fake it.

"So what can I help you with? Break in? Someone get beat up? What's the emergency?"

Rob knew that he came across hard, and was sure that this was not the best way for him to make a first impression. He knew he shouldn't be acting that way, but he just couldn't stop himself. He was too damned tired to care, and he really didn't care about what the Father had to tell him.

"I need you to do me a favor. I've been trying to get hold of the Taylors. Samantha didn't come to work at the food drive last Thursday, and she also didn't show up yesterday for mass. Since I took over here, she has never missed either. She's been one of my most loyal parishioners, and I have a bad feeling that something's wrong."

Rob eased himself into a seat in the smaller couch directly across from Father William.

"Have you called her family, to see what they had to say?"

"Samantha and John Taylor don't have any family. They had a son, but he died five years ago at the age of ten. The only family besides John that Samantha has is the Church."

"Okay, so what do you want from me? I'm not a detective. You need to file a missing person's report which I can fax in to the County, and they can investigate from there."

Rob could tell that the priest was getting frustrated, his body had become tense and his face was starting to redden. The preacher looked around the room, avoiding Rob's stare. Rob just wanted the man to hurry up, his bed was calling from upstairs and he was ready to answer it.

"I just want you to walk down to their house with me. They live only a couple houses away. I've already tried knocking on the door, but..." Father William's emotion could be heard in his voice. Rob could tell that the preacher really cared for the Taylors and was genuinely concerned about them. Rob almost wished he could feel some kind of empathy for the man, and could tell how frustrating it was for the preacher that he didn't.

The preacher turned to glare at Rob, staring him down. In the end, Rob was too tired to put up much of a fight and lowered his eyes. What the hell, it would only take a couple of minutes. Rob looked up at Father William.

"We can take a look around the house, but we can't do anything more." Rob said as he stood. "I'll go down there with you, but after that, we'll have to call the County and file a missing person's report with them."

Father William stood and followed Rob, who was already walking to the front door.

"That's fine. I appreciate anything you can do." Father William looked over at Robyn who had been standing in the front hallway. He smiled and nodded to her. "I do hope that I'm just being over protective of my flock. Speaking of which, by the way, we would love to see all of you at our mass next Sunday. We'll be having an excellent picnic lunch afterward and would love to see as many faces there as we can."

Rob stood near the door, looking frustrated at the pastor as he stood, smiling at Rob's wife. Robyn caught Rob's glare and smiled at him as she winked. Father William caught the motion and looked over to see Rob recovering.

"I do hope you can make it, but will understand if you can't."

Rob turned and walked out into the morning sun, leaving Father William to shake Robyn's hand briefly before following behind.

Father William caught up with Rob outside and they walked down the street. Rob looked around at the houses as they passed. Everything was quiet. The sun was high in the sky, but Rob remembered the houses from the night before. He expected eyes staring at him, watching as they walked down the sidewalk. While he couldn't see them now, he could feel them still, hidden behind the windows. He wondered if it was real, or his imagination getting the best of him. He chanced another quick glance. There was nothing there, no monsters staring at them as they walked; they were alone on the street.

Father William led as they moved down the street, Rob walking behind him, wondering where they were going. Father William was walking to the dead end, where the hell was he taking him? Then he remembered the fourth house, the one where everything had been dark and no one had been watching. . He'd thought the house was empty.

He walked behind Father William, his back growing stiff from trying to move so quickly. The pain grew sharper, and it felt like his spine was going to lock up on him. He could feel his vertebrae grinding together, making it hard for him to move his lower back.

Father William stopped in front of the fourth house and looked back at Rob. He was moving as fast as he could, but was now limping in a painful wobble.

"You okay?"

Rob looked at Father William with a deep scowl and nodded.

"Yeah, I'm fine." He wasn't, but he sure as hell didn't want the pastor to know it. He didn't want to give him any more reason to dig into Rob's life.

Rob moved past the pastor and made his way to the front door, looking around to see if there was anything unusual. He saw there were two cars in the driveway. So wherever they are, they didn't drive there? That was unless they had a third vehicle, but as an older couple with no kids, he doubted it. Well, maybe a collector's car in the garage, but nothing they would be using on a day to day basis.

Rob turned to look at the mailbox by the door. There were a couple of newspapers, and a few more that had fallen out of the box, scattered along the porch. He looked at the yard and the rose bushes on the front porch. They were brown and decaying. The roses, which should have been in full bloom at this time of year, were dried out, and their petals were scattered along the ground. The grass was dead, with large patches where it had completely disappeared.

"How long have they been missing?" Rob asked, as he walked to the front door, noticing how loud the wood floor boards on the porch creaked under his weight.

"Since last Thursday."

Rob knocked on the door and tried to peer into the house. He couldn't see much more than shapes with the thin curtains on the door. Still, nothing was moving inside, it was completely quiet.

"How long has everything been dying?" Rob asked, as he turned to look at the pastor. The pastor stared at him, confused, until Rob nodded at the rose bush.

"Those roses were in full bloom just last week."

Rob looked back at Father William, his brow furrowed with a questioning look. He wondered if someone had maybe poisoned the bushes. How long would it take for poison to seep into the soil and do that, though? Damn, he hoped that it wasn't done by one of his other neighbors. The last thing he needed was to get caught up in some neighborhood squabble.

Rob walked off the porch and around to the back of the house. All the plants around the house were like the rose bushes, dead and disintegrating into the ground. There was a large living room window on the side, and Rob could see plants inside. They were dead as well. Rob looked over at Father William was following behind him; Father William didn't seem to notice the plants.

"You might be right; the window in the back door is broken. How long did you say nobody's heard anything from them?"

"Last week."

Rob walked up to the back door. The window was broken. It was completely smashed in, and not just a small hole to get at the knob inside. No, this window was bashed in with a lot of aggression. The wooden frame was splintered as though someone had tried to put their foot through it. Someone had wanted in badly, and they forced their way in without any worry as to who might have heard them.

Rob looked back at the preacher who stood close to the side of the house, but not venturing off the gravel driveway. Rob motioned for him to come closer and watched as he tentatively did so. He could tell that the man was nervous, but couldn't tell if it had something to do with the broken door, or if it was just that they were actually now trespassing on another's property.

"Stay outside. Do you have a cell phone?"

"Yes."

"If you hear anything, call 911 and tell them 'officer down,' and the address."

Rob eased open the door, and it creaked in protest. It was partly off its hinges and he had to push hard against it, breaking it off the rest of the way. Finally he was able to get it moved wide enough for him to enter.

"Are you sure it's safe, or should I call someone now."

"I doubt whoever did this stuck around, but just in case, be ready with the phone." Rob said, looking back at the little man as he said it. He didn't like the idea of stepping into the house without back up either, but once again, as he kept reminding himself, this wasn't Chicago.

Once inside, he stood in the kitchen. It was dark and smelled of cinnamon. There was a sliver of light shining in from the window over the kitchen sink, and it caught a couple of dishes sitting there. They were filled with water and had a thick layer of mold growing on top. Rob wrinkled his noise, and turned away, looking into the hallway leading away from the kitchen.

He walked lightly across the floor, crossing the room. Glass broke under his feet, though he stepped carefully and tried to avoid it. When he got all the way across the kitchen, he lowered himself slowly, so that he didn't fall, or put too much pressure on his back. On the other side of the door where most of the glass had fallen, there were large puddles of dried blood.

"Shit," he said under his breath as he reached for the kitchen counter and used it to push himself up. His back cracked in defiance, as he stood and looked around for more blood. Luckily the blood was dry, and looked like it had been for a while. And with the dishes in the sink, he was pretty sure that no matter what had happened, it had happened a while ago.

Still, he wished he had his revolver. He'd thought that the pastor was just another religious nut knocking at his door with the whole 'worried about his flock' routine. He should have taken him a hell of a lot more seriously. He should have brought it, he knew that feeling the cold steel would have calmed his nerves.

Rob stepped over the last of the glass and eased into the hallway. It was lit only by the small amount of light that reflected from the kitchen behind him, and even less coming from the rooms up ahead.

He walked into the gloom, and his chest grew tighter with every step. The smell of the cinnamon grew stronger the closer he got to the stairs.

Rob reached the first of the front rooms. The house seemed to have the same design as his. He made his way through the first floor, knowing the layout, and then made his way back to the stairs. So far, other than the window on the back door, he hadn't found anything out of place. Everything was coated in a thick coat of dust yes, but there was no sign of a struggle.

Maybe the Taylor's had been able to get out okay. Maybe they heard the back door break, and were able to make it out the front door. Sure, maybe they did, but where would they had gone that no one had seen them in over a week?

Rob stood at the bottom of the stairs and looked up to the second floor. Memories of being the Chicago cop who had rushed up a flight of stairs and broke into a meth lab were flooding back. He could feel the heat of the fire around him, reaching for, and grabbing him. He thought of the flames licking him, burning his skin until it melted; the screams all around him, destroying his sanity.

"Deep breaths. Just keep taking deep breaths buddy boy," he said to himself quietly. He concentrated on taking in a long torturous breath, fighting against lungs that were trying to squeeze shut.

He put his hand onto the stair rail but had to pull it away. The heat was intense. He looked around, and he was back in the meth lab, back in the burning flames; the walls had completely disappeared in the fire. The flames were raging through his mind, burning into him. He tried to breathe deep, to close his eyes and make it all disappear.

Suddenly the nightmare was over and he was standing at the top of the stairs. The smoke receded, leaving only a slight stench hanging in the air. However, a fog lingered in his head, leaving him confused and unsteady.

Everything was unsteady; his whole life was currently unsteady. Maybe he shouldn't have returned to work so quickly, because if he kept seeing flashbacks everywhere he went, he would eventually become more of a liability than a good police officer.

He took a step forward. His leg wobbled as he stepped, and he quickly had to reach out for the railing. With a loud creak from the wood straining under his weight, he leaned over, trying to catch some fresh air. He really needed to get some air. He needed to clear his head. There was something else in the air. The smell of the smoke now gone, but it had been replaced by something much more foul. It was like raw meat gone bad.

His head was like a tornado, confusion swirling and the smell was so rancid he fought to keep rom gagging. He desperately tried to regain control, and he took short breaths to lessen the stench. He wanted to vomit, but kept himself in check. The last thing he needed to do was to make the rookie mistake of screwing up a crime scene if indeed something had happened.

The smell got clinging to him, and getting into his skin.

He looked up and saw that the first door at the top of the stairs was open a small crack. He quickly dashed for it, running through the smell until he burst inside and closed the door behind him.

If this were his house, this would have been Jake's room, but in the Taylor's it looked like it had been used as a guest bedroom. There was very little there other than a single bed, positioned against the wall. Just over the bed, two small windows were left open, allowing the fresh air to blow into the room. He gratefully breathed deeply, relishing it in his lungs.

He stood in the room, not paying too much attention to anything but his own breath. Something loud accompanied by the sound of breaking glass, crashed in another room upstairs.

Rob held his breath, suddenly trying to pinpoint the location. It was close, he was sure of that.

Rob stood still, listening.

CHAPTER 9

Coolidge was tired, his clothes were ripped, he was dirty, and he knew even though he couldn't smell himself, he smelled like crap. How couldn't he. It was the middle of summer, he was wearing a long sleeve shirt, and it was drenched it with his sweat.

So what was he going to do? He didn't like being ill prepared, but he was stuck without a change of clothes. It was never good to go into a town and not look presentable. It would make it hard for him to find any day work. Small towns weren't easy to find day work in anymore as it was, they often were skeptical of people they didn't know, and who were only going to be around for a day or two. Outsiders were baby snatchers, perverts, or even the occasional terrorist. Outsiders could be anybody, and couldn't be trusted.

It was strange, but people in cities could be more trusting. Not of the person, but of the need for work. In most cities a person could be mugged and the remaining citizens would barely take notice. They just didn't care. But as for work, people in cities knew how to use people. Using someone for day work was like they were disposable. It was something they practiced every day, both in personal relationships and in business.

Coolidge knew that trying to find work was probably out of the question, so what could he do?

He looked at the little town from his vantage point of the field. He had walked through the little wooded area, along the creek, and now stood at its edge. The town looked vaguely like it did long ago, but had grown a little since he'd left.

Still, from so far away, he could see the five corn silos standing tall. They were much smaller than most of the buildings he had seen in large cities, but compared to all the other buildings in the little town, they were the skyscrapers of the area, and he remembered the day he saw a man fall from the top of one of those buildings.

That was back when his dad owned them. His dad had owned half the town then, and had just bought him a brand new car for his sixteenth birthday. Two weeks later, his dad had come home early from work, had chased Coolidge down, and beaten him into unconsciousness. His dad must have thought he was dead when he left him lying there, and then gone upstairs and strangled Coolidge's mother before hanging himself.

Within two weeks of Coolidge turning sixteen, his dad had caused a man to fall to his death, killed his mother, and then killed himself.

Coolidge had never wanted to return.

He continued to feel the same, but something was drawing him back. The town and the house he grew up in were cursed, he had always known that, but he'd thought he had escaped. He'd kept running, always praying that whatever curse ran through the soil of the town would never catch up to him. Deep down, however, he'd known he hadn't escaped it. He knew the curse was part of him, and there was no way he'd ever be free of.

He should have died there over thirty years ago, but now he was being drawn back. His stomach rumbled, and he realized he was hungry. He didn't know where he would find something to eat.

Coolidge started along one of the back roads leading into the town. It was time to face his devil, and to give it its due.

* * * *

The streets were empty for the most part, as he made his way through town. He had passed what had once been his high school and seen the painted mustang on the large sign out in front. "Good ol' Home of the Mustangs, Go Mustangs Go!" had been chalked on the cement walkway leading to the school. Other than that faded glory, the school was quiet, abandoned for summer.

He kept walking, and within a few blocks had reached the main street. On his way, he had seen a couple of cars driving around, but compared to when he had lived there, it was very peaceful. The town seemed as though it had died off, no real life to it anymore. Even the air smelled stale, with the passing wind kicking up dust.

Coolidge crossed from the eastern side of town, over the main street to the west side, where businesses were stretched out in the same long one building fashion he remembered from growing up. The paint was faded from age, and bricks were crumbling from disrepair, but the town was basically the same one he'd left.

He had been dreading it, but as he neared the front door to the sweet shop, he dared one look over at the silos. In that quick glance, he imagined seeing a man fall from the top, and landing near the front of the main offices, but in a blink the image was gone.

Coolidge looked up at the top of the tower. The tree was still there. His father had asked a man to climb up and take down that Christmas tree shaped light nearly thirty years ago, only to have that man fall to his death. Coolidge never knew what had made his father go nuts that day. Before that, his dad had always seemed to enjoy the tree up there. It was his way of having "Christmas everyday" he had once said.

Then the money from the grain bin had begun to multiply. They bought themselves their own street, and at the end of it, back in the woods far away from everyone else, his father had a house built. The house wasn't huge, never meant to be a mansion, but it was larger than anything else in town, its architecture colonial.

That was when his father had begun to change.

* * * *

Coolidge reached what had at one time been a street leading off to the private entryway to his home. He had to stop and look around; making sure that he was in the right place. The street was now lined with four houses along the right side, and at the end where it should have led to the private entrance through the woods, there was a large railing blocking the way. The entrance to the driveway was sealed off.

On the left side of the street, where there had once been open fields and a long stretch of farm land, there was now a man-made lake, with a large fence bordering what he guessed by the low hum of constant traffic was an interstate, or some highway that now ran along the outside of the town.

Coolidge walked up the street. He hadn't been there in so long; it felt like a dream as he tried to take it all in. He kept turning around as he went; it was all so different to him. It felt like he was back in time, but not. So much looked the same; but it had been thirty years ago, and so much was different as well.

Coolidge made it to the end of the street and looked at the railing. The metal was aged, so it had been there for a while. Not that it was the only evidence that a lot of time had passed since the last time he had been there. The gravel surface of the private driveway was long overgrown, and not even visible from the street. The house that his father had thought so smart to build way back in the woods was now hidden permanently.

Coolidge climbed over the metal railing and then felt a chill race through him as he stood there. It felt like he had climbed over another barrier, much more sinister than just the metal railing. His skin felt cold, and the hair along his arms stood on end. Goosebumps rose on his skin, and he smelled something familiar in the air. It was somewhat sweet, something that he hadn't smelled in a long time. It was on the tip of his tongue, but he couldn't remember what it was. He recognized it somewhat though, from the slight smell of cinnamon.

The smell should have calmed him, when he did begin to recall it. He had flashes of a memory, his mother, with her apron on, standing in the kitchen as she washed her hands, and the results of her hard work sitting on the top of the stove. It was the smell of freshly cooked cinnamon rolls. He would begin to smell it on his way home from school, when got to about this point on the drive. They would be cooling, fresh from the oven when he ran in through the back door. The smell should have soothed him with pleasant memories, but instead a large lump formed in the pit of his stomach. He thought he'd made peace long ago with never again having one of his mother's cinnamon rolls, or any of her cooking.

He took one last look at the peaceful street behind him, taking note as to the house nearest him and the dying grass out front. It made him look around at all the trees, bushes and grass around him. They were all brown and discolored. He looked at the bark on the closest tree, and reached out to touch it. It peeled off in his hand, crumbling under his touch. Everything around him was dying and rotting away.

He looked back at the street, and could see where healthy grass faded to dead grass. It was near the third house, almost reaching the fourth, as if whatever was killing the grass was spreading, infecting all plant life along the street.

The lump in the pit of his stomach was starting to grow, making the need to vomit even more pressing. He could feel it starting to tickle at his throat. He knew that whatever was killing the grass must be the same thing that drew him back there, and whatever it was, it was pure evil. It wanted nothing more than to kill, and it wasn't satisfied with just him and his family; it wanted the lives of everyone on the little street.

He held his breath for a moment, and stood listening to the silence. He hadn't thought of it before, but it dawned on him now that he couldn't hear anything. Nothing in the woods, and other than the highway beyond the barrier, nothing toward the town either. The day was silent. If he closed his eyes, he could imagine that he was totally alone, the last person on earth.

Coolidge reached down and picked up a rock from the edge of the road and threw it hard against the metal. It made a clanging sound as it hit, and then the rock thudded back to the ground. The small sound in the dense silence of the fog relieved him as he took one last look at the street.

For a moment he thought he saw a woman standing at the far end, but before he could be sure of what he was seeing, he blinked and she was gone.

With a long sigh, he turned away and walked deeper into the woods. He was done with putting it off. As much as he'd like to avoid walking along the barely visible remnants of the driveway, it was time to face it. Face his past and get it buried, to put to rest whatever evil was waiting, trapped inside that house.

His skin felt hot, but a cold wind began to blow on him as he walked toward the old house. The day grew dark, and the trees shook around him with an incredible force. It felt like the land didn't want him there, while at the same time, the evil inside his former home drew him nearer.

As he walked, the foliage thinned, till it faded to near nothing at the house. It ended in a large clearing, one larger than it had been when the house had first been built for them long ago. At the front of the house, all vegetation was long since dead, grass gone, and the bones of wild life that had once dared to get too close to the house, were strewn about.

Coolidge stepped over a pile of bones that looked like it had once been a dog, on his way to the front door. The windows on the first floor of the house were all broken, and faded spray paint coated the outer siding. Nothing was recent, however, and he doubted that the house was even a memory among many of the town people now. It was a memory best lost and a part of history that a town had tried desperately to forget. He didn't blame them, and he had left long ago trying to forget as well.

Coolidge pushed on the door. It fought against him, but then slowly opened, allowing thirty years to come crashing in on him as he stepped into the front hallway. He remembered running through that door every day, and his mother, the angel that she was, waiting for him without fail. He remembered every single day, including her last.

* * * *

Father William stood just outside the back door, waiting for Rob to come down, and hoping that he came back with some good news. He prayed silently that the Taylors had only gone on a trip, and that the break in had happened after they left. He didn't want to think of some of the more unpleasant things that could have happened, so instead he concentrated on the positive, on places they might be. Samantha had some family in Peoria, maybe something had happened to them, and they had gone down to see them. Maybe it was something medical, so they didn't have time to let anyone know before they left. They might have had to leave in a hurry. He didn't know anything yet, so shouldn't allow himself to get worked up.

So why was his heart pounding and his pulse racing?

"My heart is in anguish within me; the terrors of death assail me. Fear and trembling have beset me… please Lord, my heavenly Father, be with me. Be with me in this time of need," he thought, as he paced around to the side of the house. He knew Rob hadn't been inside for more than five minutes, but waiting made him antsy. He didn't know what to do, and he didn't like to think about what Rob might find.

Father William stood by one of the rose bushes alongside the back porch. The roses had withered and the branches themselves had become dry and brittle. They disintegrated under his touch, turning to dust and falling to the ground.

He gazed about, and noticed that everything else in the yard was dead as well. The grass was brown, and stiff beneath his shoes. The apple trees, two of them, that had once stood tall and healthy with much fruit, were bare, the leaves had fallen and the apples rotted at the base of the trees. Dead birds surrounded the trees, probably caused by consuming what had been hidden deep within the rotted apples. Even the birds hadn't been able to the death that surrounded the house.

Father William took a long look at the house. For the first time, it had an evil presence, a pulsing heat that emanated from it. He backed away, feeling he should stay as far away from it as he could.

But he couldn't leave Officer Alletto alone in there.

Father William looked around at the woods that bordered the house and yard. It was still and quiet, but he could feel something watching, and but he couldn't shake it. He was convinced something was there, and it wanted him.

* * * *

There was such hatred burning here.

The comforting words of Psalm ran through his head.

"The Lord is my shepherd; I shall not want. He maketh me to lie down in green pastures: he leadeth me beside the still waters. He restoreth my soul: he leadeth me in the paths of righteousness for his name's sake. Yea, though I walk through the valley of the shadow of death, I will fear no evil: for thou art with me; thy rod and thy staff they comfort me."

A car sped into the driveway of the house next door. Father William looked over in time to see it squeal to a stop, inches from the neighbor's garage door. A man jumped out of the car, slamming the door closed with his foot, and then proceeded to kick the garage door. He attacked it with both feet and fists, working himself into a horrible rage. With a final kick, he stepped back, and then rushed to the door beside he garage. He kicked in that door, and ran into the darkness of the garage.

Father William watched in horror, and then looked back at the damage that had been done to the garage door. How could someone have so much rage? He wondered if he should go and tell Officer Alletto, or if he should try and talk to the man. He seemed vaguely familiar; he knew that he had seen him before, he just couldn't place him. It was hard to tell, the man was so enraged. His hair was wild and dirty; he obviously hadn't shaved or showered in days. It probably would have been hard for his own mother to recognize him. Maybe he should go and talk to him.

Father William walked toward the neighboring yard. He could hear crashing in the garage, objects were being thrown about. He looked back at the car and wondered if he was doing the right thing.

"Dear Lord, if you have ever been with me, be with me now, and give me strength," he said to himself.

He heard another loud crash inside the garage. Metal connected with metal loudly. Something was dragged across the cement, accompanied by metal randomly falling on the floor along the way. Father William neared the door, but his chest tightened, and he slowed as he got closer. He stepped to the side, hoping to steal a glance before committing to enter.

He stopped when he saw the man standing over a small lock box. The box had been ripped open, and the man had pulled out a small revolver. He stared at the revolver for a second before pushing the lock box off the workbench. It fell loudly to the floor, waking Father William from his brief daze.

He quickly backed away from the door, rushing to get out of the way of the man walking toward him.

"Hello, may… may...I?"

The man didn't stop but hurried past him and began to walk toward the yard. He didn't even acknowledge Father William, didn't even see him.

The man hurried to the back of the home and pulled hard on the screen door. It crashed open, but when he reached in to open the back door, it didn't budge, it was locked up tight.

He stood a moment, seemingly stunned. A cloud passed over his face, and then it was gone, replaced by rage. In one powerful move, he raised his leg and kicked the door inward.

Father William watched in horror, appalled at the violence that emanated from him, at the anger and hatred inside. He had torn the solid wooden door nearly off its frame without effort. Father William watched as the man stormed into the house, and out of sight.

"Please Lord!" Father William said, to himself as he raced back to the Taylor's yard.

"Officer Alletto! Officer Alletto!" Father William screamed out as he hurried. He didn't take his eyes off the back door of the neighbor's house as he ran.

"Officer Alletto!"

Father William finally turned away from the neighboring yard and concentrated on getting back to the Taylor's. As he turned, his foot snagged on something, and he landed hard, cracking his head on the ground. The world spun, and faded to darkness.

* * * *

Coolidge eased into the front hallway of his old home, the fresh breeze that blew in through the door tickling at his nose and shifting layers of dust. He sneezed loudly, the sound out of place in the silent hallway, and raised his arm to cover his nose. His eyes itched from the long undisturbed dust and mold. He could still smell the faint aroma of cinnamon but it was mixed with the smell of mold and the stale air undisturbed for many years. Though most of the windows were broken, fresh air seemed never to have entered until it followed Coolidge through the front door.

He took a breath and catching himself, slowly lowered his arm. His eyes watered, but whether from tears or allergens, he didn't know. He looked around the entryway and the memories of his childhood flooded back. He had avoided them for so long, but there was no stopping them as he stood at the threshold of what was once his life.

The house, for the most part, was destroyed both inside and out. As he stepped past the mirror in the entryway, he looked to his left at the sitting room. The brick of the fireplace on the back wall had caved in, making a fire no longer possible. He couldn't really remember them actually ever using it. Before they'd had this house built, the family had always enjoyed little dinner parties with friends and family. Then after dinner, the sitting room was where everyone gathered for an after dinner brandy. However, once they moved into the larger home, his mother decided she just didn't have the energy anymore. His father became more and more reclusive, spending time with no one but himself.

He vaguely remembered what he thought was the last time they'd used the room for a dinner party. Everyone had criticized his father for his ostentation in building the house, and discussed how there was something about it that made them uncomfortable. Coolidge wondered if the cessation of gatherings had more to do with people no longer wanting to come rather than his mom not wanting to cook for them.

There had been a large family portrait above the fireplace. His father was all about appearances, and loved to show that they were the richest people in town. Not that the town was really large enough to make being the richest impressive.

The portrait still stood above the fireplace, but there were slashes running across it. The paint, weathered by time and nature, made the portrait visible only in places. The only part that could even be remotely recognized was his father's face. Long and pale, it looked more like a skull than a man, a skull with dark piercing eyes that had the power to look straight into his soul.

"I'm home now, you bastard. Do what you want to me," Coolidge said to the portrait. He waited; half expecting it to respond, but only a slight breeze stirring the trees outside answered. Then even the breeze was gone and the house was again silent.

Coolidge walked to the stairs, slowly working his way up the circular staircase. He reached the second floor, only the sound of his feet on the carpeting accompanying him. Reaching the top, he stood at the end of a long hallway.

He continued forward and then stopped in front of his old room, which waited, unopened for over thirty years. He reached for the door knob but then stopped. His hands were shaking, his heart pounding, and his eyes filled with tears. Warmth emanated from the doorknob as he reached for it. His hand actually felt like it was starting to burn, getting hotter the closer it got. He reached out his other hand, to try and steady the other. A wave of heat pushed him away from the door and he stumbled.

Down the hallway, a door at the far end opened slowly, and the light from the sun outside struggled to break through to the dusty hallway.

Coolidge turned and looked. It was the door to his parent's room. His heart seized, and then stuttered, as it skipped a beat.

He took a step toward the room, though he didn't really want to. He suddenly felt tired and wanted to just sit down where he was. He was ready to let whatever was waiting for him come and get him. He wanted to stretch out on the floor and wish it all away. More than anything, he wanted to avoid that room. Memories that for years he had buried and had endured only in nightmares now seemed as though they'd happened just yesterday. The colors, the smells, the wallpaper, and the memory of the look in his father's eyes all seemed fresh. He was right back there, still running from his father. His father, who'd come charging home with a gun in his hand. Coolidge, whose name was Luke back then, watched as the madman ripped the family portrait downstairs to shreds. He took a knife from the kitchen and played slice and dice with both his and his mother's likeness.

That was how Luke first saw him that day. Of all the things that happened, of all the images he had seen that day, the one with his father standing in front of the portrait with the knife was always the clearest. He had been coming down the stairs from his room when he heard someone crashing through the back door. He reached the first floor to see that what he at first had thought was a burglar, but turned out to be his dad. His father stormed down the back hallway to the front of the house, one hand holding a revolver that Luke never knew he owned, and the other a butcher knife.

His father went past him without even seeing him standing there on the stairs. He was a man on a mission, a mission of destruction, hurrying to the painting above the fireplace and slashing at the images hanging there. . When his father was done, he threw the knife on the couch, stumbled back, and stood there, admiring his handiwork.

He then turned and looked into Luke's eyes. It was at that moment, Luke didn't recognize his father. He had a crazed look in his eyes, and though Luke could have been imagining it, he swore he saw a red glow there as well.

His father raised the gun and fired at him, but Luke was already running up the stairs. His feet flew, racing time and bullets. He heard them hit the wall and felt chunks of the plaster hit him. He made it to the second floor, and could hear his father stomping loudly across the living room, stumbling over what had once been their coffee table. He was screaming obscenities, telling Luke to get back down there for his medicine. For every few curses that his father threw at him, they were followed by another bullet.

Luke ran to his mother's room. He found her, sitting in front of the mirror, but she didn't look up when he came crashing into the room. She was oblivious to the gun shots and the screaming and to the pounding footsteps. She sat, running her brush through her hair, eyes locked on the mirror, seemingly mesmerized by her reflection. Luke ran to her and pulled on the hairbrush, but she wouldn't let go. The always beautiful but weak little flower that had been his mother now somehow had the strength to resist him without effort. "Come on, we have to hide!" Luke cried, gritting his teeth. However, no matter how hard he pulled, she was glued to the chair, brushing her hair, as if he weren't even there.

Luke could hear his father. He was smashing the railing as he climbed the stairs but it sounded like he was unsteady, tripping and falling over himself as he went. When reached the head of the stairs, Luke heard him connect with, and take out the upper banister.

"Come here boy!" Luke heard him yelling as he clumsily made his way down the hallway. It was the phrase that would continue to haunt him for the next thirty years. Luke looked over at his mother, it was the last time he ever saw her alive; still sitting at that damned mirror, smiling as she brushed her hair.

Luke turned away, and rushed into the closet, hiding deep in the recesses of the large space.

CHAPTER 10

Coolidge stood outside the door, with memories that had been buried for thirty years still burning fresh. His head felt too heavy for his shoulders and he wanted to lean over and let it fall. He could still smell the cinnamon flowing through the hallway.

He looked down, surprised to see his hand on the doorknob, and let it go.

He stepped away from the door, but didn't take his eyes off of it, still leery of what might appear. He could imagine his father ripping open the door and pulling him into the room, ready to finish what he'd started. He could visualize his father's eyes burning with hell's flames as they tore into his soul and his teeth into Coolidge's flesh. The vision of it, so quick, burned in his eyes, and he blinked to try to erase the image.

Coolidge took another step back from the door.

His father didn't emerge to try and take him. The door remained open the same half inch, and the sliver of light still spilled across the hallway.

Coolidge turned and walked back down the hall. He had come home, pulled by some unknown evil force, but he was going to be damned if he was going to allow it to pull him back into that room. It didn't seem to have as much hold over him now as it had before. Ever since he entered the house, he could feel the evil there, thick in the air that he breathed, but it was powerless. He couldn't' explain it, but he felt on the edge of a cliff, one he he'd been about to jump off, but now was stepping away from the ledge.

He was back at the top of the stairs when the light from the open door behind him increase very briefly. Then he heard the door slam shut. The force of it shook the walls and a picture that had somehow stood the test of time on the wall, slipped and crashed to the floor. The glass shattered in the frame and scattered.

Coolidge looked briefly back at the picture, wondering what had survived all this time, but just beyond it, he could see someone standing in the darkness in front of the door. "Where do you think you're going, boy?" His father's voice echoed through the hallway and reverberated in his head. The voice was so loud it was painful. He felt moisture on his upper lip, and when he reached up to touch it; his hand came away dripping blood from his dripping nose.

Coolidge didn't wait for his father to come after him; instead he shot down the stairs, as fast as he could. He made it to the front door, which, though he didn't remember closing it, now stood closed in front of him. He quickly pulled on the handle, but it didn't budge. He somehow knew that nothing he did would open it. It reminded him of long ago, when he'd tried to move his mother. He realized something else was at work, something evil was holding the door shut.

Coolidge turned around, and looked up the stairs, expecting his father come barreling down any minute, but the house was silent, and there was no sign of him.

Coolidge took a step away from the door. He could still feel the evil and knew it wasn't over. Whatever was after him, whatever it was that had drawn him back to the place, it was still there. It wouldn't let him go. It had a plan for him, perhaps a task? "Yessssss......." He heard the voice in his head. It was reading his thoughts, trying to get to him.

His mind was swimming. A fog grew around him, and he had a hard time breathing. He gasped and struggled for every breath, to take in any of the moldy air that was actually poisoning him. He began cough, lungs closing and fighting against the putrid air around him. He bent low, trying to find fresh air, but without success. The fog turned to dark, black smoke swirling around him, smothering him.

"KILL THEM!" The voice echoed in his head. He couldn't tell anymore if it was his father's voice or his own. It repeated over and over until there was no distinction between to the two, and they became one.

Coolidge stood, his head starting to clear.

Out of the corner of his eye, he could see the hallway mirror. In the reflection, he saw himself, his reflection combined with his father's but then the image faded away, and he didn't see even his own reflection anymore. He saw a bedroom. A bedroom covered in blood, swimming in it; looking just as his parent's room had looked after they'd died.

He was surprised to realize it wasn't theirs. It was a different room, with different people. He could see a woman in a chair on the other side of the mirror, facing him as though she were looking at her own reflection. However, her head was cocked to the side, and she was slumped over in the seat. She wasn't breathing, and there were purple hand prints around her neck. Her lips were blue, and her eyes bulged. Behind her, there was a man on the floor, covered in blood, and Coolidge guessed that it was his blood that was splattered all over the wall behind him.

Coolidge turned to look at the room behind him. It was totally unlike the bedroom that he saw in the reflection. It was still the same room he'd known for so many years, the same dining room, with a chandelier hanging in the middle of the ceiling.

He turned back to the mirror and the bedroom, covered in blood was there, but there was also a man, a skeleton faced man, standing in the center of the room. His eyes burned as they stared straight into his soul.

The skeleton faced man, the Grim, as Coolidge had grown accustomed to thinking of him, walked toward the mirror. He reached the glass and stopped, a large grin stretching from ear to ear, revealing yellow teeth.

The Grim reached through the mirror, and grabbed Coolidge, pulling him through before he had a chance to fight back.

* * * *

Rob had only been gone for a few minutes when there had been another knocking at Robyn's door. She'd gone back to the kitchen, and was continuing to put away the pots and pans that were scattered across the kitchen island. She occasionally glanced through the window at Jake, running and playing in the back yard.

"Who now?" she thought to herself, as she placed a large metal pot in one of the lower cupboards. There was a loud clang of metal on metal as another pan fell against it, and she slammed the cupboard shut before anything could fall out. She made a mental note as she stood, that they needed more cupboard space, or even better yet, one of those hanging things to put over the island so that she could hang the pans.

Robyn answered the door, pulling it open and stopping to stare at the man on the porch. It took her a few seconds to take in the company logo on his uniform before she changed from the frustrated, constantly interrupted housewife, to a much more inviting one. A smile crossed her lips.

"Hello."

"Hello, I'm here to install your triple play package. I'm with the cable company."

"Yes, come on in."

The man entered with his clipboard and she quickly showed him the rooms where the televisions were going to go, and where she wanted the internet hooked up. She already had her laptop ready to go, and was jonesin' to get back online and see what was being said about Perez Hilton. As well, there had been that girl missing down in Florida, and she wanted to know if they'd found her yet.

Robyn left the man to do his work, and went into the front hallway. Her cell phone was on the front table and she wanted to call Rob and let him know they had come to hook up the cable. Maybe if she could get online, she could get hold of her friend Ruth back in the city. Ruth was always trying to get Robyn to join her in selling jewelry, but Robyn had always felt it was some kind of pyramid scam. Still, Ruth seemed to make good money at it, and with Rob not able to work full time, she needed to find something.

She would email Ruth as soon as she got online.

Robyn went to grab her cell phone, but stopped when she saw that Rob's cell phone was right next to hers. Damn! She wouldn't be able to call him.

* * * *

Father William stumbled to his feet and staggered to the Taylor's house. He wanted to start screaming for Officer Alletto to come quick, because the man was going into the neighbor's house carrying a gun, but he didn't want the man coming back out to shoot him. So instead he hurried into the house, and even then, as he rushed through the kitchen, he kept his voice to a whisper, going from room to room.

"Officer Alletto!" he said. His whisper was barely audible, even to himself. He didn't know what he'd gotten himself into. What was going on with the people living on this street? The Taylors, even when they were at the last mass he had performed, had been not their usual selves. Sam had seemed distant, and when she'd talked to him after mass, congratulating him on what she'd said was "another excellent sermon in a long line of excellent sermons," she had been talking through him. She was looking at him, but he felt more as if she were looking through him, talking to the air.

John had come with her for a change. He didn't attend nearly as often as Sam did. In fact, he usually only came for the holidays, the really big sermons. Father William guessed that it was the best Samantha could get out of him, and he didn't press the matter. He would let her take some of the leftovers home to him when they were done with their Christmas luncheons, and tell her that he looked forward to seeing them both the next week. She would nod, but they both knew that John would never come.

However, that day he did, and Father William was thrown off by it. Not only because he had shown up, but by the glare that he'd given the Father. If he hadn't known better, he would have thought that John wanted to hit him. Father William wondered if it had anything to do with how much time Samantha spent working on different church related functions. It wasn't as if Father William asked her to work on projects, she was just always the first one to volunteer.

The glare that John gave him as he shook the his hand still gave him a chill. He didn't want to tell Officer Alletto, but it had scared him, and made him fear that something might have happened to Sam.

If Father William didn't know better, he could have sworn that he'd seen fire burning in John's eyes that day. Actual fire burning in the man's eyes, like some kind of evil in the man's soul.

He worried that Samantha was a victim of it. Wherever she was, her soul was in danger.

Father William finished searching the first floor of the Taylor's house. He went back to the center hallway, near the front door. He heard a noise upstairs and looked up to see Rob exiting one of the rooms, and starting to work his way down the hallway.

Father William quickly hurried up the stairs, calling out to him. "Officer Alletto! Officer Alletto!"

* * * *

Rob hurried out of the side room when he heard a crash in one of the other upstairs rooms. The hallway was just as he had left it, but there was no overpowering smell of smoke, no suffocating ash trying to fill his lungs with poison. He half expected the hallway to be billowing with fire again, and find himself in agony from the blaze; it was a relief to find it just as it should be. There was light coming through a small skylight overhead that consisted of a large stained glass mosaic of Jesus Christ. As well, a little light came into the hallway from the open door behind him.

It was enough for him to see that he was alone in the hallway. So where in the hell did that noise come from? It had sounded close, so had to be something upstairs.

He heard another sound, not loud like the first, but more like someone stumbling around downstairs. He made his way around the top of the stairs, to the room at the end.

"Officer Alletto!"

He could hear Father William starting up the stairs, and he hurried to the railing and looked down at the pastor who was already on the third step, repeating "Officer Alletto!" all the way up. Rob quickly lifted his finger to his lips, motioning him to be quiet.

Father William froze in place on the steps, and Rob quickly looked back at the door at the end of the hall. He could see shadows moving across the light under the door. He watched for a moment, also keeping an eye on the pastor, until he thought it was safe, and that the door wasn't going to open revealing some crazed maniac.

He turned to Father William and leaned over the railing to speak in a voice that only the priest could hear.

"Go back to my house. Call the County, there's a list of numbers on the refrigerator. Tell them an officer is on the scene, and that we don't know the full situation as of yet, but there's been a break in with a possible suspect still on the premises."

Father William looked at Rob. He had a confused look on his face, like he had something to say, but had momentarily forgotten what it was. He just stood there. Rob looked back to the room, to make sure that no one had come out, and the door was still closed. Reassured, he turned back to Father William.

"Go!"

"But-!"

"I need you to hurry!"

Father William quickly shuffled back down the stairs and down the hallway to the back door. Rob waited until he heard the priest make his way over the broken glass and out the door, before he straightened again to look at the door.

He could still hear someone shifting around in there.

Slowly, Rob walked toward the door. He moved quietly, staying on tip-toe, trying not to make his presence known as he approached.

He stopped just outside the door and listened to the sounds of the house. A gentle breeze had kicked up, causing branches to scrape against the walls. He heard his own breath, but on the other side of the door there was only silence now. It was as though whoever was on the other side of the door had paused in anticipation.

Rob realized that he was holding his own breath, and his lungs started to burn. He slowly and silently exhaled. As he breathed in, the smell of cinnamon drifted under the door. He recognized it from the other night; that sweet smell mixed with a musty smell of decay. It was nearly suffocating, and he had the sudden urge to vomit.

He couldn't hold it off anymore, and gagged. Knowing his presence was obvious, he hurried through the door, nearly falling into the room.

He stopped suddenly at the threshold, stopping in his tracks at the sight.

He had only met the Taylors once, but he instantly recognized them both. Samantha was on the floor, she'd fallen out of her chair, but her body was still frozen by rigor mortis in a sitting position. There was dark bruising around her neck that appeared to have been made by human hands.

It was her husband though, that nearly sent Rob flying back out of the room. John was on the floor, and Rob could only see the upper half of his body. Blood covered the floor as well as the walls behind him, and tiny pieces of brain matter were scattered around the room. The worst part, however, was the cat. The window was open a little, and it had gotten into the room. The cat was eating away at the flesh on John's face, pulling and tearing away at it like a wild beast tearing the flesh of its prey.

The cat looked up at Rob standing in the threshold, and gave a long warning growl.

Rob was about to back away, to get away from the madness in the room, when something moved. There'd been a small movement in the reflection of the mirror. He had to step further into the room to get a better look, and he turned quickly, coming face to face with the man standing there.

He was covered in blood, and standing in front of some writing scrawled on the wall in the victim's blood. "KILL THEM ALL" was written in large letters behind him. The man himself wore a long sleeved shirt in the summer heat, and his shirt and pants were covered in dirt and badly torn He looked like a bum from the streets of Chicago. He was a little taller than Rob, and his graying hair made him look older. However, the man had only a five o'clock shadow, not a full beard like most homeless men. He was rough; however, there was something off. He was just a little too clean cut.

Rob had always found dealing with the "homeless" one of the worst parts of his job when he worked in the city, but he was far from there. He didn't have to handle this one with kid gloves. No, the gloves were off.

The man stumbled back.

"Hold it right there."

The man looked at the two bodies and then at Rob.

"Don't hurt me," he stammered. He stumbled back into the corner. Rob reached out his hand, palm out, body turned away. Typically he would be reaching back with his other hand for his revolver, however, when his hand hit his hip, he was reminded once again that his it was still in its lock box at the house.

Rob looked at the blood on the wall, and then at the man now cowering in the corner. It was obvious to him that the man was dangerous. The blood on the wall, and the malicious strangling of Samantha proved that.

"I'm Officer Alletto. I'm with the Standard Police Department." Rob was easing closer to the man, who looked again at the two bodies and then back at Rob. He was frightened, but Rob couldn't tell if he was afraid of him, or of something else. He kept looking at the mirror, and it bothered Rob. He wanted to look over his shoulder to see what the man kept looking at, but he was afraid to take his eyes off him.

The cat gave out another growl that sounded more like a dog, rather than a cat, and it made Rob jump a little. The man and Rob both turned to look as the cat released its hold on the flesh of John's cheek. Slowly, it strutted over to the man, and then pressed itself up against his leg. It purred as it rubbed against him, smearing blood along his pants leg. The cat then turned and looked at Rob. It glared with green and black eyes, making Rob's heart skip a beat, and he felt darkness cross over his soul.

The cat growled at Rob again, and he couldn't keep himself from backing up a step.

Rob looked pointedly at the man and motioned for him to come to him.

"Come with me, I'm taking you into custody until we can get this straightened out."

The man tried to step forward, moving slowly toward Rob, but the cat kept working his way between his legs and under his feet. It wouldn't leave him alone, weaving in and out and around, until finally; the man had to kick it away. It landed on the other side of the bed, and then turned to look at the two of them. It hissed, and then scurried away under the bed.

The man looked at Rob, and slowly he lifted his shaking hands in surrender. "Step this way."

He inched closer, and Rob backed away to open a path to the open doorway. He backed around Rob and turned to leave the room.

Rob kept the man in front of him until they were downstairs, then pushed him against the wall and took the handcuffs from his back pocket. The man didn't resist as Rob locked the cuffs into place and pulled him away from the wall. With Rob holding onto the cuffs, they walked outside.

As Rob stepped onto the porch, he heard a growl behind him and turned to see the cat standing at the top of the stairs. It howled, and it sent a small tremor through the entire house. The house groaned in protest, and then in an instant, as Rob blinked, the cat was gone, and the house settled. He noticed that the wood of the porch seemed much more decayed, than when he had first arrived. The paint had peeled away, and the wood underneath looked like it was rotting before his eyes.

Rob pushed the man forward, and down the steps. He could see Father William down the street, already hurrying back.

"What's your name?" Rob asked the man, as he walked him down the sidewalk back to his house. He really didn't want this man anywhere near his family, or to know where his family lived, but the squad car was there, and he needed to get the man secured in the back seat.

"Most people call me Coolidge," the man said. His voice was quiet, like a whisper under his breath. Rob tried to see his face as they walked, but didn't want to get too close. Still, he was pretty sure that the man was crying.

"Okay Coolidge, what's your real name? None of this street name shit."

"Luke. Luke Collins."

"Okay. Good. We're talking. That's good. So do you want to tell me why you killed those two?"

"I... I didn't." The man stammered. His accent seemed Midwestern, so Rob figured he had to be from the area, or relatively close. "I just got there"

"How? Were you the one who broke through the back door?"

"No."

Father William was almost upon them, bridging the gap quickly as they walked toward each other.

"Then how did you get in?"

"You wouldn't believe me."

"Try me."

"I came in through the mirror."

"You mean you broke in through the window?"

"No, I came in through the mirror."

Father William met up with them, slightly out of breath, and Rob could tell that this was more activity than the pastor had seen in a long time. Rob could sympathize. It was the most action he'd seen in a long time as well. His back was aching badly but he was trying to ignore it until he was able to get through this.

"The County is on its way. They said they'll have a patrol here in thirty minutes."

"Thirty minutes?"

"Did you find out what happened to the Taylors?"

Rob considered telling him, but didn't want the priest to have any more on his plate. It was already too much for the man. Even then, as they stood there, he   was wheezing, and Rob was sure he must have a heart condition on top of everything else. Judging by man's weight, he could see it being a problem.

They walked the rest of the way to the squad car, and Rob opened the door, lowering Coolidge into the back seat. He didn't like the idea of sitting on this guy for the next half hour. He would call the County. Maybe if he prioritized it as a murder over a robbery, they could get a team out there a little faster. Damn he hated playing small town politics when it came to a damn crime scene. Where were his med lab and the damn investigators? He was probably going to get stuck with some County road jockey whose only experience consisted of writing speeding tickets. The only thing he would know about a murder scene was training he'd had over a decade ago.

Rob turned to look at the priest who was trying to look over Rob's shoulder and get a look at Coolidge sitting in the back seat. Rob had to gently push the priest away, and thankfully, the he took the hint and stepped back on his own.

"I want to thank you for your help today. I'll take care of everything. I want you to go back to your parish. We'll come by later to get a statement." Rob worked to get the priest's attention, to get him to look him in the eye. When he finally did, Rob could see just how worried and scared the man was. His face was sagging, and there was a sad and helpless look in his eyes that worried Rob. Even more reason the man shouldn't know about the two bodies up in that bedroom.

"What's going on?" Robyn said as she hurried down the front porch steps. Rob looked in her direction, frustrated that they were already attracting attention.

"Just stay inside. Okay honey?"

Rob watched as she went back into the house and then turned back to the priest.

"Is something wrong with the Taylors?"

Rob put his arm around Father William and walked him back to his car, making sure to keep an eye on his prisoner over his shoulder. The

Father kept his head down as they walked to his car. Rob knew the man had already figured out what had happened.

* * * *

Robyn stepped inside. She didn't get a chance to tell him, and she was worried he might have seen the cable man leave. She had to tell him. If she didn't, he was sure to find out, and then it would be another fight.

She was getting so tired of fighting with him. Ever since they had moved, it seemed they were at each other. It was getting worse and it and they fought about absolutely everything. All she'd wanted was to have the internet hooked up so she could find out if they had found that little girl down in Florida, and to email Ruth and see if she could set her up with that jewelry sales thing. It would be a way for them to make money. Still, she knew that Rob would never understand.

Robyn stopped in the hallway, trying to think of where she was going, Her mind was confused and she felt like her body was on auto pilot. She tried to pull herself out of it, to concentrate, but without success. The house was quiet, and seemed to be closing in on her.

Where was Jake? Oh, yeah, he was playing in the backyard. She should probably have him come in. He should really come in and go to his room. His father would be home soon, and he'd have something special for Luke. Luke, who's Luke? She meant Jake. His dad would be home, and he would have a surprise for all of them.

She could see her hand reach out for the stair rail, and she began to walk up. She didn't know where she was going, but felt there was somewhere she had to be. Something she should be doing.

Oh yeah, she had to get herself ready. She had to go comb her hair and get ready. Tonight would be her big night. Rob would be home soon, and he would bring home a fun surprise for the whole family.

Robyn walked to her room, and sat down in front of the vanity mirror. She hadn't had a way to sit in front of the mirror since they'd moved in, but recently, while unpacking, she'd discovered a stool to put to use. She sat down, staring at herself, lost in her own reflection.

Casually, she turned, and noticed the brush on the top of the vanity. It didn't look like her brush. It was strange and old. Still, it would do. She needed her hair to be perfect; Rob was coming home, and he had a surprise for all of them.

* * * *

"I'll come by your parish in a few hours." Rob said. He forced a smile, knowing that he needed to calm the man down a little, he was way too worked up. "Hey, you'll finally get me inside the church! How about I swing by around four? As soon as I finish up here I'll head over."

Father William eased himself into his car and looked up to meet Rob's gaze. His eyes glistened with tears but he had a slight smile on his face. Rob could tell it was taking all of the priest's energy to keep it up.

"You come to my church. We'll pray together."

"You can count on it. Maybe you'll even get me to bring my family in Sunday morning."

The priest nodded and started his car.

"I'll see you soon." Father William said. He turned away and put the car in gear. Rob stepped back and watched as the car pulled away from the curb. He sure as hell hoped that the Father was going to be okay. He doubted that many people in town had experienced murder, or anything more stressful than a natural death.

Rob turned away and was in mid step when he nearly walked into Todd. He'd somehow snuck up behind him, been almost touching his back, when Rob turned around. He'd nearly jumped out of his skin.

"Holy Shit! What the hell are you doing home so early in the day? Don't you have a shop to run?" Todd just stood there, looming over Rob. He hadn't noticed before how much taller than him Todd was. Then again, he had really only met him a couple of times, and the last time, Todd had been sitting on a picnic table for nearly the whole time.

"I came home early. I felt it was time to spend some time at home." Todd turned and looked at Coolidge sitting in the backseat of the squad car. Coolidge watched them, with a strange, fearful expression on his face. "Besides, it looks like I would have missed all the fun. So what's going on?"

There was something odd about Todd's voice. It was unnatural, emotionless and cautious, as though he chose each word very carefully and made extra effort in pronouncing each syllable. He wore a large, unnatural smile from ear to ear. It revealed large yellow teeth. It was strange, but Rob never remembered Todd's teeth so yellow and dark. With the man being a pharmacist, he would have expected him to take much better care of them.

"Come on, you can tell me neighbor." Todd said. Rob could swear that in that instant he saw a flicker of flame in Todd's eyes.

Rob backed around Todd on his way to the squad car, making sure not to turn his back on him. Something crazy was going on here, and it was spooking the hell out of him.

A gun shot pierced the eerie silence that had grown between Rob and Todd.

"Uh oh," Todd said, his voice distant and robotic. He turned and looked down the street, in the direction of the Pacifico's house. It was next to Todd's place and the one closest to the Taylors. "That sounded like trouble."

"Get back to your house!" Rob shouted, as he hurried to the front seat of the squad car, nearly pulling the door off its hinges as he pulled it open and slid in. What in the Sam hell was going on? He had one possible murderer in custody, and now he was hearing gun shots from another house on the street. This couldn't be possible! He didn't move his family to the ghetto; he moved them to a small sleepy town in the Midwest. Murders should happen there once every fifty years, not every other damned day. If he wanted to live in an area with that much crime, he would have stayed in Chicago.

Todd watched him for a moment before he turned and casually walked back to his house. Rob stared after him for a second, shaking his head, then turned to look in the rearview mirror at the man sitting in the back seat. He wanted to ask him what was going on, but he didn't have the time. He needed to call in back-up ASAP, and he needed to get to that house and see who was shooting and who (what?) was being shot at. Right then, keeping Coolidge or whatever the man wanted to call himself, tucked away in the back seat was the best he could do.

Rob reached for the police radio, but he'd barely gotten his hand around the handset, when something reached into his mind. He felt a great weight dragging him down, and slumped over in his seat. His vision became hazy, and before long his eyes closed completely, enveloping him in darkness. Strangely, he wasn't afraid, but felt a calm come over him as he drifted off, letting his body fall completely over on the front seat.

CHAPTER 11

Rob stood in the center of a large corn field. The wind tossed the six foot high corn stalks to and fro, whipping against him, slashing at him. He felt the burn of the leaves as they hit, but they didn't pierce the skin, and he knew they wouldn't. He had a feeling of comfort and safety there. His anger had lifted, anger that had been growing inside him that he hadn't realized was there. There'd been a darkness increasing in him since they had moved to the small town. Now it was gone. In the corn field, he was safe; and he could feel the darkness was gone. Instead, a strange calm had washed over him. He realized that something was different, missing. It was the absence of pain. Even his legs didn't hurt. He was completely relaxed.

Rob began to walk aimlessly through the stalks of corn. He didn't know where he was going, but felt he was being pulled somewhere. Up ahead, he saw a scarecrow, and realized it was his destination. He picked up his pace; wanting to see what had brought him there, what it was all about.

The scarecrow stood in the center of a large clearing. He reached its edge, and without a moment's hesitation, stepped away from the cover of the corn and into the open space.

Instantly warmth and comfort flowed over him. He felt he was home. Around him, the was calm, and there was a peaceful stillness.

Everything was quiet

A rustling sound came from the corn, and Rob turned to see Coolidge emerge beside him. It was Coolidge, but not. His clothes were no longer worn and tattered, but looked brand new. The man was clean shaven and freshly showered, definitely not the dirty mess that had been sitting in the back of Rob's squad car.

Rob wanted to ask him if he knew how they had gotten there, or where they were, but he couldn't talk. When he opened his mouth nothing escaped. Coolidge turned to look to him; and there was a small look of recognition, before his gaze shifted to the center of the clearing.

Rob turned to see what Coolidge was looking at.

a Native American woman stood the center of the clearing. She looked to be in her mid-thirties, and Rob had a vague sense that he had seen her before. She was dressed differently now, wearing traditional shaman ceremonial dress, but he recognized her face.

He realized she was the girl from the store, the one he'd thought he had seen on the street just the other night. She was with them now, all dressed up as though she was going to do some kind of rain dance or something.

Coolidge stepped up to stand at Rob's side. Rob wanted to flash him a warning look, since he'd moved well into Rob's personal space, but he couldn't take his eyes off her.

"You must stop him," she finally said.

"Stop who?"

"My father," said the man beside him.

Rob looked at Coolidge, questions already starting to form in his mind, but he felt that now was not the time or the place.

"He's getting stronger. You don't have much time. You are already close to losing yourself to him" she said as she looked directly into Coolidge's eyes.

"My father is already dead. How do you stop a ghost?"

"There is not much time. The house that your father built is built upon evil. I was the guardian who was to keep that evil from escaping the land, but it got inside your father somehow. It has been using him, and is now spreading through your father's spirit."

"Okay. So how do we stop it?" Coolidge was quick to ask.

Rob stood there, unable to fully absorb what she was saying.

"You must separate him from the evil. The darkness will always be a part of that land, but it is your father, and his corrupted soul, allowing it to spread. Legend speaks of two warriors. One must make a sacrifice; the other must accept the sacrifice. You must do this quickly, before the evil spreads. Darkness takes life, feeds and grows strong."

Thunder rumbled and the sky darkened. Lightning streaked through the sky and struck the scarecrow that stood high above the woman. Blue flame ignited it, but in moments was quelled, and left it untouched.

The scarecrow moved its head, turning to face the two of them. There was nothing but black where its eyes should be, yet it looked directly at them. It swung its arms and then leapt from the platform where it stood, to the ground, right behind the woman.

The scarecrow's face and its long stitched mouth, running completely across its canvas face gave Rob the creeps. He remembered that look from somewhere, remembered that face; suddenly, he placed it. He remembered that evil face coming at him in his nightmares. The eyes were dark in this scarecrow, but he knew well that fire burned behind them.

The scarecrow grabbed the woman's sleeve, pulling her around to face it. The hide fell away in its grasp, and a crow emerged and hovered beyond the scarecrow's reach. It squawked at the scarecrow as it flailed its wings. The bird pecked wildly, working desperately to reach the scarecrow's eyes.

A breeze blew toward Rob and Coolidge as they watched the fight escalating before them. On the wind, a voice, her voice, carried to them.

"Run!"

It took a moment for it to register for Rob, but Coolidge was already looking at him, and reaching for him. They took off into the corn field. For as old as Coolidge was, he could run faster than Rob.

Rob realized why. The pain that had left him was coming back again. The stabbing pain in his back blossomed, and the slight limp that he had been fighting to get rid of was back. Pain shot down his leg, and he winced, but he was afraid to stop running.

Coolidge got farther and farther ahead of him, and Rob began to panic. He could feel the air behind him getting cold, as though death were breathing down his neck. The light was fading fast, making it harder to see where they were going, and Coolidge was getting harder to spot in the whipping corn stalks.

He could hear the corn being trampled behind him. Something large and powerful was gaining on him. Instead of running through the cornstalks, something was crushing them as it followed behind, and drew closer with every step. Rob wanted to look back, but didn't dare take the time.

He pushed himself even harder. His back was in agony and he almost cried out. He wanted to lie down and give in to whatever chased him; the pain of running was growing more and more unbearable. He closed his eyes, and pushed himself even harder.

He could feel something reaching into his mind. The darkness was trying to take control of him. It pulled at him, trying to slow him, to stop him. It would make all the pain go away. He wouldn't feel a thing; all he had to do was to stop and let it in,

Rob could hear the voice in his head. It was his own, telling him to let go and give in. He didn't know how he could resist it, wasn't even sure he wanted to. The idea of just giving in and letting the darkness take over seemed so appealing.

Rob's legs gave out on him, and he landed hard on his knees.

The darkness swirled around him; scraping like sandpaper on his skin. It slid over him, trying to push its way into his mind. He knew that the scarecrow couldn't be far behind. He was coming, and Rob didn't think he could walk. With the pain shooting through his knees, he was convinced they were both broken. He was helpless.

He was losing the fight, and with his will crumbling, he knew it would soon have complete control.

At the same time, anger was building inside him. He smashed the earth with his fists, over and over, until he felt blood leaching into the soil. He had no control over it. The anger came from the darkness, and it spread quickly through him. He was losing himself to it.

A small light broke through the darkness and grew. It was blinding at first, but then began to take shape. It morphed into human form and came to stand in front of him.

"Dad! Dad!" He heard Jake shouting. "Dad, are you okay!?"

Jake was breaking through the darkness, and the light around him seemed to push it away. Rob felt the anger pushing back. "Dad!"

Rob looked at his son, still standing in the center of the light, now expanding, and where it had expanded Coolidge rushed through, reaching out for Rob's hand.

"Grab it!" Coolidge cried.

Rob reached up, his hand mangled and bleeding. Coolidge took it, and pulled. Rob struggled against him at first, but then let Coolidge help him stand. Rob could feel his knees, grinding as he moved.

He stood slowly and stepped into the light.

* * * *

"Dad!"

Rob started awake, and found himself in his squad car. He tossed the radio receiver that had been in his hand. It clattered against the floor as he turned to see Jake slamming his fists against the windshield. Jake stopped when he saw that his father was coming around.

Rob eased back into his seat, and looked around at the neighborhood as he sat up. It was quiet, with no movement, not even a bird flying overhead. An onlooker would assume the street abandoned; nearly all the grass was brown, and the shrubbery and flowers along the driveways were withered and dry, their petals colorless.

Rob didn't remember the street looking that way when he'd walked down it early this morning. He could have sworn it'd been full of color when he'd walked down to the Taylor's just a little over an hour ago. Hell, had it even been an hour?

Jake looked at the man in the back seat, and Rob turned as well, looking back at Coolidge. Coolidge was sitting up. Rob couldn't imagine that the man in the back seat had actually been in his dream with him, but it was odd that he too was just waking up.

Rob turned and looked at Jake.

"What's up? You should be in the house with your mother."

"You okay?" Jake said. Jake couldn't take his eyes off Coolidge. "Who's he?"

Rob felt light headed and groggy, but he was beginning to remember putting Coolidge into the back seat of the car.

"Hey buddy. Go back inside okay?" Rob answered. He shook his head, trying to force out the cobwebs. As Jake turned to go back inside, Rob remembered what he had been reaching for. He'd heard a gunshot. He'd been about to call it in, to get the damn County boys involved. Shit! How could he have fallen asleep? He needed to check on it, to see what the hell was going on.

Rob reached for the door handle to get out of the car.

"Hey, where are you going?" Coolidge said, watching Rob as he exited the vehicle. Rob turned to look back at him.   "County will be here for you in a minute."

"I didn't do anything, and you heard her. We have to do something!"

"Heard who?"

"The Shaman!"

Rob slammed the car door shut. How the hell did he always find these kooks? Still, something seemed wrong with the street, and he remembered the odd feelings he'd had earlier. Something wasn't right. His neighbor, Todd, was still standing on his porch, watching every move Rob made, yet Rob felt like it wasn't really Todd who was actually watching him. He stood stiffly, again Rob thought of the word 'robot' when he tried to describe him. He stood like a robot, not so much watching Rob, but more like he recording his movements…

Rob walked by him quickly and hurried down the street to the next house over. He didn't know how the hell he had passed out after hearing the gun shot go off, but he was pretty sure that it had come from this house. In fact, Todd had been standing by his car at the time, and had even mentioned that it was the Pacifico's. Even though Todd had been acting pretty strangely, Rob had to agree.

He hurried up the front steps, across the porch, and pounded on the front door. He waited, but nothing stirred on the other side. Rob looked over his shoulder and saw that Todd had moved to the side of the porch closest to Rob. He glared at Rob, sending a chill down his spine. He was starting to feel like he was in a horror movie. He was the stranger who had come to the town where everyone was possessed, and they were all just waiting until they could grab him and serve him up for lunch.

Rob turned back and continued to pound on the door, with no result

"Hello! Anyone home?" He knew he probably had sufficient cause to break down the door, but he didn't want to if he didn't have to. He remembered how the back door was at the Taylor's and decided it might be best if he went around back to check out the back door.

As he'd suspected, he found the back door smashed in, just like the one at that Taylor's. He rushed in, a heavy lump forming in the pit of his stomach. As he stepped over the broken glass, the view was eerily reminiscent. He prayed he wouldn't find the same thing all over again. However, as he made his way up the stair case toward the master bedroom, he grew more sure of what he would see.

Rob rushed into the bedroom, steeling himself for what might be inside. The house had been quiet but for his own footsteps, but with both cars in the driveway, he knew the owners were both more than likely at home. At the very least, one of them should be there.

As he entered, his worst nightmare became reality. The woman, Rob thought her name was Terry, had been sitting at the mirror. She was slumped over in her chair, with a circle of bruising around her neck. It was obvious that she had been strangled. There was fresh blood still soaking into the carpet. Rob could see a foot hanging on the side of the bed, and he was sure that if he stepped around to look, it would be Ron. He wondered if he'd once again see what appeared to be a self-inflicted gunshot wound.

How?

Okay, so the man he had down in his squad car obviously didn't commit the other murder, since this one happened after he had him in custody. Questions were coming at Rob faster than he could even comprehend them. He wanted answers, and so far, all he had was a dream and a crazy bum in the back of his squad car. He'd had rough days in Chicago with plenty of crazy shit happening, but nothing like this.

Rob turned to leave the room. He just wanted to get out of there, put in a call to County, and let them take this over, he was done with it. Maybe it wasn't too late to sell the house and go back to Chicago. Right then, a desk job wasn't sounding too damn bad.

In the corner, out of reach of the mirror, the Native American girl stood, still, and frightened. "One must sacrifice."

Rob reached for his hip, surprised to see her and reacting on instinct was frustrated once again at not having his gun with him.

Still, he wouldn't have actually pulled it on her. There was something about her, he could still remember her from his strange dream, and the calming effect she had on him.

"Sacrifice?"

"One must sacrifice. You both must work together. Be quick, before he becomes too strong. The evil is growing, the earth is dying. One must sacrifice."

Rob stood looking at her. She seemed so stoic and distant, like she was looking through him, and not at him at all.

Then her gaze changed, and she seemed even more frightened. She looked directly into his eyes, and it sent a chill through him. Her eyes were bright blue, but they were starting to reflect an orange fire.

"He's coming! You must go!"

Loud, crowing laughter, deep and menacing, shook the room. The mirror rattled in its frame, and make up and cologne scattered across the top of the dresser. Some fell, and shattered on the floor. The fragrance of different colognes, mingling in the air did very little to disguise the stench that was starting to fill the room. The cinnamon and mold stench was becoming strong as darkness came out of the mirror. Like smoke escaping a fire, it flowed into the room. However, unlike smoke, it didn't rise to the ceiling. It emerged from the mirror and took shape as a man, who then stood in front of the mirror.

Rob watched the thick black smoke as it took human form. He turned to look at the woman in the corner. She was gone, vanished by some magic of her own, leaving him there to face it.

"Why in the hell should I help her?" he thought to himself as he stood there. He wasn't sure what to do. He backed away from the smoke toward the door, but then wondered if he should run or stay and see what happened? He had the feeling that whatever came was not going to be good.

Rob turned and grabbed the handle of the door. The knob was hot, and he screamed in pain.

A voice behind him asked, "Why in the hell should you help her?"

Rob didn't want to look. The smiling man had come to him a few times in his dreams, each time terrifying him. Now, however, the man spoke softly. His voice was soothing and easy on the ear. He was no longer trying to scare, but to soothe him. "Come on, Rob. Turn around."

The voices were back, whispering, urging him to give in, to turn, and face the man. To let him in, and accept him.

Rob slammed his hand into the door, enjoying the pain that flashed through his hand.

"That's it. Give in to the anger." The voice said from behind him.

It wasn't the anger however, that Rob wanted to feel. It was the pain. When he hit the door, he felt the man's hold on him slip a little. The darkness in his mind pulled back slightly as the pain throbbed in his knuckles. Rob had hit many objects and people in the past, but never as hard as he had pitched his fist against that door. He was sure he'd broken something, and this time it wasn't a dream. He wouldn't be waking up with a perfectly working and pain free appendage. This pain was real, and he was going to use it.

With his mind now clear, he reached again for the knob on the door. He ripped it open, and hurried from the room, not looking back.

"Come back! You will come back! After all, it's your turn."

Rob didn't have to look back to know that the man was smiling his toothy smile from ear to ear. He just kept running, holding his broken hand.

* * * *

Rob hurried out the front door of the house, not willing to retrace his steps over broken glass, and out the back. Once outside, the afternoon sun assailed him, and he threw up his hand to shield his vision.

What the hell was he going to do? Where the hell had he moved his family? He wanted to get out of there. They could move back to Chicago; take their house off the market and move back in. He was definitely going to put the wacko rat trap they were in back on the market. He could try to get that desk job at one of the precincts. The layoffs were nasty, and it would be difficult, but it would sure be better than this crap. If he didn't get a job in the police department, he could always go into security. There was always something. Besides, he could try to pull Social Security due to his injury or stay on the worker's comp for a while and then possibly get on unemployment. They would be better off. Just move back to the city, get back to Chicago. Then all this shit would fade away, and Standard would be just a distant nightmare.

He liked the idea more and more the closer he got to home. Coolidge was still cooling his heels in the back of the squad car. Rob barely looked in his direction as he walked past. He didn't want anything to do with him. County would be there soon, and then Rob would go and rent himself another moving truck. Robyn could start packing. They still had most of the boxes from the move stored down in the basement, so it shouldn't take too long. They could possibly get on the road just after rush hour. They would be sleeping in their old rooms that night.

It was all starting to make sense to him. Just get out of town, get out of Dodge before the high noon showdown.

Coolidge pounded away on the squad car window, trying to get Rob's attention.

Rob heard it, and turned to look. Coolidge stopped pounding on the window and motioned for Rob.

"What the hell does he want?" Rob thought to himself. He took a quick look at his house. It was strange, but he was sure that the rose bushes in front were starting to turn brown. He didn't like the thought of that. They had to hurry.

Rob walked to the car, figuring he would calm the nut down quickly and then get inside and talk to Robyn. He opened the driver's door so he could talk through the screen between the front and back seats.

"Yeah?"

"Yeah, what? You were there. We have to stop this!"

"Stop what? Is that your accomplice, that little Indian girl?" Rob believed Coolidge knew more than he wanted to show. If he admitted it, he would have to do something about it. He just wanted to get on the road. Maybe they would even leave right away, come back for their stuff later. It's not like they had anything valuable that they couldn't replace. They wouldn't be leaving their life behind; they'd be going back to it, saving themselves.

"Dad!"

Rob turned quickly, and saw Jake running down the front steps of the house. He was out of breath and pale. His eyes were open wide, and he nearly tripped over his own feet as he ran to catch up to Rob at the squad car.

"Dad!"

"I thought I told you to go in and stay with your mother!"

"Something's wrong! She's sitting in your room, staring at the mirror. She just sits there, combing her hair. I tried to talk to her, I even screamed at her. I tried to pull her out of the chair. It's like she's a statue, she won't move!"

Rob literally felt the blood leaving his face, and his heart froze as it skipped a beat. Tears formed in his eyes and he realized that he was trapped, and there was no escape. The cycle had started. He thought about what the smiling man had said. "It's your turn." It rang in his ears.

Rob turned to look at Coolidge.

"Did you kill those people?"

"No."

"What happened?"

"I don't know what happened to them. If it's what I think, the man came home, strangled his wife, and then found a way to kill himself. Most people in this town own a gun of some kind. He probably shot himself. I didn't look around to make sure."

"How do you know this?"

"Because it's what my dad did. Over thirty years ago."

Rob turned to look at Todd, who was still standing there, watching from the porch.

"Then why hasn't Todd killed his wife? What makes them different?"

"I'm thinking that my dad, as he gets stronger, has more control. At first it was just a cycle of violence, now, he's in no rush. I think he's keeping Todd alive to keep an eye on us. We're the unknown element.   Rob opened the door, inviting Coolidge to step out of the back of the car.

"How is he doing this?"

"When my dad made all his money, and he built this street and he built his house, he was warned by an old man in town. The man didn't say much; just that the plot of land my dad was building on was a 'host of a great evil'. My dad, with all his money didn't care what anyone had to say though, and built it anyway."

"Jake! I want you to run to that priest's church. Do you remember which one he said he was from?"

Jake nodded his head, followed by a stammered

"Y-y-yes, I do."

"Good, I want you to go there and stay there till I come and get you. I want you safe, understand me? Get there, and stay put. Have him stay with you. I'll feel a lot better knowing you're in a church."

Rob hugged Jake as hard as he could, fearing that it might be the last time he would. He let go, and found that Jake was crying, his tears flowing freely. Rob wiped them away with his thumb, trying hard to keep his own waterworks under control. Then he pointed in the direction of the church, and Jake took off running.

"I'll be right back. You stay here," Rob said to Coolidge.

He rushed inside; he had made the mistake earlier of not having his sidearm with him. He was not going to make that mistake again.

CHAPTER 12

Rob was back within five minutes, however, his chest hurt, and he was sickened by what he had seen. He'd believed Jake when he told him about Robyn, but until he had seen it himself; he had chosen not to believe it. The sight of her there, combing her hair without any sign of awareness was sickening, and had made Rob want to vomit.

He'd wanted to pull her away, to get her to wake up and go with him. They could still have gone to get Jake from the church and take off. However, he knew it would have done little good. He could see by her blank stare that she was gone, and unless he did something, she wasn't ever coming back. She was lost.

He had hurried to his lock box, pulled out his revolver and tucked it into the small of his back. He knew he should put on his holster as well, but he didn't want to walk down the street in full gear. He thought it would be best for now to keep his gun tucked away in what he had often joked with Jake about as "gangster style."

Outside, Coolidge had been waiting for him by the squad car. He was still handcuffed with his hands behind his back, but had stayed put. Rob decided that must mean the man was truly innocent, and all this crazy shit was actually happening.

In a way, Rob had almost hoped that Coolidge had run off. Then he might be able to pretend none of this was real, at least a little longer.

Rob walked behind Coolidge so that he could undo the cuffs. Coolidge pulled his hands in front of him, rubbing his wrists. As one, they looked over at Todd, still watching from his porch. He was smiling from ear to ear, and Rob swore that even from where he was, he could see orange flames burning in Todd's eyes.

"So where do we go from here?" Rob said. He was talking to Coolidge, but kept his eyes on Todd. Coolidge did the same.

"The source, I guess."

"Any ideas on what we are going to do?"

"Some."

"Care to share?"

"I don't think you want to know."

Rob didn't like the sound of that and couldn't imagine what was going through Coolidge's mind. He didn't know him well enough to guess what was going on in his mind.

Together, they started walking along the street. The silence was really beginning to wear Rob down. It gnawed at his nerves. Even the sounds of the nearby freeway seemed muted, and the birds and insects were silent. Rob hoped they were all just waiting, like an audience, for some epic battle between good and evil, and that they weren't all dead. In his heart, however, he doubted that much along the street was still alive. The evil was sucking away at everything and everyone, and it was becoming stronger. What was worse, it seemed to be spreading even faster.

But how was he not affected? What was keeping it out of his mind?

They got to the end of the street, and Rob peeked back at Todd, only to find him still standing on his porch watching them. Rob hoped that when this was done, Todd, and his wife, Bonnie would be okay. That is, if he and Coolidge were quick.

They stepped over the guard rail and stood on the gravel road leading into the woods.

"This whole street used to be just an entrance to our house. The rail is where the road turned to gravel. My dad wanted to be as far away from the 'idiots in town' as he could. He liked the idea of having the woods around him. It made it feel like we were even farther away. We had a whole forest between us and the town, a forest that more than half the town was afraid to go into. A forest that the moment you entered it, you could feel the air change and a chill that bore straight into your bones. It made you feel like you had to take a hot shower and huddle under the covers, on even the hottest summer day."

Rob felt it. As soon as they'd crossed the rail, something about the air made him shiver. It was as though the sun's rays couldn't penetrate, and he'd felt like they were in a meat freezer.

"Didn't have many friends in school did you?" Rob said. He wanted desperately to get his mind off of the sudden cold.

"Yeah, well, at the time we were of the belief that we could buy whatever we wanted, even friends."

Coolidge walked in front of Rob, leading the way through the dying trees. It seemed as they walked, that every time they were about to step into a patch of sun, the trees shifted, keeping any hope of warmth away. They stepped into the clearing where Coolidge's house stood just as a cloud passed over the sun. Rob looked up, taking notice of the dark core of the cloud. A gentle breeze flowed through them and it stung like ice.

Rob's limbs felt like rubber, and every step that he took in the direction of the house, was more difficult than the last. The air grew thick, and hard to breathe. The smell of cinnamon and rotten meat almost suffocated him, but Rob was sure he could smell the thick smoke of a burning building as well. His lungs were starting to burn, and he reached out for Coolidge to pull him back.

Coolidge turned around and looked at Rob.

"I smell smoke."

"I don't."

"No?"

Rob bent over, he couldn't' breathe and tried frantically to pull air into his lungs. The world started to spin, and he began to cough, hacking until blood spattered the ground.   Coolidge rushed back and pounded on Rob's back with one hand, grabbing him for support with the other.

"Come on, man! Come on!"

The smoke lifted slowly, but the world still felt unstable around him. The feeling of not knowing which way was up was disorienting, and he had to fall forward to his knees to keep from being sick. Last night's supper was beginning to work its way up. He leaned on his hands for support, and used all his strength to keep his food down.

Laughter. Rob could hear laughter from inside the house. It was the same laughter that he'd heard back in the Pacifico's bedroom, and he knew who was there. Somewhere in that house, the smiling man was waiting for them, and the evil inside him knew they were there to try and stop it. The laughter was cocky, confident. It assaulted his senses and Rob felt a lump forming in his stomach. They didn't have a chance against it.

"Why am I not affected? Todd and the rest of them, but not me. My wife. Why not me?"

Coolidge reached out his hand for Rob's and pulled him up.

"I don't know. If I had to guess, I would say it probably has something to do with the water."

Rob released Coolidge's hand, chuckling to himself, at the insanity of it all.

"Isn't that what they always say? Craziness is in the water."

"Yeah, but the pipes all run under the woods. The street that you all live on, remember is an add-on. To get running water, they probably ran a line off of the one running to this house. The sickness that has been killing everything has probably been seeping through the land; the people along your street have been drinking it. Have you been home much since you moved in?"

Rob rocked a little as he stood. The world was still unsteady, but it was quickly equalizing.

"My head still feels like it's been through a blender."

"Just because you haven't had as much of the water, doesn't mean you haven't been exposed to it. It's still trying to take over your soul, trying to find a way in."

"Why aren't you affected?"

"I've had to live with it for over thirty years."

Coolidge turned away from Rob and walked to the front door. One must sacrifice, that was what the woman had said, but he didn't like the idea of that. He knew it would probably have to be Coolidge, or Luke, or whatever the man called him. After all, Rob had a family to think about. He wasn't about to sacrifice himself. He left Chicago to live somewhere safe, with his family, and he wasn't about to give that up here in this little hell hole.

The laughter grew louder as they neared the front door. It rang through Rob's ears, like church bells rattling his ear drums.

Coolidge reached out and pushed the door open, showing Rob the wreck beyond the threshold.

"Ready to dance with the devil?"

Rob was winced at the pain, and Coolidge seemed to notice for the first time that something was wrong with him.

"What's wrong?"

"The laughter. It's so loud!"

"It's in your head. He's getting in your head. Push him out. Push him out!"

Rob was near tears. The laughter grew in intensity and pushed at his thoughts.

"Push it OUT!" Coolidge shouted at him. Rob could barely hear him over the laughter. All he heard was, 'out.' Out what? And why wasn't Coolidge in agony?

Rob looked up at Coolidge. His head was throbbing and his brain felt like it was in a vice. Still, through his blurred vision he could see the flames in Coolidge's eyes. They were burning, and he could see Coolidge begin to smile. The smile stretched his skin, and went from ear to ear.

"Push him out!"

Out! Coolidge wanted this! He wanted the smiling man to push him out!

Tears were streaking down his cheeks. At first he thought they were from the pain, but it was from thoughts he was starting to have. He envisioned seeing his son dead, strangled in his room. Then he could see his wife; she was sitting in front of her mirror. He watched himself as he put his hands around her neck and choked the life out of her. He could see the light fade from her eyes as he watched them in the mirror. Then her life was gone, and her body went limp in his hands. She slumped forward and he looked up to see himself in the mirror, his eyes aflame. He watched his reflection as he reached behind his back and slowly pulled out his gun. He stepped back slowly, to the center of the room as he brought the gun to rest just under his chin. He continued to watch as he slowly pulled the trigger.

His vision cleared, and the room around him disappeared. He was standing outside the house, in the woods at the end of his street. Coolidge stood in front of him, reaching out for the gun. Rob noticed that he still had it under his chin, and looked down at it in confusion. He knew he had brought it along, but had no idea why he was holding it.

He looked at Coolidge and saw his eyes were blazing, and Rob swore he could see the smiling man's face staring at him through those eyes.

Rob stretched out his arm, and pointed the gun at Coolidge. "It's got to be you!"

* * * *

Coolidge looked at the gun pointed at his head, and saw his life pass before his eyes. Why did he have to come back home? How in the world, did he allow something, anything to ever bring him back here? He had been running away from it for so long. Now he was back, and staring down the service revolver that just under an hour ago had been used to arrest him for murder.

"Push it out. You have to get yourself under control," Coolidge said quietly, hoping he wouldn't spook Rob into blowing his brains out.

Coolidge kept his arms outstretched, reaching out to the officer, praying that the evil that had control of him would let go.

The cop was staring at him, and his glare was terrifying. He had a crazed look, and his eyes pulsed back and forth between their natural brown and a burning orange.

"Push it out!" Coolidge eased in to the cop a little more, within reach of the gun. He didn't know what he was going to do. He didn't like the gun pointed to his head, but the idea of what would happen if he tried to grab it and it went off wasn't comforting either.

"I'm not going to let you kill my family you murdering bastard. Get away from me, you're with him!" the cop yelled at Coolidge.

Great! He thought that Coolidge was after him. The Grim was really screwing around with the cop's head. Coolidge itched to get that gun out of his hands.

Coolidge looked around to see if there was anything he could use to distract the cop. He even debated how quickly he could make it to the closest tree. He dismissed the thought, as he realized he was way too close to him to do anything other than grab at the gun.

Coolidge slid a half step forward, too afraid to actually lift his foot, so it was more like a slight shuffle. The gravel made popping sounds under his foot that sounded like dynamite going off in the quiet woods.

The cop steadied his grip on the gun and pointed it directly at Coolidge's left eye, his hand no longer shaking.

Coolidge realized that the only chance he had was gone, there'd been a sudden change, and the cop was now sure of himself. Unfortunately that could just spell out the end for ol' Coolidge.

* * * *

Rob stood there, his sights set on Coolidge's left eye. He didn't know if one shot would kill him, but he figured if he was fast enough and got both eyes, he would be able to take out the evil. Then maybe this would all be over and he could get his family out of there.

He slowly began to squeeze the trigger. The cold steel against his finger was a feeling he hadn't felt in a long time. The pistol itself was heavy in his hand. He watched the hammer as it slowly move backward almost to the point of release, which would send the bullet straight into Coolidge's left eye.

Just before he reached the point of no return, he suddenly stopped. His hand was locked in place; and he no longer had control. His finger on the trigger held Coolidge just a hair away from death.

A warm light surrounded him. It flowed over everything around him, shining so brightly that it was all he could see. He couldn't tell where it was coming from; but it enveloped everything; the woods, Coolidge, everything disappeared.   A figure emerged; it was his father. He stepped out of the light and walk toward Rob.

"Put down the gun son. You don't want to do this."

"I have to. I have to save my family."

"This isn't saving them. That man isn't the problem." His father walked up to Rob and reached out, running his hand along Rob's cheek. He found a tear sliding slowly down, and wiped it with his thumb. "The problem is inside of you. The evil is blinding you. You must fight it! You have to find it, and push it away."

"How?"

"Find what you truly care about."

The light faded, taking with it the warmth that had surrounded him, but he noticed that the eternal chill of the woods didn't come rushing back into his bones. The air felt different. He could still feel the chill of the air around him, but only on his skin, no deeper.

He looked around, trying to find traces of the light, not taking his gun off of Coolidge, but looking in all directions. Only the woods and the darkness remained.

The wind began to build in the trees, and Rob watched as it grew in strength and speed as it came at him. His mind urged him to run, but his legs had their own idea, and wouldn't budge. He remained in place, as it blew closer, and then swept over him. And on the wind came the laughter. It exploded in his head like fireworks. The pain was so intense that light bloomed behind his eyes.

He grabbed at his head, screaming as the pain took over.

Then he was standing in his bedroom. His wife sat in front of their mirror, brushing her hair. She paid no attention to him at all.

He could hear Jake downstairs. It sounded like he was playing a video game. This felt much like his previous vision, and Rob felt the anger build inside. The veins were popping up on his arms and his fists were clenched. He wanted to hit something, badly, to hit it so hard that it would explode.

"Jake!" He called out. He could hear the anger in his voice. Jake heard it as well, and the boy's voice trembled as it travelled down the hall.

"What?"

"Come here."

He could hear Jake set down his controller in the other room. The boy's bedroom door opened and closed, and Rob could hear the boy slowly making his way to the bedroom. He stood outside the room for a couple of seconds before Rob heard the door knob turn.

The door creaked open, and Jake eased into the room. He kept his gaze downward, and somehow seemed to know that he was in trouble, and was prepared to take the punishment that was about to come.

Rob looked at him. The anger, no, the rage, made him want to hit the boy, just pound into him. He wanted to slam him into the wall, and then pound his head on it repeatedly until blood stains became the new wallpaper. Rob's breath was quick and growing quicker.

Then he stopped, and took a moment to look at himself in the mirror. He saw his eyes, burning a bright orange and flames shooting through them. The anger burned straight from his soul.

He turned to look at Jake, realizing what he had planned to do, what he had urged himself to do. The gun was still in the small of his back, but his hand had already begun to reach for it.

He was planning to shoot his own flesh and blood, to take the life of his own son; the life that he had brought into the world; the life that he had waited for, and sat in labor with his wife for, for nearly eight hours as she screamed in pain. The life that he watched come from her womb and be placed into her arms by a lovely young nurse. That life that he had sworn to protect, that he had taken his stand and walked his beat on the streets of Chicago for so long, serving to protecting.

Rob looked at his wife as she sat in front of the mirror. She was so beautiful. She had always been and always would be the love of his life. He remembered when he had stood by her when she was in the hospital after Jake was born. When the complications happened, he sat by her hospital bed, while she screamed in pain. He was there when the doctors told her that she would never have another child, and he held her in his arms as she cried into his chest.

He saw that same woman, trapped in the mirror, running her brush through her hair. He looked up at his own reflection in the glass. Behind him was the smiling man, speaking into his ear. Rob couldn't hear him, but he could imagine what the man was trying to say. He didn't want to hear it. He was done listening, done being told what to do. He was done doing what it said would be good for his family.

Rob bent over at his wife's side, but continued to stand, and the smiling man continuing to whisper. Rob turned from his reflection and looked at his wife. He looked into her eyes, not into her reflection, but still there was no change, she still didn't see him.

Rob reached out, and ran his hand along the side of her face, slowly caressing her cheek. He could feel a fresh tear at the corner of his eye. Without wiping it away, he leaned forward and put his arms around her. He began to cry on her shoulder.

He looked over and saw Jake still standing by the door. Rob reached out and motioned for him to come to him. Jake gingerly walked over, and Rob put out his arm to pull him into a hug.

Rob had made a decision. He wasn't going to let this monster destroy his family.

Rob looked at the mirror. The smiling man stood alone in the reflection, looking at them. His smile was gone, replaced with a look of pure hatred. Behind the man, Rob could see Robyn, dead in the reflection, and that the Rob in the mirror was about to shoot himself.

Rob turned away, and held his family even tighter. He closed his eyes, feeling the comfort of their combined warmth soothing his soul.

They suddenly disappeared, but he could still feel their warmth.

Rob opened his eyes, and found he still had his service revolver aimed at Coolidge. He dropped it, and felt both his world and his legs sway; his legs threatened to give out on him.

* * * *

Coolidge quickly reached forward and grabbed Rob before he went down. He had watched as the flames had dimmed from Rob's eyes, and the shaking had returned to Rob's hands. Coolidge breathed a deep sigh of relief when he saw the gun fall, and Rob start to falter.

Now, maybe they could get inside and get this whole thing over with. His hand was tingling, which meant he had been somewhere too long already and it was time to get back on the road. Then again, the tingling also usually meant something bad was coming and it was time for him to get away. This time though, he knew there was no running away. He was there for the fight, no more running, he was there to end it, and finally put his father's ghost to rest.

Coolidge helped steady Rob, and led him toward the house. The sky was growing dark, and if Coolidge didn't know any better, he would guess a storm was coming. But that isn't what he smelled on the breeze. It wasn't rain that was coming.

Coolidge made it to the front door, and Rob worked on standing on his own. That was good, as Coolidge hadn't planned to have to carry him all the way through the house. Coolidge hoped that once they got inside, all they'd have to do would be to break the mirror, thus, severing the ties his father had to this world.

Coolidge remembered a girl he had once traveled the rails with. She'd been extremely scared. She would never ride the rails at night, always made sure to find somewhere to sleep that was well lit and away from any mirrors. She'd been afraid of mirrors. For most of their travels, Coolidge had thought that she was afraid of her own reflection. Most people on the rails, especially the ones that started out as runaways, all had some issue. It usually had a lot to do with why they were on the rails.

That was surely true for the girl. Alice, yes, Coolidge was pretty sure her name was Alice. Alice once told him a story. With Alice's parents, it wasn't that they were mean to her, or had done anything to her. In fact, they tried to save Alice. Or so they'd thought.

When Alice was just a little girl, as she told the story, her family moved into a large house, most would have called it a plantation, down in ol' Mississippi. Alice loved to run around the house and explore. Unfortunately, it was a haunted house. That was part of the reason her family had gotten it so cheap.

The ghost had grown fascinated with Alice and she would see him everywhere. She called him John, and would sit before mirrors all throughout her house, just talking to him. No one other than Alice could ever see anyone talking back. They began to think that she had an imaginary friend.

However, as Alice got older, John didn't go away. In fact, it seemed like she was even more captivated by talking to him. She would sometimes sit mesmerized by the mirror, as if nothing else existed.

Her parent's finally decided it was time to move. Her father wasn't doing well at the job he had taken, and had decided it was better if they moved back home where he could get his old job back. So they packed up their things and moved back to their old neighborhood.

Alice had insisted on bringing one of the mirrors from the house with them. It was a beautiful mirror, so her mother didn't think too much of it at the time.

They settled in, and life continued as always, because of course, John had come back with them. Alice was still always in front of her mirror, and whenever she was asked what she was doing, she simply said she was talking to John.

Her parents got her a cat, in an effort to try to draw her attention away from the mirror. The cat however, knew something was wrong. It hissed and attacked the mirror whenever Alice sat in front of it. It would claw at it as though something was trying to come through and the cat meant to stop it. A few days later, her parents found her cat. It had been killed, brutally cut open. When they asked Alice what had happened, she said John had done it.

Her father went berserk, and threatened to break the mirror if she ever mentioned John again.

That night, her father died in his sleep.

The next morning, after finding her husband dead beside her, her mother destroyed the mirror.

John never came back. Alice ran away after that. It had scarred her for life.

Coolidge thought about it as he and Rob eased into the front entryway. Everything had to be connected to that mirror. Break the mirror, break the cycle.

Rob stopped after entering the front hallway. Coolidge looked at him, and then turned to follow his gaze to the family portrait above the fireplace.

The portrait had changed. All traces of Coolidge and his mother were gone. The only person left was his father, a disfigured and grim version of him, in the center of the painting. He stood smiling at them. Beneath him, in large calligraphic letters written in blood, it said,

"Welcome Home"

CHAPTER 13

"Faded pictures on the wall, it's like they talk to me."

"What's that?" Coolidge said. He turned to Rob and saw that the color had drained from his face after seeing the picture.

"Just some lyrics from a song my son listens to all the time. Just came to my mind."

Rob looked at the picture again, and felt a chill. Damn, what was it with this place that kept giving him the chills?

"So, now what?" Rob looked at Coolidge. Coolidge said he had a plan, but he was slow to let Rob in on it. He almost felt like he was just along for the ride.

Rob reached back; itching for the comfort of the revolver still nestled there. A moment of alarm flashed through him when he didn't feel it, then he remembered dropping it outside. He didn't like being unarmed. Not when he didn't have the slightest clue as to what they were going up against.

The rooms around them darkened.

Rob turned to look at the nearest window. With no electricity, all the light in the house came from outside. Rob figured it had to do with clouds passing over the sun, but when he looked at the window, there was a shape there, blocking the light. It was a human form, with burning eyes.

Rob turned looked over at another window. A young woman stood in that one, her eyes blazing orange as well. The room kept getting darker and as Rob went from room to room, each window was occupied by different people, all with eyes alive with orange flame.

Rob could barely see, as he hurried from the room to room. Coolidge stayed at the entrance watching Rob as he went. He made it back around to Coolidge who was still looking at the woman in the living room window. Coolidge seemed be transfixed.

Rob walked over to him, while turning his attention the stairs. There was still some light coming in from the upstairs windows, just enough for him to see the front entryway and the stairway.

Rob turned to see Coolidge still looking at the woman.

"Coming?"

"It's my mom."

Rob stopped on the second step and stood, watching. He looked back and forth from Coolidge to the woman. The woman looked to be ten years younger than Coolidge, no way older than her mid to late thirties. How could she have given birth to the mid-forties man there with Rob?

Ghosts.

Rob didn't like that even more.

"Come on. She's dead already."

Rob turned from Coolidge and continued up the stairs. He didn't look back to see if Coolidge was behind him, but could hear his footsteps following. He had faith that it was Coolidge and not one of the spirits who'd been watching them.

He made it to the top of the stairs and looked around at the hallway. The floor was covered in debris from plaster that had fallen away. The railing was rotted, and pieces had fallen to the stairs below.

Rob walked down the hallway, being careful to step over the clutter. He looked over his shoulder and saw that Coolidge was still behind him, but was moving slowly.

"So what are we going to do?"

"We are going to break the mirror."

Rob reached to turn the doorknob. Coolidge came up behind him as Rob pushed the door, letting it swing open.

"Sounds simple."

"Yeah."

Rob stepped into the room, and was instantly bombarded with smoke. He doubled over coughing, and his eyes filled with tears. His back seized up and he felt like he was hacking up a lung.   A voice spoke to him, and he recognized it as the smiling man's.

"Do you really think you are here? That you survived that fire?"

The smiling man's face filled Rob's vision, his smile still carved from ear to ear. Rob blinked, hoping to get rid of it, but he was still there.

"You're still in the fire. You're still in Chicago, and always have been. You're still trapped in that room. The chemicals are still exploding all around you, and if you listen, you can hear the screams. Some of them are from the women that were there when you came in. Their flesh is still burning away, and the meat is being cooked well done, can't you smell it? And do you want to know the most sickening part?"

Rob wrapped his arms around himself, bending over as the pain intensified and moved to his stomach. His eyes and mouth burned and dried from the smoke, and his skin felt red hot.

"The loudest of the screams that you hear, or would if you still had ears, if they hadn't burned away, are your own. They're so high pitched that many would mistake you for a woman, should they hear them. Your skin is peeling away from muscle, and muscle from bone. You're on the floor, dying. No one is coming for you. You're hallucinating and about to die. So why fight it? Why fight death? It's already too late."

Rob coughed harder. His breath was coming in small gasps, tasting more and more like charcoal.

He fell hard to the floor.

* * * *

Coolidge watched Rob as he stepped across the threshold into the room and within seconds fell to the floor. There hadn't been any time to react, it had happened so suddenly. Rob lay there, grabbing at his stomach and gasping for air. His eyes were bugged out and both they and his skin were burning red. Coolidge wasn't sure, but he thought he could even see smoke coming off of his skin. He was burning from the inside out, and as Coolidge stood there, he couldn't think of a thing he could do for him.

Coolidge turned and looked down the hall. He debated running to the bathroom for water to douse Rob, but he was sure that with the house being abandoned for over thirty years that the water would have been turned off long ago. Even if it wasn't, he figured there was a good chance the pipes would have rusted through.

Coolidge looked back at Rob, who'd started to scream; it terrified him. He looked at the threshold, and realized that Rob was barely across it. Maybe if could pull him back out of the room, he would be fine.

"No," he said to himself quietly. The room wasn't doing causing it. Coolidge had to break the mirror. He could see it from the hallway.

He thought if he ran in fast, and grabbed his mother's chair from in front of the mirror, he might be able to smash the mirror before his father got to him. He would have to jump over Rob, and not get caught or hit by the door, but it shouldn't take more than ten seconds to do it.

But it would be less than five seconds before Rob was reduced to a burning pile on the floor. Maybe if he stayed close to the walls, and avoided the reflections in the mirror, he could make better time to the mirror. He wasn't sure if it would work. He didn't know why he was even there. He'd run away once before, why not run away now?

He knew why. Because it would just bring him back. It would always bring him back. It wanted something from him, and he needed to break the cycle.

Well, it wasn't going to get what it wanted.

Coolidge braced himself near the threshold, taking several long, deep breaths.

"This is one hell of a mistake," he thought to himself, and then took off.

As fast as he could, he jumped over Rob's body, and then bounced back behind the door, careful to dodge the reflection of the mirror. He took a moment to suck in another breath and then quickly rushed around along the wall until he was directly beside the mirror.

He'd made it, and so far, nothing was after him. He looked over at Rob. He wasn't looking good. He still gasped for breath, but his face was starting to lose its color. Coolidge closed his eyes for a brief second to collect himself and build up his will.

"Damn it," he said to himself, and he quickly leapt out to grab the chair in front of the mirror. He lifted it and without looking, turned and put all his strength into his swing. The chair smashed into the mirror, and he stepped back to avoid the flying shards of silvered glass.

Nothing.

Coolidge didn't hear anything shatter, or even hear the chair when it slammed against the mirror.

He turned around, and saw that the mirror was still intact. However, no one was on the other side, and the same chair inside the mirror was thrown against the bed, while the original one he'd thrown was still in its place in front of the mirror.

* * * *

In the center of the room stood his father, as he'd been thirty years ago, not the evil Grim that had been torturing him on the rails ever since. He wore a sweater, one that Coolidge recognized. It was the one that his father had worn when Coolidge graduated from grade school. It had been his good sweater, the one that he only wore on special occasions. He remembered it was his holiday sweater, and he would wear it every Christmas and Thanksgiving.

Coolidge had given him that sweater for Christmas when he was nine years old. Of course, Coolidge's mother had picked it out and paid for it, but they told his father that Coolidge was the brains behind it. His father had fallen in love with it, and it became his favorite.

Coolidge couldn't think about it. He quickly dashed at the mirror, running at it with full force, and just as he neared it, he raised his arms, bracing for the impact.

At the moment he should have smashed into the mirror, he fell through it, and landed on the other side, was now a part of it.

He quickly stood to look around. The chair was still where he had thrown it. The light was brighter inside the mirror, and when he looked at the window, the sun shone brightly through it. The whole room felt fresh. It was as if he'd gone back in time, to when his parents were alive, and none of the bad stuff had happened.

His father stood in the center of the room, watching him, with a smile on his face. He was his normal self, back before all the death. He was even much taller than Coolidge.

Coolidge looked down at himself and realized that he was his boyhood self, wearing his favorite leather bomber jacket, plaid shirt, and his favorite dirty jeans. From what he could tell, he was about ten years old again. He was back to the time he'd been the happiest as a child. How was that even possible? He was home, he was young, and he was happy. No way.

"Hey you two, the cinnamon rolls are almost done." His mother's voice came from downstairs. Coolidge took a deep breath, noticing for the first time the strong smell of cinnamon that wafted up from the kitchen downstairs. He heard the sound of the oven open, and knew that soon the smell would increase, with his mother taking out the rolls to cool on the stove top.

Coolidge looked at the door. A tear formed at the corner of his eye, and he knew that many more were on the verge of flowing. This, none of this, was possible. This couldn't' be happening. It was perfect, and he wished he could stay and things could be this way forever, but he knew there was no way he could be here.

"Luke." His father spoke. Coolidge turned to look up at him, and saw that his father was still smiling as he looked down at him.

"Luke, you're home now. You've always been home. Everything has been a bad dream. Just minutes ago, you came running in to tell me about your bad dream."

Coolidge looked down at the clothes he was wearing. His favorite clothes were gone,and he was wearing his pajamas. He still looked like he was about ten, but he hadn't worn pajamas since he was eight years old.

"Remember, your grandmother got you those pajamas for Christmas?"

Coolidge looked back down at the pajamas. They were indeed, the ones he had gotten from his grandmother that Christmas. He would change into them every once in a while when he would wet the bed half way through the night; these would be a quick change in the dark. It wasn't possible. There was no way. Yet, there he stood, ten years old again, standing in front of his father.

Coolidge tried to turn to look in the mirror, but his father reached out and pulled him toward him. Coolidge let him, and looked up at his father's face.

"Why don't you go downstairs and steal us a roll?"

Coolidge let go of his father and stepped away. This was all so perfect, the smell, the warm glow of the summer sun coming in through the window. The smell of the cinnamon as it flowed upstairs. He didn't want to let any of it go, he didn't want to risk any of it.

But he had to know.

Coolidge looked at the window. The warm glow felt fantastic on his skin, and he wanted to bask in it. It was the innocent warmth you could only feel as a kid. When it was okay to sit alone in your room and enjoy life, and never having to worry about a thing.

Coolidge stopped suddenly when he saw the reflection in the glass. If he were to turn and look at the large mirror, he knew that he would see the other side, would see reality. However, when he looked into the reflection, he saw this world for what it really was. He saw his father standing behind him as he really looked, as the smiling man, his orange eyes burning like his eternally hateful soul. He saw himself, too, his true, forty year old self, staring there back.

Coolidge had known it wasn't true, but the idea of it was wonderful. For the chance to see his mother again, to give her a hug and tell her how much he loved and missed her, he'd been willing to believe almost anything. He looked at the mirror and through to the other side. Rob laid on the floor, still gasping for air, his breaths becoming shallower and farther apart. His father looked from Coolidge to Rob and back at again. Coolidge took his attention off Rob and met his father's gaze.

His father's smile, impossibly, widened further, his face cracking and breaking along the lines of his mouth until it literally stretched from ear to ear. He opened his mouth, and the cackling laughter Coolidge had heard many times on his journey there, echoed through the room.

"Come to me, BOY!" He heard the Grim say. It was the same voice that had followed him along the rails. Anger bloomed in Coolidge. This man, this devil that was once his father, stood mocking him after all the torture he had put him through. Coolidge felt hatred rise up alongside his rage. Heat burned in his chest as he remembered. The man in front of him had killed his mother, tried to kill him, and had killed many more, had ruined his life, destroyed any happiness he had as a child and now mocked him with it.

Coolidge didn't know what made him do it, but suddenly, he found himself rushing toward the Grim, his hands reaching for the devil's throat. In a flash, his hands were around his, no, it's throat, and squeezing with all his might. The Grim reached up, trying to pull him away, but Coolidge put all his rage into holding tightly to the Grim's throat.

To Coolidge's surprise, the Grim weakened in his grasp. He gasped for air, and his eyes began to lose their intensity. The flames began to dim. The smile disappeared. Coolidge held strong to his rage, and squeezed even harder.

* * * *

Rob felt it, a sudden change. It was as if a vacuum began to suck the smoke out of the air, pulling all trace of it from his lungs. Air, fresh and clean, filled his lungs, letting his gasping coughs bring up massive amounts of soot and phlegm. The after-taste of charcoal and ash was strong. He turned over on his hands and knees clearing his airways and easing his burning chest.

"I'm going…to…kill…you!" Rob heard Coolidge say, through clenched teeth. He looked up at the mirror and saw Coolidge on the other side, his hands around the smiling man's throat. The eyes of both men were blazing orange, and Coolidge seemed to have the man in a death grip, the hands around his throat squeezing tightly.

Great, now what was Rob supposed to do. He sure as hell wasn't crossing over after him.

He looked around the room, trying to find a way to end this. The room was empty, for the most part, but he noticed that the closet was open just a crack. He walked over and opened it. Inside, he found an old wooden bat. The bat looked pretty beat up, but he picked it up. As he did, he remembered what the young woman had said. One of them must sacrifice himself.

Rob looked at the mirror. Rob doubted that Coolidge had meant to sacrifice himself, but with the smiling man's attention diverted, it seemed like the only chance he might have to end it all. It was what Coolidge had said, and had been trying to do - to break the mirror. That was the smiling man's connection, his portal, and it needed to be destroyed.

Rob didn't hesitate. He ran to the mirror, bat poised, and when he reached it, he put all his weight into the swing. As a boy, Rob had never been athletic, but he tried to make up for it now. The bat hit the glass, and instantly upon impact, the mirror shattered, glass shards flying throughout the room.

Rob didn't take any chances. He reached for the top of the mirror frame and pulled it forward. The weight of the large dresser fought him, but he pulled harder, and it finally tipped forward and crashed to the floor. The mirror was still attached to the dresser and didn't hit the floor, so Rob wasted no time, he pounded on the back side, breaking through the wooden backing and smashing every last piece of glass to the floor. Even then he continued to beat on the mirror. While he was sure it was shattered, it felt good just to take out his frustration on it; his anger at what the smiling man had almost made him do.

After a few minutes, when he was sure he didn't hear any more yelling from the other side, he finally dropped the bat. He was done.

He walked toward the door, a huge weight lifted from his chest. He figured his next step should be to burn the damn placed down, that the trees were far enough back that the fire wouldn't jump. If he called the fire department quickly enough, they would be able to control the blaze. The house was old, and hadn't been taken care of, so it should burn fast, All he would have to do was go to the Taylor's, their house was closest, and he would probably be able to find a can of gasoline. They no doubt had one, since they owned a large riding lawn mower. There should be some gas in the garden shed.

* * * *

Rob poured all the gasoline he'd found in the Taylor's shed along one side of the house. He didn't think it would be hard to start the fire, and it would spread quickly. He had picked up his gun on the way, and it was now tucked safely in the small of his back. The last thing he wanted was anyone coming to put the fire out and finding his service revolver just sitting on the ground. That would bring more questions than he wanted to answer.

He was sure that the County police would get there quickly. They would have a lot of questions, and though he wanted to do nothing else but spend the rest of the day with his family, he knew in all likelihood he would be spending it with County as they tried to figure out what happened here. There wasn't a chance that he was going to tell them the truth. The last thing they would understand would be some evil entity bouncing through mirrors and killing off half the street.

He sure as hell hoped that Todd and his family were okay.

Rob lit a piece of paper that he'd found in Todd's garage, and tossed it on the gas soaked wall. Instantly, it turned into a towering blaze, reaching toward the sky. It took less than moments for it to spread beyond the accelerant, taking firm hold on the building. He knew if investigated, they would find arson, and would launch an investigation. He was counting on them not looking too closely. Hopefully, because it was so old, they wouldn't think twice about it burning down.

Rob walked around to the front of the building. He knew he wouldn't get to watch it for too long… It would be suspicious, him being there, but he did want to take some satisfaction in the sight of the burning house.

He leaned against a tree, and a slight smile touched his lips. Who would have ever thought that he would be enjoying a house fire? He actually began to enjoy the smell of the burning wood.

He heard something shatter at the back of the house, and thought the flames had blasted out one of the windows. Amazingly, the front door opened, and Coolidge rushed out, escaping the billowing smoke.

Rob hurried to him, and helped him get away from the house. He put Coolidge's arm around him, and rushed him to the closest tree so Coolidge could lean against it.

"How the hell did you get out?"

Coolidge was coughing, trying to clear his lungs of smoke.

"I saw you break the mirror. I don't know how, but when it shattered, I felt this huge pulling sensation. Next thing I knew, I came to, beside the bed, and the place was on fire." Coolidge looked up at Rob, "Nice touch by the way."

Rob looked at the man leaning against the tree. He sure as hell hoped that didn't mean that the smiling man had escaped as well. Rob stepped back to give Coolidge some breathing room, and to look again at the house. The fire was burning strongly, people would have seen the smoke by now, and the fire department had probably been called.

"We'd better go." Rob said.

"Yeah."

Rob put his arm around Coolidge and helped him walk along the path. They could hear the fire blazing behind them and the building starting to self-destruct.

In town, the fire siren sounded. It blasted through the air, drowning out even the noise from the blazing building. Coolidge nearly collapsed as he pulled away from Rob, putting both his hands against his ears. His eyes closed in agony and he cried out.

Coolidge looked up Rob.

"He's inside of me. You have to kill me. You have to-." Coolidge said through gritted teeth. His voice cut out, his eyes began to blaze orange, and he began to smile.

Rob nearly fell as he tried to back away too quickly, and slid on the gravel. In town, the fire siren faded away, and the smiling man uncovered his ears. He stood up straight, and Rob was reminded how much taller Coolidge was than he. The man stood menacingly, his eyes blazing at Rob.

"What's a matter boy? You afraid of your new friend?" The smiling man said. "It was so nice to have my own flesh and blood come visit me."

Rob walked backward, trying to keep out of reach. He pulled the gun from behind his back and pointed it at Coolidge. He didn't want to have to shoot him. It was much easier to think of him as a sacrifice when it was just breaking a mirror, but to actually shoot him? Rob didn't know if he could do it.

Coolidge nodded. It was slight, but Rob saw it. He didn't think it was the smiling man nodding to him; he doubted he even realized he was doing it. It meant Coolidge was still in there, and that the smiling man wasn't fully in control yet, but Rob doubted that it was going to be that way for too long.

Rob pulled the trigger. The bullet struck Coolidge between the eyes.

The flames quickly faded from his eyes and his smile was gone. He continued to stand for what seemed like minutes, but Rob knew it couldn't have been. Finally, he fell to the ground.

Rob eased himself back against one of the trees. He should get out of there, he should run, he should start thinking of his cover story. Plant a piece on Coolidge and put all the blame on him. What was he thinking? He had always been a good cop. He never kept a backup piece. As for making up a cover story, he'd never been good at it.

He didn't know what the hell he was going to do, and suddenly wasn't in any hurry to do it. For right now, he was just going to sit there. It was over, his family saved.

Exhaustion seeped in, and he could feel himself slipping off to sleep. Maybe if he was lucky, he would wake up not remembering any of it. That would be nice. That would be very nice, he thought, as he let his eyelids close.

Just let it all go away, all the bad memories.

EPILOGUE

Rob's living room finally quieted, hours after he'd left what was once Coolidge's family home. He was tired, hurt, and all he wanted was a good night sleep. He realized that was something he hadn't had in a long time.

He hadn't noticed it right away, but he felt more himself, as if he had been asleep for a long time, and now, while still a tired SOB, he was awake. Very awake, and ready to spend his nights just sleeping, without someone controlling his dreams, for the first time in a long time.

He watched as Robyn closed the door. The last few hours had been filled with questions and confusion. He had lied when answering many of them, had told them all that he had no idea what happened. He went with Father Williams story when he could, filling in some of the gaps regarding the dead bodies.

He'd had to put much of the blame on Coolidge, but then, since many people in the town had seen him, it didn't take too much convincing. Small towns, remembered the past, and they feared it. Stories spread, and the one about his parents getting killed when he was a teenager was well remembered, and many blamed him. It wasn't far-fetched for them to believe he'd come back to do more.

Rob looked up as Robyn walked toward him.

Sure, they were hurting. They would be hurting for a long time, but they loved each other, and that was what mattered. They would get through it. As she reached out her hand to him, he took it and matched her smile.

They both felt it. It was over.

Word from the Author

Hello Everyone.

I hope that you enjoyed this re-release of my first novel, "Inside the Mirrors." I am extremely happy to bring it to you. When Mirrors was first released, I will admit, I had rushed it to release, and while I was sure about the story, and thought I had been sure about the editing, I was wrong. By the way, this "Word from the Author" is going out unedited. Please don't hold this against me.

I quickly got the reviews back, and it was quickly pointed out to me that the old adage is true, writers make their own worst editors. I screwed up, and while everyone loved the content within the pages, all the reviews pointed out the editing. In fact, it quickly made me a little embarrassed about it, and I actually have not promoted the book as strongly as I would have.

So, when the opportunity came up, and I was given the chance to go back and make things right, get the book re-edited and prepare it for a rerelease, I jumped at the chance.

In doing so, I also re-read a lot of this book, and I, as a reader, liked it. I hope all of you do as well. There are a lot of fun moments in here, and I hope some truly creepy ones for you.

So where did this book come from? Well, the original story for this book came from two different ideas or general ideas with a third element. Huh? yeah,

First, it came from a true story that involved my little girl having an issue where she had the traditional imaginary friend. However, her friend, who's name was Bob, would talk to her through the mirror, and whenever anything bad would happen, she would tell us that Bob did it. What made this very creepy was when she started to talk with a deep "Bob" voice for when Bob was talking to us.

The other creepy element to that story was where the mirror she would talk to Bob actually came from a haunted Mississippi plantation that my wife had moved back to Illinois with. While we don't know if there was a Bob that had been haunting the plantation, when it came time for us to move, we decided that the mirror was not coming with us. After we moved, and the mirror was gone, so was Bob...

The other idea that was a center piece to this novel, and this comes from one of my mantras. I write about what scares me. Right before I wrote this novel, I had a brief spell in a very dark place. In that place, while I was driving with my wife and family in the car, her and I had gotten into an argument and while I can't remember what, I remember that I did something stupid to "prove a point." In essence, I put everyones life in danger.

Where does this come into play. When I thought about it later, as I was pulling myself out of that dark place, one of the things that scare me more than anything else on this planet, is that something I would do, something I did, caused my family to be hurt.

And with those two elements, "Inside the Mirrors" was born.

I do hope that you enjoyed the novel. Please, continue reading. "Hatched" my next novel is almost done. I am working on finishing the edit and revisions now and this time will send it to an editor before it is published. I have, however, already gotten the first chapter edited, and have included it here. I hope that you enjoy.

Thank You,

Jason R. Davis

ROADSIDE ASSISTANCE
(Short story from the DEADHEAD MILES Anthology)

The world around him was a dark place, lost in an endless nothingness of gray. Miles of road had faded away and vanished beyond the short glow of headlights, but the fog never seemed to end. Yellow lines stayed to his left, coming from nowhere and disappearing back to where they began. The white line to his right was a steady beacon that guided him, and kept him on the path. Neither could be seen for more than a couple of feet beyond the hood of his truck.

The fog seemed to just go on, and he had no idea how many hours he had been captured in it. Curves would suddenly appear, and try to catch him off guard. They would twist left and then right, and before he realized it, he would be going up another hill. His truck would go at the challenge of the harsh rise in the earth and he could hear the roar of the diesel engine as it growled under his feet.

The latest hill was a long stretch that curved in and out. His engine was fighting with fury as the RPM's slowly lowered, until it could go no further without shuddering. Then, with the engine screaming, he downshifted, the higher gear released, and there was the quick grab as the lower gear engaged. The engine steadied, and he continued up the rise.

His speedometer showed that he was now down to thirty miles per hour. With the heavy weight in the trailer behind him, it was a fight just to keep the large semi on the road, even at that speed. His transmission, only an 8-speed, along with the lower horse-powered engine of his company truck, made the climb almost unbearable. Even with the throttle open all the way, he was still inching along at what felt like a crawl. He wondered if he could walk faster.

He reached forward and grabbed his coffee. The taste was bitter and it had lost much of its heat. He had filled the cup when he'd started out that morning, but the warm, soothing liquid had soured as it cooled. He put it back into the holder, and rested his hand back on the gear shift.

He hoped that the mountain would crest soon, and he would be able to shift back into higher gear.

He blinked his eyes, and could feel the sleep crusting at the corners. The night seemed like it would last forever, and the fog made the road disappear into nothing. Fog always felt like that to him. Even in daylight, whenever he had to drive through fog he would have to fight to keep his eyes from betraying him. At night, they felt like they were more closed than open.

He wished he could just pull off somewhere and step back into the bunk to get a few additional hours of sleep. He had time yet, and he could afford to do it. It wasn't time that kept him from getting more sleep. No, it was the damned fog.

He would stop at one of the little emergency pull offs and tuck himself away. His eyes needed it. The lines were moving on him, swaying back and forth, making it harder for him to stay between them. He would love to just pull off into the haze. It seemed like it was calling to him, pulling at him. Sleep was beckoning him and he desired it more than anything.

He just never saw any place to pull off in time for him to stop. His load was too heavy, and it would take a lot of braking distance. Being barely able to see past his hood, he wouldn't be able to stop until he was long past the turn to any of the pull-outs.

Another one came and went, and he watched it pass with a raw hunger. He never thought he could crave anything this badly, after all, it was just sleep. All he had to do was close his eyes and it would come; he'd be lost to it.

If he closed his eyes, he'd be dead, and if he was lucky, he would only get himself killed. All it would take would be for his eyes to stay closed too long, a gentle drift of the wheel, and he would be either rolled over in the center median, or barreling down the side of the mountain. His rig would take out the guard rail like it wasn't even there, he was sure of that. He was riding an eighty thousand pound missile, and the thin piece of metal that made up the guard railing would do little to stop it.

He finally reached the top of the long ascent, and the rig started to speed up as his foot still held the accelerator to the floor. He got it to the right RPM's and then slammed it into the next higher gear. He hurried his way through the gears, getting back to speed now that he was on level ground. When he finally reached his last gear, he could already feel the truck starting to head back down.

With a flick of a switch, the engine brake roared to life, trying to slow his momentum. Now with the truck not going uphill, he had to fight it from going too fast on the downward slope. His load was heavy. His engine brake was already calling out in frustration, trying to slow the truck down. He wasn't sure if he'd missed the sign, or if this state just didn't post the percentage of the grade. He didn't know how bad a fight he was in for. The truck was already speeding faster than he would have liked, and he had no idea just how far the slope descended.

Maybe he would get lucky and it would be a short, straight hill and he would have nothing to worry about. His wife had always told him he needed to think more positively. Maybe he would. Maybe this hill would start a change in his life. A new him, and when he reached the bottom he could call her and tell her everything was going to be okay.

His ex-wife.

Things were not okay. They were not okay then, and they weren't ever going to be okay. A long way up usually meant a long way back down, and he had been climbing that hill for what seemed like an eternity. Of course in the fog his perception of time was warped, but he was still pretty confident that it was a long drop.

The truck quickly pushed itself well past the speed he wanted her to go, and John pressed down on the brake. He didn't want to push down too hard or too fast. If the road turned out to be slicker than he'd thought, all it would take would be for the rig's brakes to slow down too fast, before the air brakes on the trailer had even started to slow. Then the nightmare would truly begin. The rig would jackknife; the trailer sliding down the road would pass his track and pull him into a spin. It would be unrecoverable, and his life would be left to the fates. The semi would truly become an 80,000 pound missile, deadly to any vehicle in its path.

If he was lucky, he would see the trailer sliding around him in time. If he did, he would have two options. He could try and save it by flooring the accelerator and trying to outrace the trailer. He would be going at break neck speed down a mountain that he didn't know, and still a danger to those around him and himself, but he would have a chance to regain control. With any luck, he would come to a runaway ramp, see it in time, and be able to turn off into it. If so, he and his load would be saved.

There was still a lot of risk though, and he could be speeding at 80 miles per hour, or more.

The other option was sacrifice. The moment he saw the trailer coming up alongside him in his long side mirrors he could ditch the truck. He could try going left to the median, but that would probably put him in a much faster spin. If he sacrificed himself by turning the wheel to the right, he would take out the rail, but no one else would get hurt. That is, unless there was a house at the bottom of whatever mountain he was going down.

No, the brakes were a bad option unless he did it just right, so instead of applying hard pressure to slow his speed, he eased his foot down on the brake.

It took a second for the air to rush through the lines and the brakes to engage before the tractor slowed. He counted for five seconds, watching as the speedometer roughly matched him. He slowed one mph for every second he applied the brake. Once he hit five, he released the brake.

The truck quickly accelerated forward again, picking up speed nearly as fast as he had let go of the brake. The engine brake whined loudly into the night sky, but John doubted that it could be heard far beyond the fog. It was easy to think that the fog muted the sound as well as his sight. It was easy to believe he was the last man on earth. Was he? It had been so long since he had seen another vehicle.

He applied the brakes again before the truck could get up too much speed, and again counted to five and watched the speedometer fall. He released the brakes and again the truck lurched faster down the mountain.

He should have started his descent in a lower gear, he thought. He knew better. In this weather, he never should have tried to get the truck back up near the speed limit. Even if he didn't know how bad the downgrade was going to be, he should have been in a lower gear for just that reason. It was stupid to act like everything was fine and he could just float down the hill. It wasn't like he was hauling a light load. No, he was nearly overweight; there was no way he could take too large of a downgrade without having to take off down a runaway ramp at some point.

He also couldn't keep applying his brakes this heavily. He was getting back up to speed nearly as fast as he was taking his foot off the brake. His brakes would be smoking soon, and if he was lucky, they wouldn't catch fire. In a way, he would be lucky if he didn't see anything at all, just let the flames leap out, let them blow one or more of the tires and that would be the end of it.

What did he have anyway? What did he have left? Christine? How long ago had it been when she told him she didn't ever want to see him again? Two weeks? Or had it been three since he had come home and found her with another man, having sex in his bed?

He'd come home and caught her, and yet she still had the audacity to kick him out of their house.

He knew it was because she blamed him. Somehow, somewhere through the years, her love for him had soured into hatred. He had seen it in her eyes as she screamed at him and chased him out, as though he had been the intruder.

The image of the two together still lingered on the back of his eyes every time he closed them. He saw how she looked at him, first like a trapped animal. Then her face had changed, and he had seen the hurt in her eyes. He knew that somewhere inside, she still loved him, but that hadn't been enough for her. She had needed something else, and she hadn't been getting it from him. The look had been replaced with one of satisfaction, and cold hate. All the years of their life together had shown through in that instant and he knew that they were done.

He didn't want to think about it, and right now, he sure as hell didn't want the images to invade his thoughts.

He let his boot pull back on the brake, not sure if he could see a flicker of light in his mirror. With the fog, he had no way of seeing the back lights of the trailer. If it was sliding around him, he wouldn't see it until it was too late.

"Fuck it," he said to the empty truck.

He kept his foot off the brake. He quickly picked up speed. He could feel the truck becoming the deadly missile it could be. It was becoming a weapon, that, if he decided to target it, he wasn't one hundred percent sure he had enough control left to aim it.

He wouldn't aim it though. He was just tired. He felt like he just wanted to be done. He just wanted to sleep and to let his head fall forward and stay there. He just wanted his eyes to close and to stay closed. He wanted the nothingness, the void outside, to suck him up into it and take him.

He felt the ground beneath him change. His descent was slowing. His speed was still excessive, but was no longer increasing.

His eyes grew heavier. He hadn't realized just how much the acceleration had actually revived him. He reached for his coffee and again tasted the acrid flavor of what had once been a rich full bodied extreme blend from one of the truck stops. Extreme blend was such a joke. It would get his heart racing sometimes like it was going to explode, but his eyelids would still feel like they were tied to anvils, making him fight against them.

The truck reached the speed limit and he allowed his foot to move back to the gas pedal. He wasn't going back up another hill, which was good.

He thought maybe he should just pull off to the shoulder for a while. He could get fifteen minutes. That would be enough to keep him going. He just needed a quick power nap, and he could even stay in his seat.

He watched along the side of the road. His weariness hungered for rest. It was a tiger wanting to be fed; he wanted nothing but to fall into a quick coma.

He could too. The shoulder had become wide enough for him to pull off. He doubted he would see any state patrols stopping by in this fog, and he wouldn't be there long. Why not?

Why? For the same reason that he never allowed himself to when he was tired at night or whenever there was fog pressing in on him. Because if he did, and some idiot four wheeler happened to hit him, he was still at fault. Even parked along the side of the road, the truck driver was always at fault. The other driver could be asleep at the wheel, or just a bad driver, the truck driver was to blame, even if he was lucky, and there were no injuries. Injuries meant criminal charges, and deaths meant involuntary homicide if the driver had a record. It wasn't fair, but it was the life of a truck driver.

Drivers lived with the constant fear of mistreatment by the law. Either it was a patrol officer who had a chip on his shoulder, or it was someone out to make their unofficial quota for the month, truck drivers were always the ones to be targeted.

John was thankful for the anger that was starting to push back some of the drowsiness. The thoughts, while they distracted him from the road, made the weariness lift a little, and he could think about some of the wrongs they had done him. He could think of why he had to be working for the company he was with now, because of his high CSA score with the DOT.

Who were they to get on him for his past? Some pieces of it he hadn't even thought of in years, why should they come back to haunt him all this time later?

The company he was forced to work for now, one of the few that didn't look too closely at driving records and infractions, was also the company that was pushing him to go far beyond what his body was telling him that he could.

He reached a hand up to his eyes, wiping away some of the sleep that had crusted there. He knew it would be back soon, but he wiped it away anyways. He wanted the sleep gone, and he wanted his life gone. He wanted---

He'd just pulled his hand away from his eyes in time to see the large alligator teeth standing tall across the lanes of the interstate. There they were, the twisted and gnarled shapes of rubber and metal that would bite into his own tires and tear them into shreds. He didn't have much time to react, and there wasn't much he could do. The blown tire in the road was fresh, and if he hit it wrong, his own tires might go as well. He wasn't too worried about the tires on his own truck, he thought they could take damage, but the tires on the trailer would barely pass a trailer inspection. They were already filled with notches, and the tread on them was barely at the legal minimum. If they hit a tire directly, who could say if it would blow? It wasn't a chance he wanted to take.

He swerved to the right side of the road, trying to keep an eye on his trailer. He didn't have much time, and he knew that if he was going to keep the tires from hitting the warped rubber and metal debris in the road, he had to get as far over onto the shoulder as he could. The debris was well over both lanes so there was no point in trying to go to the left, and even though he had the road all to himself, his instinct was to always go right. It was precaution. If he did go left and someone just happened to be passing him, he'd slam them into the median, and in a worst case scenario, send them spiraling onto the other side of the interstate and into oncoming traffic.

He looked away from the mirror, not sure if he was going to miss the tire or not. The fog stole his view of the rear of the trailer, and he wasn't sure from the angle if he was going to miss it or not. It looked like he should, but it was hard to tell for sure.

"Damn! Damn! Damn! Damn!"

He turned his gaze forward and looked at the shoulder, just in time to see the source of the blown tire in the road.'

He was heading straight for it.

"Fuck!"

On the shoulder of the road was a large passenger bus. It was pulled off at a bad angle, and its flashers were trying to penetrate the fog around them. They weren't doing a good job, and he barely saw it in time to veer back to the left.

His right mirror clipped the back left corner of the bus. It shattered, and the glass blew out, striking his passenger window. Hundreds of little shards shot out in a whine of protest as they left the frame of the mirror and crashed against the passenger window. Little scratches formed a mosaic patchwork of the world outside, lasting for less than a second. Then there was a loud crack, and he barely saw the mirror frame as it smashed into the window. It suddenly became a spider web, barely able to hold itself together

He could hear the squeal as the corner of his trailer grazed the corner of the bus. The view to his left had disappeared.

With the window a mess, and the mirror gone, he had no way of seeing how hard he was about to hit the bus. He also had no way of knowing if his trailer was going to slide around him, jack-knifing along his flank. If that happened, the bus would be lost; the trailer would slam against it, and push it through the guard rail.

Another sound blasted into the morning air. His imagination flared with the image of the bus falling, with the thought that they were still on a mountain top, and that the bus was going over a great cliff. In his mind's eye, he saw the bus teeter back and forth on the edge for a few moments, and then, like some grotesque cartoon, slip over the edge.

The tractor made it back onto the road, but he still didn't have much control over it, and he was turning the wheel frantically, now back to the right. His foot was off the accelerator, he had somehow remembered to switch off the engine brake. Now he was easing it with the air brake, just putting slight pressure on it to keep from causing any more of a skid.

He chanced a look into the remaining driver's side mirror. His trailer was still behind him, but it was swaying badly. It was leaning to the left and looked like it was on the verge of rolling over. If it did that, the tractor would be taken with it, and he'd have to rely on good luck to keep him from going over himself. The truck would be on its side, and he would be left to the fates when it eventually slid to a stop.

A lane opened up to him on the right, onto the shoulder past the bus. He had to fight the truck to get it there, to not lose control, or let the truck speed over the side. The road was slanting back up. His speed decreased greatly, and he was thankful that he could slow the truck down and inch up the slope.

The truck came to a stop. The smell of burnt rubber and burning metal on metal brakes raced to fill his nostrils. He didn't let himself relax though. He quickly pulled the two knobs on the dash, and heard the air hiss as it escaped from the lines and allowed the parking brake to grab the rig and keep it from going back down the hill.

Then he was out the driver's side door and landing on the ground. He hadn't even tried to lower himself. He didn't have time. He had hit that bus, and his heart was racing with the thought of all those people falling in a twisted metal coffin of death.

His lungs burned and his chest felt like it wanted to collapse in on itself. It hurt to breathe, and there were tears escaping the corners of his eyes. He wasn't sure if it was from the pain, the worry, or just from the exhaustion that was threatening to come back.

Part of him still felt like this may be a hallucination. The fog still pushed in from all around him. Somehow it felt like that fog was even in his mind.

Maybe he hadn't even hit a bus, maybe he had imagined all of it and he was actually asleep, still at the wheel, rolling over, or falling now, to his own death.

He made it to the back of his trailer, and after seeing nothing wrong with his driver's side tires, hurried over to the other side. So far everything was fine. Maybe it was all a dream?

He stopped when he rounded the back corner of the trailer and saw the shredded tires. Not just one of them, but both the outside tires had blown, and now had only fragments of rubber clinging to the metal of the rim.

"Fuck," he said to himself, as he had a pang of selfish thought, and knew that his career was probably over.

He reached into his pants pocket to grab his phone. He needed to call it in, he needed to get the repair crews out there, and get both tires fixed. He needed the emergency crews out there in case someone was injured, or even dead inside the bus.

He patted his pants and was momentarily surprised that he didn't feel the small hump that was his flip phone. It wasn't there. Of course it wasn't. He had been driving. He always emptied his pockets on long trips. Wallets dug into his ass, and his cell phone, well it was hard to answer a phone that was in your pants pocket. He often kept both of them in the little recess under his stereo. They were both still there. He hadn't thought to grab them.

What about the people in the bus? He still hadn't heard anyone call out to him. He didn't know if they were okay. He would have to go back for his cell phone later. Right now, he had to make sure everyone in the bus was all right.

He could barely see it, when he turned in its direction.

The thick fog kept it well hidden, but he could just faintly see the flashing lights that marked its location on the side of the road.

"Hello!" he called out, as he started to walk back to the bus.

His heart was lowering itself out of his throat, and as he walked toward the bus, his lungs weren't hurting as much. He still felt like there was a large weight pressing down on him, but he no longer felt like he was going to pass out.

"Hello! Is everyone okay?" he called out again.

As he yelled, it felt like the fog around him seemed to soak up the sound. He never heard the echo that he would have expected, and around them there were no morning sounds. He didn't hear any birds singing, there were no car sounds along the interstate, even along the other side of the road. Most valleys through the mountains often times had rivers or towns in them, and even these were now silent. There was no sound at all.

Even his truck, left idling behind him was growing faint. The sound of the diesel engine sounded like it was moving farther and farther away.

The hair on the back of his neck told them that he was going somewhere he shouldn't be. He felt like he was drifting into an episode of the Twilight Zone, and that somehow, around him the world was changing. Like maybe he was walking into, what was that they called it? Another dimension.

He tried to laugh to himself at the thought, but could barely crack a smile.

Something was not right here.

He had to work hard to ignore it. What was he? He wasn't some little boy that let childhood fears take control of him.

Yeah, just keep thinking that, he told himself.

He reached the bus, glad that it hadn't been pushed over the railing. It hadn't even been pushed near the railing. The loud sound he had heard must have been the explosion of his own tires. That was at least some good news; he was already starting to feel a little better.

"Hello? Is everyone all right?" He yelled again as he looked from the back of the bus to the open door. Fog swirled around him, and somehow, it was actually thicker there. The fog seemed like it was billowing out from the bus itself, as inside was a massive wall of gray.

He tried to look through the windows, but couldn't see a thing. Lighter spots spun and twirled within darker gray, and moved in and out of each other.

It was like watching a container of water as food coloring was added. The colors would at first swirl around each other before they mixed together. The fog, however, wasn't mixing together.

Where was everyone?

Well, just because it was a passenger bus didn't mean it had been full. The bus could have been empty. Okay, but then where was the driver? The door was open, so someone had to have survived the accident.

Maybe the driver had been thrown when he hit the bus? He could have been thrown over the guard rail, or he could be somewhere along the pavement. He was probably hurt. Maybe he had passed out. If he'd been thrown when John's truck had hit the bus, then he probably had a nasty head injury.

John turned away from the open door of the bus and looked briefly around at the surroundings. Well, he might as well get the worst possibility out of the way first.

He stepped over to the guard rail. It took him a couple of steps to reach it, making him doubt that the driver could have been thrown that far. If he had though, John didn't think he would have survived. When John got to the side, he saw that it wasn't a metal guard rail, but a cement barrier, which meant that more than likely they were on a bridge. If they were on a bridge that also meant that it was a long way down, hundreds of feet, most likely. It wasn't something anyone could have survived, unless they had wings.

Yeah, it was too far to be thrown. The front of the bus hadn't been hit that hard, and even if he was propelled out of it, the furthest he would have traveled would have been to the base of the barrier.

John turned and looked around at the ground outside the bus. He couldn't see very far, but as he walked just a few feet back and forth, he didn't see any sign of blood. He guessed that if the driver had fallen out of the bus, he would have been hurt and probably bleeding.

So where the hell was he?

"Hello!"

He was surprised that there still hadn't been a single car or truck along the interstate. The fog was bad, but even in the worst conditions there were always a few idiots out driving. Tonight he had been one of them, but he couldn't imagine no one else out there.

He walked back to the open door of the bus, and reached in to grab the metal bar, fumbling to find the step below him. He couldn't believe how much thicker the fog was inside. He could even feel the coldness of it as he reached in. It was like the inside of the bus was 20 degrees cooler, with the air inside releasing its chill outward.

He stepped into the bus and a shiver went right through his bones. He fought to keep it from shaking him, stifled the feeling. He wasn't sure if it was visible, but inside him, he had actually felt his bones shake.

All of this just wasn't right.

Why was he doing this again?

He guessed that he had to make sure that if anyone was in there, he had to confirm they were okay. He hit the damned bus, he may have hurt someone. He doubted it now, after seeing how he hadn't even moved the bus, but that wasn't to say he hadn't given someone a heart attack.

Then again, wouldn't he have heard someone by now? He moved to the center platform that should have allowed him to look down the aisle of the bus. He couldn't see anything but the fog that swirled around him.

"Hello?"

He took a step toward the back, and reached his hand forward to rest it on the front barrier that separated the seats from the front of the bus. The vinyl was well padded, but felt like ice to the touch. Everything in there was so damned cold.

Just past the barrier, he felt a bone chilling breeze that pushed at him from deeper in the bus. The fog swirled with it, and for a brief second, he could see the shape of a person sitting in the front seat. Just as fast as he saw it, the shape was gone, the fog hiding it again. He was left standing there alone.

He was sure he had seen it though. It was darkened, and he hadn't been able to see any features, but he was sure he had seen it. His hand was only about two feet in front of the person, and he stood only another two feet above that. The fog didn't allow him to see anywhere near that far. The person could have been a mile away; in this mess he never would have been able to tell, unless he actually touched them.

If they were there though, then they would have been able to see him when the fog had swirled around him. Why hadn't they done anything? Why hadn't they said anything? Why hadn't anyone responded to him?

"Hello?" he said again, the goose bumps along his arm prickling in the cold, foggy breeze. The hair on his arm was stiff. He hadn't worn his coat; it hadn't been that cold, or so he'd thought. He didn't know that it was going to be like a meat locker in the bus.

He allowed himself to believe that's why the goose bumps had formed on his arm as he slowly reached forward. He leaned in as he was reaching out. He didn't want to. Some instinct, something deep inside warned him not to look any closer. It told him to go, to get out of there and run. To run back to his truck, climb back into his cab and get out of there as fast as his rig would go.

Yes, it would cost him his job. A hit and run. After this he would never be able to drive again, but somewhere inside he felt that would still be better than anything he was about to find once he looked through the fog.

He couldn't stop himself, though. The wheels were already in motion. The momentum was already propelling him, and like his truck, once it was up to speed, it was hard to get it to stop. He was too damned stubborn and bull-headed. Add that to the long list of reasons Christine had said she didn't want him anymore.

Sure it was just a long list of excuses, but he had known there'd been some truth to it.

It didn't make what she'd done any more forgivable, but maybe he had pushed her. Maybe he did share some of the responsibility.

His hand touched something hard and frozen. It felt chiseled, as though it was made out of stone and left outside. It seemed somehow moist, and yet frozen at the same time.

He ran his hand along it as he neared. It had bumps along the center, but long smooth areas on either side. The smooth part felt indented and sunken. He went back to the center and felt another impression. The smooth surface gave a little as he pressed in, and was slightly soft to the touch. It wasn't as cold as the other spots; there was actually a little warmth to it. And there was something else, something that felt doughy on the surface, but under more pressure, felt hard beneath.

Then he was close enough to see. He was touching a man's open eye, as it stared blankly up at him with the expression of death, the features frozen in place. His finger was pushing in on the iris of the eye, its softness the frozen soft gel that was the outer coating.

John fell back, away from the body. His feet tangled beneath him, and he slammed against the barrier. He bounced back, and his back slammed into the coin collector that was sticking out of the center console. He felt a stabbing pain that jarred him, and turned him so that he landed on his side on the hard, rubberized floor.

A hot pain ran along his side, and it felt like he had been clawed on the way down. He knew it hadn't been scraped, but it felt like it. The pain burned, and he wanted to scream out as it stung him. He ground his teeth together to fight it. Starbursts flashed within his eyes.

He was oblivious to everything else. The pain in his shoulder and head didn't hurt nearly as much as his side. He couldn't believe the intensity of it.

He felt along his back. He knew he wasn't cut, but putting his hand there helped a little to calm the sensation.

Slowly, it faded and he started to pull himself up. When he twisted to the side, there was a twinge of pain, but he could handle it.

He stood, and looked down the length of the bus. If the first man was dead, was there any point in going the rest of the way through? He doubted there were any survivors; if there were, someone would have called out by now. He knew he hadn't been the one to kill that man. He looked like he had frozen to death. Who knew how long the bus had been out there? Maybe they had all died from exposure.

Except, it had been a mild winter. The last day it had been cold enough to have ice on the roads was four or five days ago. There was no way these people would have gone undiscovered that long. Even so, it had been freezing, but barely, and he didn't think it had been cold enough to freeze a man. It has to be a lot colder than 32 degrees for that. He was sure of it.

How sure? Actually he was more scared than sure, and he only hoped it made sense.

John turned to leave; he was done with the place. He would get a few miles down the road and then call it in. The cops may give him hell, and he may never drive again, but that didn't matter; he wasn't going to stay around. This shit was just too damned strange. He wanted out, had to get out of there.

He saw a light out of the corner of his eye. Somehow, it shone through the darkness of the fog, and hit him, blinding him momentarily.

When he turned, he could see that it was moving back and forth, coming from the back of the bus.

Something was moving back there. He couldn't see the shape of it, but someone had to be doing it. They must be up and walking around.

"Hello. I'm here to help. Come here, I can help you," he called out toward the back of the bus. The light shifted, and though he couldn't tell if it was coming toward him or not, whoever it was had definitely heard him. It was reacting to his voice.

"Come here, I can help you. If you need it, I can get you an ambulance." He said again to the back. He was trying to keep his voice calm, though he could hear his voice cracking a little. It was higher than usual, and was almost like he was talking to, and trying to calm a baby.

The light didn't come closer. Instead, he found himself moving back towards it. It was like it was beckoning him. He didn't want to go. He had told the person to come to him, why was he going back there?

But, then again, if the person was hurt, they wouldn't be able to come to him. They had been in an accident.

He still wanted to turn and run, to get out of there and escape whatever horror movie he'd found himself in. He wasn't a hero. Why was he still walking back there?

He didn't know. His feet were no longer obeying him. He couldn't stop. The light was calling him, was pulling him, and he was helpless to turn away.

As he made it down the aisle, he saw more shapes in the fog. The passengers of the bus all sat in their seats. They were like wax figures, motionless, staring blindly off into distant space. He could see them more and more clearly. As he moved to the back of the bus, the air grew cooler, but the fog became thinner.

Halfway down, he was fighting to keep from shivering. The hair along his neck and arms was upright and frozen. Even his skin was beginning to hurt from the cold. His lips were going numb and he could feel the moisture in his eyes freezing.

He was freezing. He couldn't explain it, but he was.

The bodies were still as he moved. Some seats had just one passenger, like the man that had been at the front of the bus, but some seats had two. Most were adults, but he had seen one woman with a little girl. The little girl had been asleep in her mother's lap, with her arms under her head as a pillow. She had been sleeping when she died.

He no longer cared about what happened to those in the bus. He had never really wanted to know, but now he downright didn't care. He just wanted out. He wanted to get away. It still wasn't too late; all he had to do was turn and run. He could just turn, push off hard, and take off towards the door.

Even if he did though, he somehow knew that the door to the bus was closed. He didn't know how he knew, but some instinct told him that it was already too late. The door was closed, and he was stuck there now.

With them.

It didn't matter, he couldn't run. His legs weren't listening to him anymore.

He neared the back of the bus, and as the fog started to thin in front of him, when he expected that he would finally see the light and whoever held it, the light faded away. The fog parted all around him in a swirl of gray and dark blue. It pulled back in on itself, faster than the eye could see.

Within two unsteady heart beats, the fog around him was gone. All the fog inside the bus had disappeared. Outside, it still swirled, but inside the bus, it had been sucked away, and he was left with the darkness.

But wait, it wasn't completely dark. There was a slight red glow that ran along the runners that ran along the floor of the bus, so that passengers could make their way to the bathroom safely. He looked at them for a while; he couldn't help himself, watching how the glow disappeared the farther it went. He felt like a moth bouncing against a light, he was so attracted to it. It led straight into the back wall, and disappeared past the door to the bathroom.

"Hello?" He heard himself again calling out toward the bathroom as though someone might be in there. No one was, and he knew it, but his body seemed to ignore the fact.

Nobody was in there. No one was in the bus. He was all alone.

He was all alone with a bus full of corpses.

He thought that should have worried him more. He should have been more afraid, but all he felt was cold and numb.

Suddenly, he heard a noise behind him.

In his mind he was turning in less than half a heartbeat, whirling around to face an attacker, but his body actually moved much more slowly. His mind raced, waiting impatiently for his body to catch up. In his mind, he already knew what was there. He was ready for it.

He had already accepted it.

When he turned, he saw them.

The passengers.

All those that he had passed as he'd walked down the aisle. They were there, standing now, their dead eyes looking at him. Their cold hungry eyes were lifeless, yet showed him their desire.

The closest one stepped away from its seat, and walked down the center of the aisle. Behind her, the rest of them followed. They were all coming for him. They moved slowly, but why hurry? He wasn't going anywhere.

He was trapped. They had him. They'd waited until he was at the back of the bus. He could try to hide in the bathroom, but what would that get him? At the most he'd last a couple of hours, but more than likely they would have the door broken down in a matter of minutes. They had waited until he had no way out and there were too many of them between him and the exits.

The windows around him now seemed to steam up, and the air in the bus changed. It was no longer the ice cold chill that had been running along his skin when he had first come in. It was getting warmer. Somehow with the bodies awakened, there was heat, and it was pulsating.

He looked around frantically. There had to be something. He saw the steamed glass, and looked at the window closest to him. It was all that kept him from the outside world. He looked at one of the glass panels, and thought that it was cracked in the middle. Passengers could push open this window to let in a little air, but it wasn't meant to open far enough for someone to get out. At the most, it looked like it could open to about a six inch gap. With his size, he would need all the glass out for him to be able to get through. He was a big guy.

He looked back at the corpses walking towards him. At least they had been when he turned away. They had stopped just a couple feet away from him, and were now just watching him. He wondered what they were looking at. They had him, why not just come and finish it?

He looked back to the window, and then over to the one on the other side. There was no need to look any further than the back row. The other windows were too far away and there was no way he could make it. His only chance was these back two.

Did he really think he could make it? Somewhere, he was actually beginning to believe he did. After all, he thought he had seen… yes he had. He turned back to look at it. There was a crack in the back window to his left. If was a small one, but it had probably happened when his truck had hit the bus. It wasn't much, but with the glass already starting to weaken, maybe he could smash the window and get out that way.

It wasn't a great idea, and he wasn't relishing the idea of jumping out a bus window and landing hard onto the ground below. There were a lot of things that could go wrong. He could jump out the window and get hit by a passing vehicle. There still hadn't been any, but he figured it would make sense that another car would just happen to come by when he was getting out. Currently that seemed to be the way his luck was going.

Then there was the fall. He was a large, fat man, and he wasn't going to hit the ground softly. He would probably break an arm or a leg, and maybe a couple of ribs. It was going to hurt like hell. And then what? He'd run to his truck? He would probably barely be able to move. These things might be able to move fast, or maybe they couldn't. Even at a slow walk though, he was sure they'd be able to get out there and catch him.

But what other ideas did he have? He couldn't think of any. No matter what he chose, none of the options seemed to play out in his favor. At least if he went for the window, he would have done something.

He looked back to the corpses. They still stood there watching him. What the hell were they looking at? Why were they not rushing him?

Then it occurred to him. He was their food. They were playing with their damned food. They were watching him, enjoying his fear. They were going to wait until they knew he had given up, and then they'd get him.

Well he wasn't about to give up. Death had been a lot easier to accept when it was him choosing to die. He was sure as hell not going to let someone take that damned decision away from him.

John dashed to the window and slammed his body into it. His shoulder pounded the glass and he heard a loud crack. He reeled and bounced back. No looking behind; he didn't want to see if they were getting closer, he was purely focused on the window. The glass hadn't broken, but he had heard something give. Maybe the window was breaking away from the frame.

He smashed against the window and the sound of cracking grew louder. It was faint, but it was there. He pulled back again. He was starting to feel the pain throbbing in his arm. The glass still didn't show any further sign of damage, but there was definitely something happening.

Maybe it was the fiberglass of the outer frame giving in. He had to keep trying. He had to.

He rushed forward again. This time as he moved, he could feel the faint touch of ice cold fingertips graze his skin. They had been closing, and he'd just avoided their grasp.

He slammed into the window again, this time he heard an audible snapping sound. Then an explosion of pain shot up his arm in a blinding storm of fire. Something was wrong. Something was very wrong.

He looked as he stumbled back, and saw that the window was still undamaged. His arm wasn't. Lightning strikes of pain shot from his shoulder to his elbow. He could no longer feel past his elbow, and he could see the faint outline of bone trying to break through his skin.

He took another stumbling step backward, and then his legs gave away.

As he fell, he looked up. He could see the hands reaching out for him. Dead eyes looking down, and on the closest face, he saw a smile touch the corner of its lips. Just beyond, as he was falling, he could see something red, something that he'd missed before.

He hit the ground with teeth rattling force, just before he realized what he'd seen at the base of the window. Blood was leaking from his mouth and he could feel the stinging pain in his tongue, but it was nothing compared to the pain in his arm, and all of it was making his head swim.

What was it that he'd seen? The little red thing there by the window, what was it? Why had it seemed so familiar?

His eyes focussed for a brief second. He was able to see it again before another face passed over him and blocked his view. All of a sudden he knew. At the bottom of the window, he had seen the red handle of the emergency release. It would have dislodged the window, giving him a chance to escape.

The cold fingers tugged at him. They were pulling at his injured arm, and he felt warm liquid rather than the pain. The liquid splashed against his face, and he knew they had pulled the arm free from his body.

Somewhere he heard a scream. It was a hideous sound, somewhere in the darkness. It seemed far away, and yet echoed, and he could feel it reverberating through him.

He hoped that whoever it was, they would be okay…

Then the last of his mind slipped away.

HATCHED
(Invisible Spiders: Book 1)
PREVIEW

CHAPTER 1

John didn't know what had woken him. One moment he had been a part of the nothingness that lay behind his eyes, lost in deep sleep. The next, he found himself lying awake in his room. He was on his bed; - a mattress on the floor, and he was just barely above eye level to the floor. Outside, the glow from the streetlight shone through his cracked window, its light giving him just enough illumination to make out the familiar dark shapes of his room and its furnishings.

With the lights off, no one other than himself would ever be able to find anything, as it was all just heaps of dark shapes and odd angles. Even with the lack of light, he was familiar with the different piles of dirty and clean clothes, tossed aside pieces of half-finished art, wads of paper, tissues and toilet paper.

Not that it mattered to him. Sure it was a mess, but it was his mess, and why should he care what other's thought? It was his life, and he lived it how he wanted to.

Shadows started to dance through the window, cast by the streetlight outside shining on tree-branch fingers, pushed by the wind. It looked like a large skeletal hand was reaching across his window and down to grab him, its bony fingers outstretched…

Part of him, (the paranoid part,) feared that those bony fingers were reaching into his room, and they were going through his stuff. The hand seemed like it was searching for something, as it shifted back and forth, bouncing from one dirty pile of clothes to another.

"Yeah, like they'd ever find much worth a damn," he thought. All he had of value was his 'rent-to-own', 37 inch television, sitting in the living room, and his stash, which sat in the large bag he had just brought back from little Chicago. This was tucked nicely away in his closet, under a pair of soiled undies that would turn the most crazed away.

The bud was safe.

Ah yes, the bud was safe.

"Precious sweet bud, let you ripen so fine. Precious sweet bud, I'll make you mine," John said to the small dark bedroom. Nothing responded to him in the little apartment, which was good, as he should have been all alone. He allowed himself a little smile, as he thought about the bag. He had tried to grow his own before, but it never dried right. He wasted a lot of seed, and in the end, taught himself that it was just too much damn work, when all he had to do was take a short drive to Little Chi-Town, and he'd come back happy.

John felt a slight tingle just inside the ridge of his nose. It was like a breeze danced in his nose-hairs, and he broke out of his enjoyable thoughts to rub at it. The tingle persisted, and he rubbed harder. He pushed his finger deep along the inside of his nose, as though he were trying to pierce his way into his mind. Then he pinched both sides, hard, and pulled downward, long and slow, letting the dryness of his fingers feel the soft tissue inside.

His fingers scratched the inside of his nose, and the tingling subsided enough that it was no longer unbearable. He was able to clear his head, and felt a vague sense of relief at having prevented the tickle from working its way into a sneeze. Sneezing would have just been a waste. Who knew what would come flying out? He didn't want to lose any of the present that he'd been enjoying.

He turned his head and looked at the envelope sitting half-open on the top of his dresser. He could just see it from his spot near the floor, as it hung just ever so slightly over the edge. A slight smirk wriggled at the corner of his lips, as he remembered its contents from earlier. Not that there was much left of it, but the envelope still sat there. He was surprised he hadn't thrown it out after he had partaken of its contents.

Then again, he didn't remember anything after he'd inhaled the nose candy he'd found inside the folded up piece of paper. It had been one hell of a hit. One long snort and he now here he lay, on his bed. Who knew how many hours later it was? He sure as hell hoped it was the same day, or night of, well, whatever damn time period he was in.

"Damn bitch probably put itching powder in the shit," he thought. There were only faint traces of the white powder she had sent him earlier. It was sprinkled about, like dust that had fallen to the hardwood floor. When he'd opened it, the only thing written inside had been: "Enjoy."

He had. He'd never been a big fan of nose candy, but was never one to turn away a good high when it came to him.   He was just surprised to see it coming from the "Miss Psycho Queen" that was his ex-girlfriend. He guessed she still hadn't taken the hint he gave her, when he told her to get lost.

Damn. Why did he have to date the crazy ones? He was always stuck with the ones that would never go away. Instead, they would latch on and cling to him no matter how often he'd call them cunts and whores, or however badly he treated them.

John pushed himself up, moving into a sitting position, with his legs running along the hardwood floor. The floor was cool against his feet, which felt good in the warm stuffy heat of his place. He wished like hell he could afford a damn air conditioner. The summer wasn't even officially started yet, and already his place was getting too damn stuffy. What was he going to do once June hit, or July? There was no way he was going to be able to bear it without something.

He had thought about possibly stealing one from somebody's window. Air conditioners looked like they would be the easiest thing in the world to steal. Not that he had ever stolen one before. He'd stolen many other things, little things that no one would ever miss, but he had never tried something that big. All he would have to do was walk up to someone's window, and just pull. They looked like they would just pop right out, and then he could hurry on home with it.

Yeah, maybe he would do that. He was really starting to like the idea as he reached over to the side of his bed, and fumbled to turn on his basketball lamp. He had to fight the little push-pull switch, and grumbled as he fought with it. Finally, on his third attempt, the lamp finally clicked on, and light flooded the little bedroom.

Out of the corner of his eye, John could have sworn that he saw little black 'things,' scurrying out of sight. They had been just at the corner of his vision, making it hard for him to be sure, and by the time he had turned to look, they were gone. Probably figments of his imagination, or more hallucinations, he thought as he reached to rub the sleep from his eyes. It wouldn't have been the first time for him to be seeing things, and he still wasn't quite sure what the hell his   Ex had sent him.

If it wasn't a hallucination though, he wouldn't have been too surprised. He didn't have the cleanest of places, but at least it had never been known for roaches. Leave it to him though, to be the man who would draw them into the place.   Not that the landlord would care, or try to do anything. The place was a dump, with a reputation for being one, so there was little chance he would even call in an exterminator. After all, he might accidentally kill the termites that held up the building.

"Ugh", he thought, why the hell was he up in the middle of the damn night? He leaned forward and pulled himself up from the mattress he had plopped down onto the floor. His bedroom was never meant to entertain visitors, so he kept the barest of essentials, and the mess stretched wide. His mattress sat just on the hardwood floor, with no frame to hold it up, and his clothes were thrown about. Trash littered the floor in the general direction of the door.

The kitchen area of the apartment was just off to the side of the living room, with a short hallway that lead back to the bedroom and the bathroom. The living room, where he spent most of his time, had a heavily worn, badly tattered couch with its stuffing coming out of various seams along the back. Across from that, was the television that he was currently renting to own. That is until they decided to come get it. He hadn't made a payment in a while and they kept calling to bug him about it.

He looked through the open door of his bedroom toward the living room. The television casted a soft glow, still on, but in sleep mode. It was always the visual center-piece of the apartment. It was also the only thing that wasn't old, tattered, or a flat-out piece of crap.

However, he usually turned it off when he crashed for the night. He was surprised to see that it was still on.

John stumbled across the room, over the tossed about piles of clothes, as he made his way to the front hallway. It was dark, catching only a slight glow from the little lamp. Not that it mattered much.

His eyelids had grown heavy, and as he stumbled, he wondered why the hell he was even trying to make his way to the bathroom. The heavy pain in his lower stomach and the burning sensation coming from his lower bowels reminded him why as he stepped into the little bathroom and clicked on the light. It's fluorescent flashed a few times before coming to life.

He barely caught a glimpse of the pale reflection of himself in the mirror as he stepped past it to the toilet. The seat was up, left up living the life of a bachelor, and he didn't worry about closing the door behind him. His eyes were closed, and he just listened to the sound of water on water, and felt the release of the pressure that had been building up in his bladder. Sometimes there was no greater joy, and as the relief came, now was one of those times, as the sensation tingled through him.

As he finished, he opened his eyes to reach forward and flush, when he stopped, noticing the red liquid that filled his toilet. It was dark red, red as the crimson life force that coursed through his veins.

"That had better not have come from me." he thought to himself. He looked at the water, trying to think of a way the color could have come from anywhere else. He reached forward and flushed, but as the red liquid went spiraling down to the sewer, fresh, clear water replaced it.

"Ah, fuck me." He said to himself. Last thing he wanted was to be pissing blood again.

John stepped groggily over to the sink and looked at himself in the mirror. He was about to reach forward and wash his hands. Not that he was the most sanitary of persons, but he had been taught to do so as a child, and it was one of the few good habits he never had broken.

He was stopped though, by the pale reflection of the face that looked back at him, and the deep bloodshot eyes with dark circles under them. His hair was greasier and more ruffled than usual, and his lips and face were without a touch of color to them. He was never one to focus on himself in the mirror, but he was sure that if he had looked that way hours earlier when he'd gone to bed, he would have noticed. He looked like a dead man walking; how the hell could he have missed it?

Then there was the dried blood. It was coming from his nose; just a little trail of it from his right nostril. It was tiny, as though he'd had the start of a nose bleed, but before it had really developed, had stopped and was now all scabbed over.

John leaned forward toward the mirror, so that he could get a better look into the black opening of his nostril. He had a sudden strong itch, forcing him to start rubbing at his nose again. The itching grew stronger, a tickle that grew to a fire inside, nearly bringing tears to his eyes as he rubbed his nostrils, both inside and out. He tried again to wipe the sleep from his eyes as he peered through the darkness.

He could barely make out what looked like a long black hair sticking out of his nose at an odd angle. John reached up, readying himself to pluck it out, and for the sharp pain that would follow.

As he started to grip the hair, it twitched and began to move. John pulled his hand away and watched as it moved, and pulled itself back into his nose, disappearing into the darkness of his nostril.

"What the --?" John whispered to himself and leaned in closer, just inches from the glass. The itching sensation grew unbearable, till he felt he could rub it until it bled and the skin was raw.

He was tired, and he just wanted to get back to his mattress on the floor, and sleep his way back to the model who had been sexually assaulting his dreams.

John smiled at the thought, and started to pull himself away from the mirror, when the hair reappeared from his nose. It was longer this time, and now it shifted, coming out farther, then pulling itself back into his nostril.

He started to reach forward to open the mirrored cabinet to grab a pair of tweezers, so he could just pull the damn thing out, when the owner of the 'hair', a large spider, emerged from the inside of John's nose.

John stood there, his hand hovering just above the edge of the mirror, no longer wanting to pull it open. He was transfixed now, by his visitor, and left his hand there. He was afraid to move, to pull his hand back, while the large spider stayed perched on his upper lip. It just sat there.

John stopped watching it in the mirror, and tried to look down at it. His eyes burned from the strain of focusing on an object so close, and all he could make out was a large black shape.

How had the thing been sitting up in his damned nose? He wondered how long it could have been up there. How had it survived when he'd been squeezing and rubbing his nose when it itched? Had it gotten into his brain? Had it been digging around up there? Ugh, even worse, what would have happened had he squashed the damned thing in his nose?   His stomach belly-flopped at the thought of it, and he had to stifle a gag. He wanted to let loose into the toilet.

Without watching himself, keeping his eyes focused purely on the spider, John lowered his hand away from the edge of the mirror and moved back until he was again squarely in front of it. He could feel the spider's legs on his lip; it sort of danced there as he moved, as though it were trying to ride him like a wave as he shuffled back from the mirror.

It was one big spider; he could barely fathom how it had come out of his nose. He leaned over the sink, figuring it was time to try and knock the thing off, so that maybe he could wash it down the drain.

He turned on the tap, and fumbled for the stopper so that the sink slowly filled with water. He didn't turn the water on too fast, as the last thing he wanted was to spook the spider and have it crawling all over his face. However, so far, it seemed to be content with just sitting there, watching him.

John raised his hand, getting ready to shake his head and knock it away at the same time. He rocked back and forth briefly to get himself into a prepped stance, and then he swung.

The spider quickly ran back into John's nose, and it was again on fire with the itching sensation. This time he could actually feel it moving around in his head. It was going deeper into his nose, and then he could feel the large shape forcing its way, into his airway.

John coughed, the large lump moving up and down his throat. He was gagging in reflex, trying to get it out. He put his finger down his throat to try and force himself to throw up, and get the spider out that way, but it fought against him. He gagged again, trying to push it up but it kept running up and down his throat, to avoid coming back up. It was fighting against him in his own damn insides!

Tears came to his eyes as he tried to cough as hard as he could. His throat burned and became raw, but still nothing.

John dropped down to his knees in front of the toilet, and reached his arms out as if he'd been drinking and was now praying to the porcelain God. He tried to vomit into the toilet, hoping to clear the spider from his throat, but could only dry heave. He could barely breathe, as it stayed lodged, and he couldn't keep himself from continuing to gag.

He wanted to all-out cry, as he rested against the arm that was leaning on the toilet. His body felt like it was burning up, and he imagined he could feel the heat emanating from it. It was too hot, as though his skin was about to ignite.

He looked at his arm, expecting it to be red. It was still pasty pale.

A lump formed under his arm near his elbow. It seemed to appear from nowhere, and protruded grotesquely. It was nearly three quarters of an inch in diameter and half an inch tall, pulling the skin tight and red where it suddenly grew.

The lump broke through the skin, another spider exiting, tearing its way out, and onto his arm. Blood dripped from the hole, and the spider started to run quickly down his arm. John reached for it, trying to claw at the spider with his other hand, to kill it. He nearly got it a couple of times, but the spider was quick and kept dodging his attempts. Instead, it turned quickly, and ran back into the hole it had made in his arm, back under the skin.

John clawed at his arm, at the hole, trying to tear away the skin and get the spider out. His long, dirty nails, pulled away clumps of flesh, but the spider continued to move, under the skin, toward his hand.

It made it to his wrist, and John quickly reached around above the sink, trying to find his razor. His arm was now draped over the toilet, blood running from where he'd tried to claw the spider out.

He could barely see above the basin of the sink, or the cabinet he was reaching for, but he heard the crashing of objects falling: his tooth brush, the plastic scraping the bottom, the large heavy sound of the shaving cream as it was knocked over and rolled into the basin.

John finally felt his hand clench around the plastic handle of the razor. It was a cheap, dollar store shaver, but he hoped that digging hard enough with it, he'd be able to get the damned spider out. Damn the things, damn them, he wanted them out! He hated spiders, more than anything else, he hated spiders!

He brought the razor to his wrist and was about to start tearing away at the flesh, but there was no longer a lump. His arm and wrist were clear. They had an unhealthy, pale cast to them, but they were clear of anything hiding beneath. He still had blood trickling down his arm, but the spider seemed to be gone. It was the same with the spider in his throat; he didn't feel as though anything was blocking it, and he could breathe again.

He reached out to the sink, and used it to help him stand. He still didn't feel quite sure of himself, and he felt like he might be trapped in a nightmare, somehow. He hoped that he had never truly woken up, or that he might just be on a bad trip.

Looking at himself in the mirror, he still looked like death warmed over. He was tired and just wanted to go back to his bed. It was calling for him, like a siren song reeling him in.

His ear tickled, and he reached up to pick at it, but before his hand could reach it, he felt the familiar feeling of the spider's legs on his skin. In his reflection, he could just barely see the spider pushing back the hair that was typically draped over his ears.

He shook his head madly, trying to get the spider, as he felt it start to crawl toward his face, its legs leaving small stinging sensations along the unshaved roughness of his skin. He bobbed his head, like a swimmer trying to clear water from his ears, trying to use gravity and force to rid him of the eight legged beast. Then, after one last, hard shake, he felt it release and saw it land on the floor.

It was still there, shocked by the fall, he assumed. Before it could regain its senses, he quickly stomped down on the cursed thing. Strangely, he expected it to squish between his toes, as he was still barefoot. Instead, he barely felt anything.

He pulled his foot away, only to see black dust where the remains of the spider should have been.

www.ingramcontent.com/pod-product-compliance
Lightning Source LLC
Chambersburg PA
CBHW070614130626
46556CB00001B/363